'Petit has already established him[...] observer of modern Britain; [his ...] mood of the times on those streets beautifully' *Big Issue*

'A highly charged atmospheric novel [and] an accomplished thriller that really delivers the goods' *Books Magazine*

'This spare, stylish novel manages to be both pacy and atmospheric, humorous and full of pathos. Above all it conjures a shifting, gloomy suburban London not usually chosen as a literary backdrop' *Midweek Magazine*

'*The Hard Shoulder* is Chris Petit in fantastic form. A great London novel. There's no praise higher than that' *The Crack*

'*The Hard Shoulder* has all the qualities of a gritty and well-crafted documentary' *Tribune*

Chris Petit is a novelist and filmmaker. His work in film includes *Radio On*, *An Unsuitable Job for a Woman* and (with Iain Sinclair) *The Falconer*. His first novel, *Robinson*, is republished by Granta Books. He has also written *The Psalm Killer* (1997) and *Back from the Dead* (1999). He lives in London.

THE
HARD
SHOULDER

Chris Petit

Granta Books
London · New York

Granta Publications, 2/3 Hanover Yard,
Noel Road, London N1 8BE

First published in Great Britain by Granta Books 2001
This edition published by Granta Books 2002

A CIP catalogue record for this book
is available from the British Library.

1 3 5 7 9 10 8 6 4 2

Typeset by M Rules
Printed and bound in Great Britain by
Mackays of Chatham PLC

To Jennifer

Before

O'Grady, a big man once, stood in the empty carriage of the silver train as it moved faster through the long tunnel from St John's Wood into daylight at Finchley Road. He wore an overcoat but looked like a man that rarely did, and the battered holdall at his feet was far from full. He stood awkwardly, waiting for the doors to close, blinking at the light after so long underground.

After West Hampstead the train travelled a ridge. Slate sky bled the colour from the view. To the left he could see the tower of the Kilburn State cinema, like a small finger of Manhattan stuck into the London skyline. O'Grady felt his stomach contract and thought of riding on, but he got out at Kilburn, pausing to watch the train move away down the long, straight track. He couldn't remember if the carriages had always been silver.

He took the stairs down to the street. He was still unfamiliar with the process of everything and whatever he did felt like it was at the wrong speed, even handing in his ticket to the unmanned booth. Outside, the two railway bridges, cutting the road at an angle just above the station entrance and booming whenever a train passed over, were his first familiar landmark. To his left Shoot Up Hill ran up towards Cricklewood. To think he had once aspired to Cricklewood. O'Grady turned right.

The Kilburn High Road had been a ditch when he left, and still was from what he could see. He wondered if Morans, where he'd had his first job, was still there. It was, the same. The rest of the shops looked as fifth-rate as ever and the street had not lost its air of having long since given up. Traffic was clogging up in both directions. A white van parked half on the pavement blocked the way, its orange tail lights winking in unison. O'Grady had not seen indicators doing that before. Apart from that, everything looked the same. It was a shock to find so little changed. From what he had read there was supposed to be a boom on.

Further down on the other side was the Black Lion. He had favoured the Black Lion after being barred from the Roman Way for brawling. Inside reminded him of the iced cakes of childhood treats. It was more the size of a church than a pub, with several tall rooms. There had been music on Friday nights, Irish bands over from Belfast and Dublin singing mournful country and western. Most of them stayed at his sister's. There had been a barmaid, too, with artificial red hair, lacquered to perfection, which meant she would only let him take her on all fours so as not to muss it up. He had never found out who told his wife.

It was soon after opening and the place was empty apart from a couple of biddies in a corner chasing bottles of stout with what looked like sweet sherry. He had not meant to go in, even after he had crossed the street. The barman was a surly lad more interested in his paper than pouring Guinness. O'Grady asked for a Jameson's too, to give him something extra to do. Once they'd jumped when he stood at that bar.

He went and sat by the door, where he could watch anyone coming in or out. There was nobody he recognised. He nursed his drinks, appreciating the kick, telling himself he'd have just the one round, but when it came to leaving he had another because he had started to feel comfortable. The sun came out and brightened the room and O'Grady watched the motes of dust caught by the light. A blind man came in with an accordion and ordered a drink. His shoes were brand-new and yellow, in contrast to the grey of everything else he wore. O'Grady wondered if anyone had told him what colour his shoes were, and how you explained that to a blind man.

He was tight when he left, not drunk but getting that way. He had no expectations for the rest of the day, apart from the hurdle of Molly. He had made up his mind to go straight there when he saw a sign he had long forgotten. Tony's Are the Best Steaks in Town. He knew they weren't, but they were better than the pizzas over the road. He was in no hurry, he told himself.

He recognised Tony but Tony had no recollection of him. O'Grady felt like talking but Tony's mind was on other things. His vegetables included cabbage, which he couldn't eat, to Tony's obvious disapproval. O'Grady ordered another beer to make up for it and by the end of the meal some rapport had been established because he was offered a sticky, sweet liqueur on the house.

Everything was much more expensive than he remembered. Tickets, drink, food: he seemed to have shelled out a small fortune for not very much. From what he could see, nobody paid him any attention. Once his whole life had been about making an impression, not necessarily a good one, more a matter of leaving his mark, which was what he had understood by using his fists. Now he had grown invisible, which was how he wanted it.

He walked Kilburn's backstreets for half an hour, sobering up. Then he went back to Tony's for his bag, which he had forgotten.

He needed to get off on the right foot with Molly. She was taking him in when nobody else would. He walked past the house a couple of times. She'd had a new sign done. Maybe there was a boom on after all. The trees in the street had recently been lopped right back and in their knobbly brown hardness looked like pillars of old turd. The house was taller than he remembered. Standing before it, he felt daunted by what lay ahead. Small days of best behaviour under the disapproving eye of his sister.

He rang the bell. Molly took her time answering. Even before she opened the door O'Grady knew he was in the wrong. He was late and she would smell the drink on him.

'There's no red carpet, if that's what you're thinking' was all she said by way of a greeting.

O'Grady crossed the threshold. The mosaic floor he hadn't given a thought to since leaving. In his day it had always had two or three pieces missing, and sure enough they still were. He stood in the hall, gripping his bag. He had no explanation to speak of. Most of the time now he found he had nothing to say. Molly did not even look at him or ask how he was.

'Your old room's empty,' she said. 'It's let usually, so the electricity and heat are on a meter. Fifty pences and pounds is what it takes. I'll be leaving to visit mother at five.'

It was an instruction, not an invitation. They would take the bus as Molly disapproved of the tube.

His old room was in the eaves. There wasn't much to it, a few sticks of furniture, a view of rooftops and television aerials. He had grown up there, his mother letting rooms to lads from Ireland, most of them over on digging jobs. At some point the place had started calling itself a hotel and one or two men in suits, travelling salesmen, began to be seen in the dining room. His father, from what he could remember, had never been mentioned. All O'Grady knew was that he had gone ahead of them to England but had moved on by the time they arrived. This was what was commonly known as an Irish divorce. There were rumours of Canada.

O'Grady lay on the bed and waited for time to pass. He had taught himself not to think, stripping his mind like an engine or a gun, not bothering to put it back together.

Their mother was in a nursing home in Willesden Green. She was ninety and gave no sign of knowing him. The home stood in a long avenue, the houses grander than Kilburn though still appearing to labour under the same misapprehension. These were suburbs where nobody came out of choice.

The home was run on forced good cheer underneath which O'Grady saw it for what it was, an institution like any other with its inmates there on sufferance. Fire regulations meant there were too many doors, the carpets had swirled patterns to hide the dirt and the place smelled of overcooking. His observations struck him as more real and solid than the wispy figures they found in the day room. A television was playing *Planet of the Apes*. Several ancient people sat around it in a state of semi-stupor, pointing at the screen from time to time when something caught their attention. His mother was sitting by herself next to the window. O'Grady did not recognise her at first, a shadow of her old self, all the fight gone out of her. He could see nothing of the woman who had boxed his ears and chased him up and down the stairs of his childhood.

She seemed to have only one aim, which was to make them have a cup of tea. Molly refused, saying that it was too much trouble, but O'Grady could see what it meant to her. It was all she had left to offer.

'I'll have a cup of tea with you,' he said.

His mother focused on him for the first time and asked if he was Molly's husband. Molly explained that he had been in America. 'You remember.' His mother peered at him, none the wiser, and O'Grady saw that he had long been erased from what little was left of her memory.

'Who is that man?' she demanded again after a silence. Before Molly could answer a fracas broke out around the television and a stout woman in a blue uniform had to come in and settle the squabble, which was about someone switching channels without asking.

It was dark outside and O'Grady could see the reflections of the three of them in the window and wondered at the ties of blood, stuck between the two women he had spent most of his life trying to get away from. There he was again, and the rest felt like a dream.

They travelled in silence back down to Kilburn. It was a Saturday evening and from the top of the bus O'Grady could see the pubs starting to fill up. With Molly it was the same as ever, always what was left unsaid.

She told him there was a meal. They ate in the parlour off the kitchen which was, with her room upstairs, Molly's private space. There was a small eating table and a chair that wasn't quite an armchair by a gas fire where his mother had sat at the end of the day reading the newspaper.

'What does the doctor say?' he asked eventually.

'She'll outlive the lot of us.'

Speaking between mouthfuls, he said what he had been wanting to say. 'You'd not get another man for seventy pounds a week.'

Molly laid down her knife and fork and looked at him directly for the first time. He could not hold her gaze. 'Seventy pounds is all I can afford. Kathleen comes in mornings but the child has no brain to speak of. I've rooms that need painting. And I'll not cook for you after tonight.'

He didn't want her to, he nearly said. Something about the way she ate reduced eating to the first stage of an unpleasant process that ended with the toilet. O'Grady was pushed not to laugh for the first time in as long as he could remember.

'Peace and quiet is all I'm asking,' he mumbled, staring hard at the remains of his stew, which had looked like shit to start with.

'What's so funny?' asked Molly sharply.

The next morning was a bright blue in contrast to the grey of the day before. O'Grady made his bed, leaving neat hospital corners, before going downstairs.

The kitchen was hot from cooking and smelled of frying. A girl in a grubby white overall was wiping her brow as O'Grady walked in, and he caught a glimpse of a damp sweat patch under her arm. Cooked breakfasts were stacked on a hotplate, waiting for him to serve. The girl nodded and blew a stray hair from her forehead, as if it was him she was dismissing. Molly had said that her name was Kathleen. She was a big girl, country-looking, with red hair. Red hair, real or fake, O'Grady thought wistfully, must have featured in his life more than in the average man's.

Behind him the swing doors into the dining room banged and Molly walked in, already supervising before she was properly into the room, pointing O'Grady towards the waiting breakfasts. 'Those are for the boys by the window. If the rest are after nine they're too late. Stand no nonsense. These show bands think they can march in when they like.'

The bands played at the National. O'Grady, who had gone regularly in his youth, remembered the boys standing against the wall while the girls danced together, handbags placed carefully on the floor by their feet. Back in the early sixties Van Morrison had once stayed upstairs, when he was still playing the saxophone in local Irish bands. That was the story.

O'Grady felt self-conscious entering the dining room, like he was walking onto a stage which everyone would be staring at, but nobody paid him any attention, even when he shoved the plates under their noses. The residents were either old or very young, with little in between, beached spinsters, snagged by his sister's propriety and her long-term rates, and lads looking like they had just got off the boat.

Back in the kitchen Kathleen flipped two more breakfasts onto plates and used a cloth to hand them to him.

'There you go, mister. They're hot.' She sounded like she was from Cork or thereabouts. The sight of her reminded O'Grady how long it had been since he'd had the chance of studying a woman's arse outside of a picture. In his distraction, he ignored her warning and dropped one of the plates. It smashed and the yolk of the egg ran yellow over the faded red linoleum.

'You've hands for nothing,' said his sister.

O'Grady was vacuuming the stairs when Kathleen passed by carrying fresh linen. He stood aside for her.

'Her bite's a lot worse than her bark,' she said, smirking.

On the upstairs landing someone was whistling 'Mack the Knife', jaunty to the point of being provocative, and he reached the top of the stairs as the sun broke through the window behind. O'Grady was unable to make him out beyond his wearing a proper jacket and hands stuck in his trouser pockets.

'Morning, Kathleen,' he said, like he was addressing an assembly. 'Clean sheets today?'

The voice was full of innuendo, Irish but O'Grady could not place it directly. Kathleen replied equally loudly, joining in his game. 'Morning, Mr Shaughnessy, clean sheets today. Is that an aftershave you're wearing, Mr Shaughnessy?' They seemed to be acting for his benefit.

'Eau de toilette, Kathleen, eau de toilette. Remember that.'

There was a laugh in his voice. After watching Kathleen's departure down the landing he turned to O'Grady. '"The cement is there for the weight to bear," ' he quoted. ' "Mack the Knife". Bobby Darin, God rest his soul, streets and away the best version. So you'd be Miss O'Grady's long-lost brother.'

O'Grady nodded cautiously. The sun still prevented him from seeing the man clearly. For the first time he feared that his homecoming was not as invisible as he would have liked.

Shaughnessy sounded an unlikely guest for his sister's dowdy establishment. As he passed down the stairs O'Grady saw him properly for the first time, in his tie and checked waistcoat, and with the sort of white hair he associated with certain priests of his childhood, so fine that it was a miracle it had not fallen out. He was short but seemed to take up a lot of space. Behind his air of bonhomie O'Grady sensed something solid and calculating.

Spotting Molly walking out of the dining room into the hall, Shaughnessy leaned over the stair rail and called down smoothly, 'Good morning, Miss O'Grady, and a finer one you couldn't wish for.'

Her stiff reply did not hide her disapproval.

'Just introducing myself to your brother,' Shaughnessy added. He winked at O'Grady. Molly looked up at them suspiciously, then announced she was going to the ten-thirty Mass in a way that made it clear that she expected O'Grady to go too because it was her rules he was playing by now. O'Grady bent his head in submission, wondering whether it was forgiveness he was really after, or if his nerve had gone for good.

They walked down to Quex Road. O'Grady wore his overcoat in an effort to look respectable. The church was full. As usual most of them were there from habit, as a long-odds bet that there was an afterlife for which they could qualify through the single act of regular churchgoing. When the congregation was asked to give the sign of peace, Molly shook hands with the person on her left and the woman in front, but not with him. She went up to Communion while he sat and waited, his mind marking time as it always did in church.

Afterwards a crowd stood outside, the men in their blue suits gearing up for the pub before the Sunday roast. O'Grady could smell brutal amounts of aftershave slapped on cheeks scraped shiny and nicked by the trembling hand of that morning's hang-over. He recognised some of them but they didn't seem to notice him. There was Tommy Doyle looking prosperous. He and Doyle had been at primary school and the last he had heard Tommy had his own building firm and a mansion in Brondesbury with a drive for his cars. 'Cars, plural,' he had once boasted to O'Grady. Tommy looked like he was discussing business. Nobody was quite sure what went into some of the holes Tommy dug. The last time O'Grady had seen him was a dozen years ago at a wedding. Both of them had been sweating drink and Tommy was crowing. 'I've got my own expanding contracting business and Arabs for neighbours.'

He couldn't say if Tommy had seen him or not, but he didn't come over as he once would have done. O'Grady thought it typical of Tommy to continue coming to Quex Road rather than transferring to a smarter church. It showed everyone that he had remained a local boy. More likely, thought O'Grady, it let him lord it over the proles when he wouldn't have been given the time of day in a smarter parish, where he would have still been taken for bog Catholic, regardless of the size of his wallet.

O'Grady stood meekly behind Molly, in line to speak to the priest, who was glad-handing the women with the skill of a politician. He was tall and as handsome as a television priest. His hair looked like he spent too much time fussing over it. O'Grady had always been suspicious of good-looking priests. The father looked switched-on enough as it was, O'Grady thought, but managed to light up even more on greeting Molly, and smoothly announced that they stood at five hundred pounds for the tombola, thanks to her good work. 'And how's your mother?'

'Between you and me, Father, as fit as a fiddle.' She sounded skittish in a way that O'Grady had not seen before, but then priests, he decided, were the only men allowed to pay Molly any attention because they were considered safe.

The priest turned a terrifyingly white smile towards O'Grady. 'And this would be your brother you were telling me about. The one from America.'

'The one from America,' Molly confirmed quickly. O'Grady wondered if she would admit the lie at her next confession, along with her secret carnal thoughts for the priest. He tried not to dwell on the thought of her, three sherries down, sitting in disarray in front of the gas fire, rosary in one hand, in a vain effort to ward off the temptation, while the disobedient one did its business.

'Delighted to have you back,' said the father with a sincerity that took O'Grady by surprise. 'I'm sure Molly is. A man around the house.'

O'Grady nodded and held his tongue, thinking of Tommy Doyle and his like. To them the last place for a man was at home. Very few of his own memories featured the various places he had called home. Before going away, most of his time had been spent avoiding it.

The priest turned away to the next parishioner and O'Grady dutifully followed Molly down the steps. 'Such a fine man,' she said. 'Done wonders for the parish.'

O'Grady waited until he was walking alongside her before asking, 'And are you delighted to have me back?'

From the set of her mouth he could see she was not going to answer. He nodded back towards the church. 'Are they still teaching that charity begins at home?'

'Home!' Molly retorted, visibly stung. 'You've got a nerve coming back and calling it home.'

'And telling Mother and that priest I've been in America.'

'His name is Father O'Donovan. What would you rather I tell him?'

He had no answer to that. He saw that the lie was to protect herself. They walked the rest of the way back in silence. He left her outside the hotel, saying he wanted a walk. He didn't really. It was an effort even to think of it, but he had no desire to return to his room.

He walked down Willesden Lane and strolled round the cemetery with its well-kept air of finality and after that headed over to Queen's Park, past the rows of dreary Victorian villas, carefully avoiding the more familiar streets and any places that held memories. It would take a bomb to change Kilburn. The only difference he had noticed was a small park in Streatley Road he was sure had not been there before. He could not remember what had been in its place.

He walked mechanically, head down and noticing little, his mind in increasing turmoil. He could not tell if it was elation or rage, or what this exaggerated state referred to. He looped down past the edge of Maida Vale until he found himself on the Edgware Road and ploughed his way back up to Kilburn, fighting a north-east wind flecked with rain.

It was a woman he wanted, he realised by the time he was back in the High Road.

Staring at the cards in the window of a newsagent, he was startled by a voice at his shoulder, saying, 'I loathe a Sunday myself and this one slower than most.'

It was Shaughnessy, the dapper man from the hotel, looking conspiratorial in a spotless white trenchcoat and trilby. O'Grady felt ashamed at being caught at the massage cards.

'Are you coming for a drink?' Shaughnessy asked.

O'Grady wanted to say no but had grown unused to refusing. Seeing his hesitation, Shaughnessy cocked his head at the cards. 'Of course, if you've got other plans.'

O'Grady shrugged. The Black Lion stood across the road. Shaughnessy threw in a further prompt. 'No one's saying we have to tear the arse out of it.'

O'Grady found himself falling into step with the smaller man and they crossed the street together.

With it being a Sunday lunchtime there were more women than normal. The place was almost filled up and had that particular air of a pub in daytime, when the booze still smelled fresh and the smoke lent an allure. People's spirits were up, their voices cheerful. O'Grady looked round at the hospitable surroundings – the fire, the lit-up but silent jukebox, the heavy velvet were all a lot more welcoming than the church in Quex Road. Shaughnessy was at the bar, declaring it his shout and asking if Guinness was all right, which it was. From the way Shaughnessy was treated, O'Grady understood he was a regular.

'A damn sight more welcoming than your sister's place,' said Shaughnessy. 'Don't know how she gets away with the prices she charges.'

O'Grady wondered about Shaughnessy and whether he was being deliberately befriended and, if so, why. Again he struck O'Grady as an unlikely guest for his sister's place. For some reason he thought of his mother, along with the other wraiths in their last waiting room, meals the only punctuation left to their days.

Shaughnessy was watching the slow pour of the Guinness with approval. He leaned towards O'Grady and said out of the side of his mouth, 'Kempton Park, two thirty tomorrow, Nelson's Eye. Faster than a fart. A foregone conclusion and I have that from the horse's mouth. Fourteen to one.'

He told O'Grady to take a couple of seats that had become vacant, at the table by the door where he had sat the morning before, while he settled for the drinks. When Shaughnessy joined him he sank half his pint in one go, leaving a moustache of froth on his upper lip. 'I was a sporting jockey myself,' he announced, 'though you'd not think it to look at me now, until I fell off the horse altogether.'

He gave a wheezy laugh. O'Grady wondered what to say. Something about whatever the other man said made it hard for him to think of a reply. Shaughnessy took another gulp of his drink and looked appreciative. 'Ah, it tightens the dung in you.' He saluted O'Grady with his glass. 'To the roaring boys, and yourself back from America.'

O'Grady wondered how Shaughnessy knew, and had a picture of Molly driving up and down the High Road in one of those cars they used at election time, blaring the news through a megaphone. She would have been better off saying nothing.

'There long?' asked Shaughnessy with a raised eyebrow that suggested he was happy to go along with whatever version O'Grady chose.

'Long enough,' said O'Grady, trying to sound noncommittal. He wondered where it was that Molly imagined he had been.

'New York?' asked Shaughnessy.

'No, not New York.' He sensed a trap.

'I was there myself for a while,' went on Shaughnessy easily. 'A few years ago now.'

He appeared eager to get on with the story and O'Grady relaxed, thinking he had been too suspicious. Shaughnessy was a man who liked the sound of his own voice.

'I had an American Judy and the lot. Big bank roll, Jack Daniel's. Ah, New York! I even drove one of those cars with the big fins.'

Shaughnessy waited for O'Grady to finish his drink, telling him that they had plenty of time. While O'Grady was at the bar getting new ones Shaughnessy went to the jukebox. His choice was surprisingly maudlin and he stood doing a little shuffle in front of the record while waiting for O'Grady to fetch the drinks.

He grinned over the top of his fresh glass and asked, 'You were never there, in the Big Apple?'

O'Grady shook his head. Shaughnessy seemed to have smoothly moved up a gear, whereas the effort of getting the drinks had left him ragged. The actual transaction of paying made him nervous. He knew the value of the coins well enough but found himself hesitating when confronted with a handful of change, as if it was Albanian or Italian money rather than regular pence. He only half listened as Shaughnessy blathered on and the song in the background reached a sobbing crescendo.

'Grand town. Great women, great bazooms. Fabulous dancers.'

My eye, thought O'Grady, the man's no more been there than I have, and he doubted if he had spent more than an afternoon on the back of a horse either.

The room had grown loud with cranked-up blather and drink-induced bursts of laughter. There was more of an air of urgency now, with last drinks being ordered before going off for lunch. Most of the women had already left to attend to the final preparations for the roasts. Shaughnessy looked around the room with the air of a man who had seen more than the rest of them. 'Different speed altogether in America, and that's putting it mildly. I know it's none of my business but, if you don't mind my asking, how much is that sister of yours paying?'

O'Grady studied the top of his Guinness where the foam had thinned, thinking absurdly that it might answer for him. With the heat and the drink he was starting to feel giddy. Whatever he'd had in mind for that day hadn't involved drinking with this nosy buffoon.

'Tell me to fuck off if you want,' Shaughnessy went on. 'No offence meant, seeing how she's your sister and all – and none taken, I'm sure – but that woman is the tightest cunt this side of Sligo.'

It took O'Grady a moment to realise that what he was hearing was himself laughing. Against all expectation. Shaughnessy joined in, sounding like an old engine trying to start up, which set O'Grady off even harder.

'Of course, it's the women who crack the whip, leastways where I come from. Was she always such a misery?' asked Shaughnessy.

'She was. She was.'

O'Grady wondered if he and Shaughnessy were going to become friends.

'So what's she paying. Sixty? Seventy?'

'Eighty,' replied O'Grady wondering why he was lying.

'Eighty quid a week. Criminal, I call it.'

He stayed on without meaning to. At a certain point the background din receded and turned to a gentle lapping and he listened to Shaughnessy's tales of New York, nodding occasionally or laughing when it seemed expected of him. He was drunk, he realised, which was why he had a feeling he didn't normally have, of everything fitting together. He didn't ever want to have to leave. The clock above the bar said half-past one. The place had thinned out. It was O'Grady's round.

This time he was served by a barmaid, her cleavage in evidence, which he glanced at surreptitiously, while waiting blearily, money in hand and no longer nervous.

'I've been away in America,' he announced, to test how it felt.

'That's nice,' she replied, bored, scraping foam off the top of the drinks with a knife. So much for the art of conversation, O'Grady thought.

'And two Jameson's,' he heard himself saying. He had a flash of Molly reciting the Lord's Prayer: 'and lead us not into temptation'. 'And make them doubles,' he added. What the hell.

By quarter-past two the place had filled up again, mainly with men O'Grady recognised from before, back after their dinner. The tempo had quickened and everyone was fighting to get their word in. Shaughnessy's face was shining from the heat and he was shouting. Already great chunks of what they'd been talking about had swirled away out of the reach of O'Grady's memory. Shaughnessy kept the stories coming, and when the IRA came round with their collection tin he swapped banter with the spotty youth and slipped him fifty pence with a surreptitious air of importance, making a charade of it, as if to say that he was in reality its paymaster-general. After the lad had gone, Shaughnessy muttered to O'Grady behind the back of his hand, 'There'll be bombs before Easter, mark my words.'

Drunk or not, O'Grady was starting to make out where Shaughnessy was coming from. Kilburn had been full of his likes when O'Grady was growing up, chancers with the gift of the gab. Unlike himself. When it came to stories he could never see how to put them together. 'There's this man, see.' It always reminded him of standing on a high board being unable to jump. He never saw the words joined up in a rush as Shaughnessy did, but only the gaps in between, which left him lost between one word and the next.

Shaughnessy surprised him by more or less repeating his thoughts. 'There's this man, a pal of mine. And I know for a fact he's got a crate of Jameson's for a very fair price, considering. We could split them and have a hooley.'

O'Grady thought of Molly's disapproval while Shaughnessy tugged at his sleeve.

'Fuck the cost, man, you needn't worry about that. I'll put a tenner on Nelson's Arm for you, and we'll pay out of the winnings.

Let's watch the race on the telly, have a jar or two, and I'll intro-
duce you to some of the girls. Maureen's always willing, and
Kathleen's a fine heifer, loves a party. A stout-hearted girl, fucks
like a steeplechaser, though I've not ridden her myself.'
Shaughnessy was in his stride, O'Grady could see, and the way he
scattered his words reminded him of a boxer's jabs. Leaning
close enough for O'Grady to smell the drink coming off him,
Shaughnessy went on. 'She wears jeans so tight you can see the
crack, and not a stitch underneath. She doesn't like a VPL, as she
calls it. Do you know what that is?'

Shaughnessy nudged him. O'Grady was on the point of bluffing when he saw the other man was caught up in the telling of his
story. 'A visible panty line. And now, about this case, come in for
half. I'd float the whole thing as a welcome-home present but I'm
a bit short myself.'

O'Grady was finding it hard trying to keep up. 'Kathleen in
the kitchen?' he asked eventually.

Shaughnessy looked at him and laughed, saying nothing but
intimating that his friendship would offer up untold surprises.
'This time tomorrow Nelson's Eye will be past the winning post
and we'll be in clover.'

He woke up in his room to find it dark outside and that he had
been sleeping in his clothes. It took him a moment to realise what
had woken him, the clunk of the electric meter running out. The
one for the gas was still working because the fire was going.
O'Grady listened to its hissing and wondered what level of pain
he would feel if he grasped the lit honeycomb.

The next morning he served breakfast with a hangover, and the
sight of each yolk threatened to turn his stomach. He breathed
through his mouth in an effort to avoid the smell of frying.
Chastened was the word, he thought.

After breakfast Molly wrote him a shopping list. Past the open
swing doors he could see Kathleen hoovering in the dining room.
He looked at her arse. It was hard to tell if Shaughnessy was
right.

Molly tore the list off her pad and handed him two five-pound notes from her purse. The sober precision of her every move was like a silent reproach. The scrap of toilet paper stuck to his neck where he had been unable to stop the bleeding after cutting himself shaving felt like a dead give-away, apparently confirmed by Molly saying, 'You'll not be associating with Mr Shaughnessy if you know what's good for you. And bring back the change.'

In the Safeway on the High Road O'Grady found himself standing in front of a display of baked beans tins taller than himself. A printed card read, 'Heinz Beanz Free Offer: "World of Survival" Wildlife Kit – offer in stores now.' That was what he needed, he told himself grimly, trying to make a joke of it.

The Monday-morning shoppers were all pensioners, old women for the most part, who pushed their trolleys with a manic intensity that allowed for no detours. Several times O'Grady was nearly run over. Half of them seemed to be there for the fun of the trolleys rather than the shopping, which was depressing whichever way you added it up, buying their solitary meals for the next few days, with an Angel Delight thrown in for a treat.

While he was unpacking in the kitchen he heard Shaughnessy's voice in the hall, asking, 'Oh, Miss O'Grady, would you have seen your brother?' and his sister's curt reply, 'No, Mr Shaughnessy, I would not,' when she knew perfectly well where he was because she had been standing next to him the minute before.

Back in the kitchen, Molly briskly set about tidying away, aware that O'Grady would have heard her.

'I can look after myself,' he said.

'Famous last words. Those tins go in that cupboard there.'

He could see she was seething and could not resist goading. 'Everything in its place, eh, Molly?'

The undisguised hostility with which she banged down the tin she was holding took him by surprise. 'You walked out of here twenty years ago without so much as a word, so don't you get smart with me, mister.'

Her anger snapped back shut and she continued about her business as though he wasn't there. It was a gift of hers, he thought, being able to dismiss people like that.

Upstairs he found his door ajar and he could hear someone in his room. His first thought was that it was Molly snooping, except she was still downstairs. He felt foolish knocking before entering his own room, as if he was being superstitious.

Kathleen in yellow rubber gloves was at his basin, her cleaning cloth squeaking as she worked at the enamel. He stood awkwardly by the door, not knowing what to do. His sister apart, it was the first time he had been alone in a room with a woman for as long as he could remember. If Kathleen noticed his discomfort she gave no sign of it.

'Shaughnessy wants to know if you'll be down the pub at lunchtime.'

O'Grady's attention was taken up entirely with being stuck by the door, unable to withdraw or move forward. He watched Kathleen put another spurt of Jif on her cloth. 'I thought the two of you had a hot date,' she went on. 'Getting on famously is what I heard.'

'Not today. I can't.'

She shrugged and ran the taps, giving the basin a final rinse. 'Suit yourself, that's what I say.'

She picked up her bucket of cleaning materials and moved towards him. O'Grady felt overtaken by clumsiness. Whichever direction he went to let her pass – left or right, forward or back – he was certain it would be the wrong one. He ended up staying where he was, which meant she had to brush against him on her way past. She paused in front of him. Her eyes were bluer than most and had the look of being in on a joke she wasn't sharing.

'You don't look such a hard man to me,' she said.

O'Grady turned away, saying nothing. He must have moved too, because when he was next aware of her he was in the middle of the room and she was by the door, half hidden by it, and looking more mischievous.

'If you ever want your bed making up in the morning just whistle.'

He shook his head slowly. He suspected she was making a fool of him and it took an effort to control his anger.

'No? I thought not. First time I set eyes on you I thought to myself, there's a fellow that makes his own bed.'

Early in the afternoon he walked up to Willesden Green to see his mother. The nurse went through an elaborate reintroduction, saying, 'Look who's come to see you.' At least the nurse remembered who he was, calling him Mr O'Grady. His mother was in her room this time, a tiny overheated space not much bigger than a ship's cabin, with a bed, an armchair and a television. The book at her bedside was called *The Belstone Fox*. What possible interest it could have for her he could not fathom. She had barely seen a field in her life. Her lunch had been taken in bed and the half-eaten remains lay on an invalid tray, which the nurse took away. The television was on, showing afternoon racing.

O'Grady told her about America. 'I drove a car with big fins,' he said. 'And they have giant supermarkets and the women are fabulous dancers.'

It was an exhausting business because his mother made no contribution. He came to the conclusion that he was getting in the way of her watching the racing, so shut up. He wasn't aware until it was half over that the race on was the one Shaughnessy had been talking about. The commentator urged on the horses, his voice rising to hysteria as the two leaders went for it neck and neck. Even his mother leaned forward and paid attention, clenching her fists at the excitement. The two horses crossed the line together and they had to wait for the result which went to a photo finish.

It was Shaughnessy's horse that won, and afterwards O'Grady was left with the feeling that things were being slotted into place around him, without him understanding why. The solitary life with no expectations that he had marked down for himself was not going to be as easy to achieve as he had thought.

After the surprise and excitement of the race – O'Grady had been yelling the horse on – he resolved again to keep to himself, to do the work he was being paid a pittance for, and to visit his mother regularly, whether or not she knew who he was. Like he had told Molly, he wanted quiet, and with that might come peace. The picture he had was of himself sitting content in the warmth of his room with a newspaper, his finger marking his place as he got up to feed the meter, with no one else there to bother him. Over the years he had learned a lot about small distances and the effort it took to go through some doors. He wanted to spend the rest of his life going through fewer doors, and knowing what was on the other side. A deck chair on an empty beach would be nice.

Apart from his duties around the house he managed to avoid everyone for several days. Molly was always in the kitchen when he and Kathleen were there and Shaughnessy never took breakfast. After his work was done he went to see his mother. The thinness of her white hair, skull gleaming beneath where it had been pressed flat at the back and missed by the comb, frightened him. When someone brought a two-week-old baby into the day room the residents stared at it as though something so tiny and young was beyond their comprehension. Several times his mother had appeared to tremble on the brink of saying something but never did until after the incident with the baby, when she leaned forward, fixed O'Grady with a querulous eye, and asked, 'Why were all the others taken?'

'What others?'

She looked at him like he was stupid.

When he fell he fell fast and hard, ambushed by Shaughnessy in the street late in the morning on the way back from Safeway, shopping bags in each hand. Shaughnessy's trilby was set at a jaunty angle and it was clear straight away why O'Grady had managed to avoid him. Shaughnessy hadn't been around because he was in the middle of a bender, and jubilant.

'Where've you been? You were supposed to be with us celebrating. Kathleen's saying you're behaving like a woman in purdah. I told you we'd be in clover.' He did a little jig, then produced a wad of money from his back pocket and waved it at O'Grady. 'I'm a man of my word. See, I've been keeping it separate.'

Passers-by were starting to stare. In his excitement Shaughnessy was shouting loud enough to compete with the street preachers who used the precinct further down the High Road. Trying to refuse, O'Grady gestured with his hands to show they were full. Shaughnessy responded by stuffing the notes into his coat pocket.

'Take it, man, it's only money and yours for the price of a drink.'

O'Grady lifted the shopping bags again. 'I can't, I'm busy.'

He was unable to say why his resolve broke. It had something to do with not wanting passers-by to gawp at him, laden down with plastic bags like a housewife, and Shaughnessy treating him like a poodle. He had a flash of irritation at making himself so beholden to Molly all the time. The money felt easy and good in his pocket and Shaughnessy gave him an out by saying he could make it a quick one. O'Grady told himself that was the answer. Just the one.

It wasn't until he noticed something melting in one of the bags and leaking onto the carpet that he realised how much time had passed. The bags were to do with him, he knew that, though how exactly he could not remember. Shaughnessy's voice came at him from a long way off. 'The only real mortal sin according to my dear departed mother – gone all these years, God rest her soul – is drinking in the afternoon. Cheers! And in the middle of Lent!'

The clock slid across the wall. O'Grady shut one eye and it stopped. 'Jesus, is that the time?'

He could barely recollect the last thing they had talked about. Each time the conversation changed he lost the thread. He had no idea what they had been on about. He supposed they had end-lessly replayed the race. That would be it, he decided.

Shaughnessy seemed to be speaking with the aid of a wah-wah pedal. 'Ach, tell her where to get off, that's what I would do. You're the one that fucking came back to lend a hand, so she can bloody well respect that once in a while.'

In the toilet the sudden flushing of the urinal alarmed him and he sprayed his shoes. In his impatience to be done he finished before he was ready and felt his trousers damp. There was some-thing about pub toilets; they could never be mistaken for any other sort. He tried to keep the thought in his head so he could tell Shaughnessy. Shaughnessy would understand.

Back at the table he grew distracted by the sharp line of a shadow high on the side of a building over the road. The lower part of the pub's windows was curtained off from the street. Shaughnessy's monologues washed over him. There were little puddles round his beer mat. Next time he'd piss in the glass and drink it back down, cutting out the middle man and saving him-self a lot of money. Money frightened him in some way. Now that he had none. When he'd had it he had thought it would be there for ever, telling his daughter they'd be riding the money train.

He heard Shaughnessy saying, 'Maureen, I must say you're looking fucking great today.'

O'Grady looked up. Shaughnessy appeared to be talking to several young women – in fact only two once he had them in focus – both considerably underdressed for the weather, sunny or not. The nipples on one jutted proud through her blouse and O'Grady felt a jab of lust that reminded him of hot-wiring a car. At the same time he wanted the women to go away, but Shaughnessy had other ideas.

'Meet Maureen,' he said to O'Grady. 'And Kathleen you know in her domestic capacity. Come and park those fantastic arses here, girls. You're looking at two fellows with fat wallets.'

O'Grady fetched the drinks. He still had over a hundred pounds. He was doing well. A hundred pounds was a handy bonus and it wasn't as if he was saving up. Back at the table Shaughnessy was arguing with the women. They had been expecting to meet in another pub. It was then that O'Grady realised they were drunk. Kathleen had a glint in her eye and was recklessly dressed in a short skirt and what his mother would have called kinky boots. She was bare-legged and wasn't wearing tights. O'Grady was not sure how to equate this exotic creature – who had on black eye-liner that was flicked up at the sides and bright lipstick which he wanted to see messed – with Kathleen in the kitchen.

Maureen was complaining of the cold.

'Thin-blooded, that's your trouble,' said Shaughnessy. 'Look at me, never worn a vest in my life.'

Kathleen nudged O'Grady. 'Your sister's on the warpath.'

'Ferchrissakes!' interrupted Shaughnessy. 'Let the man enjoy his drink in peace and give me one of those fags of yours.'

Kathleen rolled her eyes at O'Grady, who was enjoying the banter. 'Given up smoking, he says. Given up buying, more like, and on the scrounge ever since.'

O'Grady badly wanted to be able to say something that would make them laugh. Shaughnessy helped himself to a cigarette with a wink to O'Grady, who puzzled over its meaning, whether it was to do with the two of them being on the same wavelength, or if it was a wink of encouragement regarding Kathleen. O'Grady gathered that Maureen was with Shaughnessy, which was a shame because he was more curious about her with her clothes peeled off than Kathleen.

'What's that?' yelped Kathleen suddenly, pointing at Shaughnessy.

'What's what?' Shaughnessy was holding his cigarette from underneath, smoking it at a jaunty angle like he was in a cocktail bar or in a fancy play.

'What you're wearing.'

At that point O'Grady's afternoon fell apart. He clung on to Kathleen and Shaughnessy's unfolding conversation as though by sheer mental effort he could force it to blot out what was happening on the other side of the pub. From the reaction in the other room, it looked like the temperance society had just marched in, but it was only Molly blazing disapproval. O'Grady heard Shaughnessy protesting loudly. 'What do you think it is? It's my fucking shirt.'

Molly had not seen him yet and Kathleen was on the attack, her voice raised. 'I can see it's your fucking shirt, you old get, but what's that under your fucking shirt?'

O'Grady took her line for a prompt, and decided to use the distraction of their argument to slide unnoticed onto all fours to pick up his shopping bags, with luck at the exact moment Molly looked over, so she'd miss him. He could sneak out while the others were still squabbling.

He heard the smile in Shaughnessy's voice as he announced smoothly, 'It's my tee-shirt, you daft bitch.'

'Get away, you old goat,' Kathleen shouted back. She was being too loud, O'Grady thought, anxious that her racket was about to wreck his plans. 'It's a fucking vest! "Never worn one in my life," he says.'

O'Grady squeezed his eyes shut, wishing they would all go away. He heard Shaughnessy chirpily asking Molly what she was having to drink, and asking loudly if anyone had seen O'Grady. He felt Kathleen dig him with her foot while trying to stifle her giggles.

'Ah, there you are, Pat,' said Shaughnessy with the air of a man who thought it quite normal that O'Grady should choose to be on his hands and knees. O'Grady turned his head and saw Molly glaring down.

'Look at the state of you. Don't let me see you again until you're sober and ready to apologise.'

He thought it might lessen his humiliation if he helped her with the shopping bags but she snatched them away and marched out, with Shaughnessy announcing loud enough for her to hear, 'Well, Pat, it looks like you've got the rest of the day off.'

The women fell about laughing and laughed even harder when O'Grady said, 'Ah fuck it, I'm fucked now.' Realising that he had said something funny helped to lessen the shame. Once he would not have given Molly the light of day. He stood, none too steadily.

'Kathleen, lend the man a hand,' said Shaughnessy.

'Help him yourself,' replied Kathleen tartly, lighting another cigarette and snatching the packet away from Shaughnessy.

'Be an angel,' Shaughnessy cajoled. 'It'll be worth your while.'

O'Grady stood swaying, watching Shaughnessy beckon Kathleen. They whispered together while Maureen gave an unfocused grin in his direction. She had said even less than he had. The white of Kathleen's blouse stretched tight across her back and O'Grady tried to imagine the feel of her skin. Shaughnessy winked again, this time at Kathleen. O'Grady knew the wink was about him and wondered how much Shaughnessy knew.

The next thing, they were in a mini-cab, just him and Kathleen. He tried to remember if they had gone on somewhere else first and what he might have told her. His head felt as though it was wrapped in cotton wool and about to explode at the same time. Kathleen was leaning against him, holding on to his arm and cramping his space. He could smell perfume on her. Her eyes were shut and he thought she had passed out. He shut his eyes, too, and tried to remember if he had asked Shaughnessy why he had been placing bets for him. If he had, he couldn't recall Shaughnessy's answer. Smooth and slippery, no doubt.

He got his arm back from Kathleen, and checked his money. He had no idea how much he had left or, come to that, where they were going. The streets were dark and the side window steamed up. At a guess he would have said Kentish Town.

He thumbed through the notes.

'You have got a fat wallet, mister,' said Kathleen. 'Where are we going?'

The driver interrupted, adding to Kathleen's question. 'You still haven't said where to.'

O'Grady noticed him properly for the first time. He was Asian, Indian or Pakistani, and spoke in a sing-song voice. Immigrants were getting more confident, he thought. The Irish, when they first came over, had all mumbled like they didn't want anyone to hear.

He had no idea where he wanted to go. All he knew was that he didn't want to get out, and didn't know how to undo the situation with the woman, whatever that was. A flash of Molly standing over him forced him to remember what he had been trying so hard to forget. He sighed and fished out a five-pound note, passing it to the driver. 'Just drive.'

A couple of large furry dice hung from the rearview mirror and the seats had shaggy covers in a tiger-skin pattern that did nothing for O'Grady's blurred vision. 'Cruising around. This is the life, eh?' said Kathleen.

Afterwards O'Grady couldn't remember exactly when they had kissed, then or after driving some more. He had been aware of wanting to but wasn't sure if that's what they were there for. She was barely more than a kid. Just before they did, she asked him to shift over and put his arm round her because she was cold. Then it was less a question of kissing than of gluing their lips together. The sensation was warm and sweet and sticky, and he could taste her drink. After so much fantasising, it was more awkward than he remembered. Their teeth scraped and her weight felt uncomfortable against him. Drink made them clumsy and O'Grady didn't know what to do with his hands.

'I've the painters in,' she whispered, 'but I could give you a good tonguing.'

O'Grady saw the driver's eyes bulge in the rearview mirror. He didn't know what to say and wondered what she wanted from him. He let her offer ride and eventually asked, 'How old are you?'

'Who's counting?' she answered, sounding sulky. 'How old are you?'

'Too old,' answered O'Grady truthfully. To the driver he said, 'Turn left at the lights, then first right.'

He directed them to an estate in Camden Town. Kathleen started to look expectant, like they might be going to a party or a drinking house. O'Grady wiped the condensation from the window and, seeing the familiar sign for Bethlehem House, told the driver to stop and wait.

It got complicated after that. He said he'd be back in five minutes. The driver insisted he settle the existing fare and they had a quarrel over how much he had paid. Kathleen interrupted, claiming O'Grady had handed over five pounds on getting in the cab. O'Grady couldn't care either way. He could see Kathleen was disappointed he wasn't standing up for himself. Once he would have stuffed the man's furry dice down his throat, but that was then. When Kathleen made to get out he told her to wait. He didn't know what on earth he was doing, if he was honest with himself, which was probably why a simple thing like paying for a taxi was so close to getting out of hand.

Some things never changed. The buildings lifts were broken. The door to one was jammed open and O'Grady could smell the piss from yards away. The flat was several flights up and he kept having to stop to catch his breath. Drunk or not, he was out of condition.

When he got there he lost his nerve and it took him several minutes to get up the courage to ring the bell. A window on the landing showed the lights of the city. O'Grady was struck by his own insignificance and how absurd the altercation in the taxi had been. For some reason the view made everything about who he was seem questionable.

He rang the bell, waited, and rang again. Someone was in, because he could hear the television. He rang a third time. He was on the point of leaving when, as an afterthought, he lifted the letter flap and found a pair of eyes staring back at him. They were hostile rather than frightened, as was the old woman's voice. 'What you want?'

O'Grady tried to sound conciliatory. 'Please, I want to talk to you, about the people who lived here before.' She continued to stare and said nothing. 'It's important,' he added, 'I find out where they are.'

The old woman cocked her head, considering, while O'Grady tried to make himself appear as plausible as the circumstances would allow. Then she said, with a venom that surprised him, 'Fuck off, you great drunken Irish git, before I call the police.'

Too tired to argue, he walked back down to the cab and gave Kathleen another five-pound note, saying, 'That should be enough to get you a ride home.'

She shrugged, dismissing him. Her fare was the least he could offer after wasting her day, her disdainful expression told him. O'Grady watched the departing cab. One of its brake lights was not working.

The next morning Kathleen looked at him when he came in the kitchen, only to make a point of ignoring him. She was the least of his problems. O'Grady's largely sleepless night had been spent deciding what he would say to Molly. Molly was giving him the silent treatment along with Kathleen, and he served breakfast trying to tell himself that there was something funny about their frostiness in a sweating hot kitchen.

Molly waited until he was done serving before announcing within Kathleen's earshot, 'I'll not say anything about yesterday except in future you keep your drinking to your own time.'

O'Grady stood twisting a dishcloth in his hands, partly as a way of trying to remember his prepared speech, while also wishing it was his sister's neck. 'I was thinking,' he said slowly, 'I should give notice or whatever you want to call it. I had no right asking you to take me back and I'm no good at what you want me for anyway.'

Molly stared at him incredulously. 'Where would you go? And what would you do?'

'Still,' he mumbled, 'you'd be better off without me.'

'I can't manage alone and that's a fact.' With that she turned away and O'Grady saw that for her it was the end of the matter. He hadn't been prepared for her refusal. His mind had gone blank, and all he wanted was for the next thing to happen so he could forget about this.

Molly paused on her way out and briskly repeated, 'I can't manage alone and that's a fact.'

Out of the corner of his eye he saw Kathleen pulling a face as Molly added, not unkindly, 'There's nothing out there for the likes of you. You could make a start painting those rooms I told you about.'

With Molly gone, Kathleen muttered, more to herself than to him, 'Worse than the nuns.'

'Worse than prison,' he responded flatly and was rewarded with a sharp look of curiosity.

There were two rooms at the back of the house Molly wanted decorated. She showed him the cupboard where the rollers and brushes were. After inspecting the rooms he said he would hire a steam cleaner as the job ought to be done properly. Molly was concerned at the extra cost and he shrugged and said he'd pay for it himself, out of the winnings Shaughnessy had given him. He wondered if she would object, saying she didn't want gambling money associated in her place, but she said nothing.

The rooms were below his. They had once been one large room, now divided into two narrow singles. At that time of year they tended not to be let. There were several layers of wallpaper, going back to when the house had been built, over a hundred years before, and there were parts where the plaster had gone. The woodwork, beneath its last couple of coatings, had been covered with a varnish that turned as sticky as treacle when he tried to strip it. He wondered how many people had used the room, and what kind of families had lived there when it was new. His guess was that they would have been the better off shop-keepers, prosperous enough not to live over the premises. The house was close to the High Road and the front had been made to look more substantial than the villas further down.

Once he had scraped down to the woodwork he sometimes found the carpenter's pencilled measurements. To do the job properly would, he reckoned, take two weeks. Molly, when he told her, looked dubious and he could see she suspected him of slacking.

'It's not just a question of slapping a coat of paint on,' he said, glad that for once her opinion counted for less than his.

He took pride in doing the job properly, making the rooms good. He wondered if anyone had been born in them, or died, and about the sex that had gone on, and what sort. Solitary for the most part, he supposed, as they had been singles since becoming lets. As a boy he had once overheard two of the cleaners complaining about the state of the sheets in the single rooms.

'Have you noticed how,' one had said, 'the stain always looks like the map of Ireland?' When he asked his mother what they had meant he got his ear cuffed and was made to wash out his mouth with salt water.

Several days passed quietly and for the first time since being back O'Grady felt a rhythm to his life. After doing the breakfast he went upstairs and got on with the rooms. It took him more than two days to get all the paper off the walls and ceilings. With the steamer the room soon became like a Turkish bath. The machine hissed and gurgled, cutting off all outside sound. Once or twice he was surprised by the sight of Molly like a ghost in a mist come up to see how he was getting on. The first time he jumped at the sight of her. The next time she knocked and asked him if he wanted a cup of tea. He was touched by the offer.

In the middle of the day he broke to eat in one of the cafés in Willesden Lane and take a bus up to his mother. He got into the habit of buying her a newspaper and taking back the one from the day before for himself to read in the evening. His mother never acknowledged his presence, in retaliation, he presumed, for all the years he had not been in touch. He knew she could still speak because he'd asked the woman running the home and was told, 'She speaks well enough when she wants.' O'Grady decided to match his mother's stubbornness. He'd come every day until she paid him attention.

After finishing work he went for a walk, regardless of the weather. It was dark by then and he took to the empty back-streets. After them the sight of the busy lit-up main road was always welcome. He avoided the pubs and in the evening sat and read the day before's paper from cover to cover.

One afternoon, after crossing the park that took him from West Hampstead back to Kilburn, O'Grady passed the big dance hall that had been a regular feature of his youth. Fridays and Saturdays, he and the other lads had spent their evenings getting legless, eyeing the girls – who were much bolder than them – and generally being useless about dancing. Even Molly had sometimes turned up for these evenings and jived with the other girls. Thinking of her now, the idea of it was almost inconceivable. Molly with her beehive and flouncy skirt, mouthing the moves to herself while overhead the big mirrored ball caught the light as it slowly turned.

O'Grady was surprised to hear music coming from the dance hall. It seemed too early. He went in, still ambushed by the sudden flood of memories. At the time he had always thought of those evenings as fraught with potential embarrassment. It jolted him to realise that he now looked back on them as one of the few good times. There had been condoms in top jacket pockets that never got used, and the misery of buying them in the first place.

There was no one in the foyer. The music coming from upstairs was formal, a waltz. He went up, curious. Voices came to him from thirty years before. 'Arey dancen, Vinnie?' The question had been asked of a red-haired lad he had never seen before or since who had shown them all up by cutting a dash on the floor with the girls, taking them one after the other, but dancing mostly with Tommy Doyle's girl, and Tommy muttering within O'Grady's hearing, 'I'll fill in his card for him, you mark my words.' O'Grady had heard that after the dance Doyle and his gang had put the boy in hospital.

'I must say you're looking fucking great tonight, Maureen.' This had been said to a girl he was trying to date, by Eileen who worked on a vegetable stall. The girls had always had a cheerful directness that the boys never managed, and a brisk assumption that boys in general, and Irish boys in particular, were useless. Part of the problem was that the girls were keen on long petting sessions which stopped short of the technicalities of mortal sin, and this required a stamina and patience most of the boys couldn't match.

O'Grady opened the door to the upstairs hall. It was as he remembered, down to the mirrored light. There were maybe twenty people in the centre of the room, most of them the same age as himself. He had stumbled across a dancing class, he realised. Nobody paid him any attention as he sat down on one of the seats along the wall.

He watched as the couples rose and fell, reminding him of ships carried by a kind sea. Standing in the middle was a short, older woman with smoked glasses and a walking stick which she used to beat time. O'Grady wondered if she would recognise him. It was one of the shameful secrets of his childhood that at the age of eleven his mother had dragged him off to dancing classes, for reasons he had never been able to fathom, and had sat in on them to make sure he had attended the full course. Miss Lantorn was the name of the teacher and he had been mortified when she had singled him out to help her demonstrate the steps. There had been six girls in the class and one other boy, a spotty, effeminate

English lad who was keen to learn. The deal O'Grady had made with his mother was that in return for going she was to promise not to tell a soul. He had resented the experience most of all because he knew it would not help him achieve what he secretly wanted, which was to be as confident and outgoing as his Uncle Harry, his mother's brother, who literally waltzed his way through life. Uncle Harry came to stay twice a year and O'Grady had memories of him dancing round the kitchen with Molly and his mother, then using a chair to demonstrate a fancy new step from South America. Uncle Harry was a travelling salesman, selling cement, whose spare time was taken up with competition dancing. There was a wife but she was always too ill to travel. 'Never trust a man that doesn't dance,' he had once announced to O'Grady, who even at his age had thought anyone would have been a fool to trust Uncle Harry. Harry sang and Harry danced and told stories, and occasionally slipped O'Grady half a crown.

Harry's approval was enlisted when it came to the dancing classes. 'In a few years' time you'll thank your mother, when you start to get interested in girls.' But it hadn't turned out like that. He had merely vowed never to dance again, and in the climate in which he had grown up that had not been a hard promise to keep.

Sitting in the dance hall, watching, he regretted his decision. It had taken him in a direction which had seemed a much tougher line then but now could be seen as the one of least resistance. He had become one of the boys.

Shaughnessy was conspicuous by his absence, and after a few days O'Grady started to think that he had moved on. The mechanical task of decorating, with its stages of visible improvement, left him feeling guardedly optimistic.

In the kitchen he and Kathleen developed a routine that involved making only general observations, and she didn't clean his room any more. Shaughnessy's name was not mentioned.

One afternoon he returned to the dance hall and found out from the office that Miss Lantorn held her classes twice a week. O'Grady doubted if he'd have the nerve to go back. As far as the thought formed in his head, it was the fluid movement of the dance he envied. His own life had been all jabs and elbows and, more recently, inertia.

The morning he went to buy the paint he thought he spotted Shaughnessy on the other side of the High Road and instinctively ducked away down a side street to avoid him. Before leaving Morans he checked carefully that the way was clear. But Shaughnessy was cleverer than he'd thought, because just as he was turning into Dyne Road the familiar voice nailed him.

'I hear your sister's got you decorating.'

O'Grady stopped. Feeling the weight of the paint cans, he thought of wrapping one round Shaughnessy's head. He walked on, but Shaughnessy was not so easily discouraged and he soon caught up and fell into step. 'By the way, I apologised for leading you astray. Bowed and scraped. What is it in particular she has against you? Is it her time of life, or what?' O'Grady refused to be drawn. 'Ah, Pat, you've a great talent for making a question sound rhetorical.' Shaughnessy gave a mirthless grin and pointed to the paint. 'Were you ever professional?' Again O'Grady said nothing. 'Were you never a pro?' Shaughnessy continued archly. 'As a matter of fact, what did you do, aside from getting your diploma in hoovering?'

O'Grady ploughed on, head down. When he next looked Shaughnessy had vanished. For a moment he wondered if he was not awake but sleeping and in a dream.

O'Grady was sure Shaughnessy was plotting something. He sensed it in their meeting and in Kathleen's sudden change of attitude. She had taken to cleaning his room again – not that he ever found her in it – and once or twice stopped and chatted while he was painting. Most of the time she said the first thing that came into her head, which O'Grady found entertaining enough. He envied her ability to talk on without getting tongue-tied, and the sound of a woman's voice was a pleasant relief from so much silence. She told him about the films she went to see and her favourite actors, and the stories of the soap operas she watched on television, which were so crammed with bizarre incident that they sounded more like *The Arabian Nights* than the East End or Manchester. She told O'Grady he reminded her of Clint Eastwood.

'In age, maybe,' he said, trying not to sound flattered.

'You can see he's a big fellow, unlike most of them. Robert Redford's a midget.'

Thanks to growing up with five elder brothers, Kathleen had a preference for Westerns and regretted their going out of fashion. 'There's *Silverado*, I suppose. It didn't open yet, but I hear it's awful, even if it has got Kevin Costner. Do you go to the pictures much?'

'Not for a while now and never much.'

'Would you come with me one evening? Maureen hates going

and I feel an idiot sitting there on my own, and at the State you end up getting pestered all the time.'

O'Grady couldn't tell if she was offering him a date or just wanted company. He decided from the way she rattled on she was saying it for the sake of saying it, rather than meaning it.

O'Grady took to cautious drinking again, starting by way of celebration on the evening he finished preparing the rooms. He stopped after two. He drank in the Black Lion, aware that there was a possibility of running into Shaughnessy, but he felt sufficiently resolved to take the risk. On the first evening Maureen and Kathleen clattered in, all dolled up, and exchanged pleasantries. He bought them a drink and made his excuses. Maureen raised her glass. 'The man's a gent. Are you sure you won't stay?'

She batted her eyes at him comically and made him laugh. He was tempted to join them. Later they were going dancing, she said.

Kathleen pulled a face. 'It's all right for her, she can dance. All I can manage is hopping from one foot to the other.'

O'Grady looked in again the next night, hoping they would be there. He could have arranged something with Kathleen, he realised, yet had preferred to leave it to chance. He suspected this might have something to do with hoping to run into Maureen on her own.

After a clean run of several nights, O'Grady had a hunch that Shaughnessy would be in the Black Lion and he went instead to the mock-Tudor pub by the gates to the cemetery. It was a Thursday night so the pub was busy. By the time he had finished his second beer there were two other couples at his table and drinkers were standing several deep at the bar. It meant he did not spot Shaughnessy until he was returning his glass. He cursed his luck – right hunch, wrong pub. He cursed himself, as well, for taking back his glass instead of walking out. Shaughnessy was deep in conversation with another man with his back to O'Grady, who quickly turned away hoping to lose himself in the crush.

He had managed only a couple of paces before Shaughnessy was pulling at his shoulder and beaming at him. 'If I wasn't so thick-skinned I'd think you were avoiding me.'

'I am,' said O'Grady curtly.

'Have you seen who's at the bar?'

O'Grady glanced reluctantly towards Shaughnessy's companion, who still had his back to him. There was something depressingly familiar about the blazer and thinning hair scraped across his scalp in an up-and-over. When the man turned O'Grady's worst suspicions were confirmed.

It was Tel, though if they had passed on the street O'Grady would have had trouble recognising him. Years of hard drinking had wrecked the few looks he'd had. More than ever his head looked like a skull on a stick. The blazer was probably the same one O'Grady remembered, from a brief stint as secretary of an Essex golf club which had been abruptly terminated after Tel and O'Grady were found passed out after a night spent drinking the bar dry.

Tel's face lit up on seeing O'Grady.

'Hello, mate,' he said. His expression was still one of dog-like devotion, which was misleading because Tel had a nasty streak and could turn vicious. He stood there, swaying, his silly drunk's grin plastered across his face, while Shaughnessy smirked as though he'd just pulled a rabbit out of a hat.

'Long time no see.' Tel stumbled slightly and used O'Grady's arm to steady himself.

'Take your fucking hand off me,' said O'Grady. He pushed him away and walked out, leaving Tel looking hurt.

The cold night air was like a slap in the face after the overheated pub. O'Grady had gone about thirty yards when he heard Shaughnessy bleating his name. Tired of being followed, he strode back to Shaughnessy. Seeing his anger, Shaughnessy came to a nervous halt and flinched in anticipation of the blow that wasn't delivered, though O'Grady made to hit him.

'Don't do anything senseless, now. Tel said you had a flaming temper.'

O'Grady pulled back. His breath showed ragged in the cold air. He carefully put his bunched fists in his coat pockets.

'Spit it out,' he said. 'What's on your mind?'

No longer in danger of being hit, Shaughnessy reverted to his usual crafty self and said, 'Oh, it's of no consequence really. Tel was telling me about this Irish geezer – the family came from Donegal, I believe.'

He shrugged to say that was all. O'Grady took his fists out of his pockets and Shaughnessy, taking the hint, went on in a rush. 'The fellow did a bank job. Donkeys years ago. With Tel and a couple of other Cockneys. Got himself picked up straight after – the others never were – and he went down for a long stretch and never got paid. He's still owed. Do you know this story?'

'Go on.'

'This is according to Tel, at any rate. The thing is, Tel's owed as well. That's the point. They diddled him, too.'

'And what's Tel done about it?' asked O'Grady, realising he was betraying a curiosity he had been trying so hard to deny.

Shaughnessy shook his head. 'Nothing. He's cleaning windows when he's sober enough to climb a ladder.'

'And blathering to anyone who'll listen.'

On the other side of the road a number eight bus raced past, all lit up and totally empty.

'Christ, man,' said Shaughnessy. 'You saw him. He's stocious most of the time, ginned out of his head. He says the Mick is out, and this big streel is coming back to claim what's his, and then we'll see the fur fly.'

O'Grady stared at his shoes. 'It's an interesting story,' he eventually said. 'But it seems to me you're missing a Mick.'

'Tel says you're the man,' said Shaughnessy, an edge of panic to his voice now the little tower of dreams he had been building with Tel was in danger of collapse.

'I was in America, remember? Ask my sister.'

He turned away and started walking down towards the High Road, ignoring Shaughnessy calling after him.

'I've seen him.' Shaughnessy raised his voice, making sure the words carried. 'The big slabber's behaving like he's put a pistol-shot through his own memory. Big man, my arse!'

O'Grady kept walking.

He got to the supermarket early, but when it came to paying there was a long queue and only one till. Then two more opened and the able-bodied shoppers scattered to join them, leaving O'Grady stuck with the dodderers. The already slow process of checking out was slowed down even more by the dodderers being too scared or cautious to get their money out until their total had been rung up. Then they fumbled with gnarled, arthritic hands, paying with agonising slowness, offering endless amounts of change, enough to fill a small bucket, which had to be recounted several times. At O'Grady's turn the checkout girl looked at his basket, pointed to a large sign overhead and recited, 'Express checkout, nine items or less.'

All the tills were open now and busy. Moving to another would add at least twenty minutes before he was clear. Sensing his indecision, those behind him let out a collective sigh, and an old man pushed past to claim his place.

'Excuse me,' said O'Grady with what was left of his patience. 'Were you not taught any manners?'

'You heard her, mate. Wrong queue.'

Perhaps because the man had the same weaselly intonation as Tel, O'Grady brought his foot down on the man's instep with enough pressure to make him whimper. The rest of the queue went goggle-eyed. O'Grady turned and banged down nine items on the checkout belt, counting each one aloud.

The checkout girl sulkily rang them up. When she was nearly done, O'Grady added another tin and stared at her, daring her not to take it. The line behind him was torn between exasperation and bored excitement at the prospect of a bit of drama. He heard the word 'bully' and the old man whose foot he had stepped on started to puff up with indignation as he sensed the others uniting.

But the checkout girl proved bloody-minded. She ignored the extra item and rang up his total. When O'Grady picked up the tin again and banged it down everyone grumbled aloud.

A tall youth in a brown uniform with 'Security' written above his breast pocket pushed through the crowd to see what the trouble was. He looked very young with his spots and sticking-out Adam's apple. O'Grady abandoned the shopping and started to walk away. When the security guard tried to stop him, O'Grady paused long enough to tell him to back off, which he had the sense to do.

Later on, O'Grady thought of the incident as a turning point. It released something, made him see that his decision not to act was eating away at him. There was no such thing as a clean break, he told himself, and it was foolish to pretend otherwise.

Kathleen was starting to give him sly looks, and he thought of her offer in the minicab. Doing breakfast he found himself studying her surreptitiously, and fantasising. From watching her eat, after they had done with serving, he guessed she would also have a healthy appetite when it came to sex. But, if there was anything between them, he did nothing about it, hoping she would give him a clearer sign. When she didn't he decided he had been fooling himself.

Waiting at the stop for the thirty-one bus, O'Grady could see Shaughnessy on the other side of the road, in the betting shop. Shaughnessy had been following him since the encounter with Tel, he was sure of it now. They had spoken only once, when O'Grady ran into him on the High Road outside Iceland. Since the altercation at Safeway O'Grady had switched to the Iceland store further up the road. Shaughnessy had raised his hat on his way past and muttered sarcastically, 'Nothing fucking ventured, nothing fucking gained.'

O'Grady waited a long time for the bus. The sun came out and lit up Shaughnessy in the betting-shop window. He made no effort to hide and even raised his hand in mock salute.

The bus took O'Grady over to Camden Town. He got off near the High Street and walked to Bethlehem House. The local newsagent still had the Irish name O'Grady remembered but the man running the shop was Indian.

'Where's old man Byrne?' asked O'Grady.

'I'm Byrne now,' said the man brightly, raising his eyes to the sky.

'Byrne's Irish,' said O'Grady, thinking the man was trying to make a fool of him.

'Yes, yes. Byrne's Newsagent and Tobacconist. I bought the whole business, lock, stock and barrel, when Mr Byrne died. His family didn't like the hours, you see.'

O'Grady said he was looking for someone from eight or nine years before, and the man shook his head gravely. 'Oh no, sir. Not that long ago. Three, four years, maybe. Sorry not to help.'

He asked around in shops and pubs, searching for anyone from the old days. In a laundrette he found a woman who had lived in the neighbourhood for years, but she didn't remember him. In the pubs he spotted background faces from the old days but they all shook their heads. A lot of the families had moved on, he was told, on account of 'the darkies'.

He made several trips to Camden Town and returned with nothing. It made him realise how few people he'd known during his time there. Most of his life had continued to centre on Kilburn and across into North Kensington.

His first significant lead came in a pub by the Euston railway line where he had drunk at one stage. It was a large place and had always had a quick turnover of staff, so he was surprised when the landlord remembered the woman who had been running the place in O'Grady's time. She was now over in a pub near the junction of Camden Road and York Way.

With Kathleen it happened without him expecting it. She was at his basin with rubber gloves on and a tin of Vim. At the sound of his coming in she looked at him in the mirror, then got on with her cleaning. O'Grady shut the door behind him and she looked up again and smiled. He stood watching her hands working at the basin, then found himself fixated by the nape of her neck. She was wearing her hair up, as she usually did when working.

Her hands paused when he touched her neck, then carried on. O'Grady was aware of the pulse of his blood and the noise of traffic outside. Part of him was scared after so long. He was just as worried that nothing happened to break the spell.

'Hadn't you better lock your door, mister?' she said, voicing his thoughts.

'Nobody'll come in,' he answered and she turned round and they kissed. Her tongue was in his mouth and he could hear her

peeling off the rubber gloves. He didn't trust himself to manoeuvre them to the bed, and she seemed to sense that, so they
used the basin to take her weight and she wrapped her legs
round him. Nor was she wearing knickers. O'Grady worried that
the whole thing was too fumbled and hurried, but she seemed
unbothered and took her pleasure with easy enjoyment, slowing
him down, telling him, steady on, it wasn't a race.

'This is the ticket,' she said and O'Grady sensed it was some
grand act of dreamy disobedience for her, her escape from the
drudgery of the everyday. All those hours he had tried to remember what it had felt like, how exactly, and now he was doing it
again he couldn't say, exactly. He thought of the blind man's
yellow shoes and other things to stop himself being too quick,
sure that Kathleen would gossip to her friends. He wondered
if she was anywhere near coming herself. By the end he still
couldn't tell. For all the relief, he wasn't sure if he wasn't more
confused than when he'd started.

For Kathleen there was little dwelling on the matter. She
gathered her cleaning materials, snapped back on the rubber
gloves and announced with a practical smirk, 'Confession for the
pair of us now.' Her briskness made O'Grady think he had failed
to satisfy and he mumbled, 'A bit quick,' to which her sure
reply, 'Practice makes perfect,' left him uncertain if he stood cor-
rected or whether it was a promise of more to come.

O'Grady went over to York Way straight afterwards, telling himself that he would make up the time to Molly in the evening. It
took him a couple of goes to find the right pub.

The woman he was looking for, he remembered holding court
on the customers' side of the bar while her husband did the
work. Her laugh was loud and frequent and helped to account
for the pub's success. It told everyone they were having a good
time. The contrast between her confident blonde hair and her
husband's dark slick-back had reminded him of old black-and-
white movies. The last time O'Grady had seen him he had
been sitting in his wife's seat, wearing carpet slippers with a

dark suit, clutching his head in his hands because she had left him for another landlord. Within three months the locals had all moved on and the man was gone as well, fired by the brewery, which brought in someone new to smarten the place up, without success.

O'Grady wasn't sure it was her, partly because she was behind the bar and not perched in front of it. The hair was now an extravagant black helmet, and her make-up looked like it had been applied in layers. It was barely noon and she was dressed for the evening, wearing a lot of gold and a jazzy silk blouse, all zigzags in copper and black, which reminded him of television interference. There were just the two of them in the pub, which from the look of it was struggling. He dithered over what to drink, as he was still uncertain if this was the woman. He asked for a bottle of lager, as a way of almost not drinking, and, while watching the woman tilt the glass and pour the beer, he asked, 'Excuse me, it's Carole, isn't it?'

'Who are you?' she answered sharply, then peered at him and did an exaggerated double take, followed by her familiar booming laugh. It had grown ragged and throaty. O'Grady reckoned she must be on at least forty a day.

'Blimey,' she said, 'time hasn't done you any favours.' The laugh was rolled out again, this time interrupted by a coughing fit. 'Join the club,' she said ruefully. 'What brings you back?'

'Just passing,' said O'Grady. She recognised him, but he doubted if she could place him. 'What are you having?' he added.

'A bit early for me, thanks, love.'

Behind the wall of perfume he could sense the loneliness coming off her. He wondered what had happened to the man she had run off with, or the man with the slick-back, come to that. She changed her mind about the drink, as O'Grady knew she would, with a pantomime of temptation getting the better of her. 'Well, just a teeny one for old times' sake.'

She fixed a vodka from one of the bottles hanging upside-down behind the bar. Those bottles and their optic measures summed up for O'Grady what was most satisfying about a pub: the promise and choice, the endless permutations and rituals to the straightforward objective of getting plastered.

Carole shovelled ice into her glass from a bucket, followed by a squirt of tonic from a hose attached to the bar. 'So, how have you been keeping?' she asked and O'Grady replied, 'Fair to middling,' and raised his glass.

'Cheers,' said Carole soberly, and O'Grady thought the day ahead looked awfully long. The conversation dried. An early regular came in and Carole went off gratefully to serve him.

Before leaving he told her what was on his mind. Carole made a great show of remembering. God help us, thought O'Grady, this was a woman who was supposed to have been a good friend. The best she could finally come up with was 'She's been gone a long time.'

'Do you know where?'

Carole gave another smoker's laugh. '"Up" was all she said, and I bet she did.'

'No Micks where she was going.'

He couldn't be bothered with the bit that tailed off into polite conversation, so he drank up and left. In the end neither had been pleased to see the other. Their meeting only emphasised how little had been achieved in the intervening years. There were no polite goodbyes beyond a brief nod.

That night O'Grady made a start on priming the woodwork, to make up for the time lost in the day. The rooms were lined with paper and in their uncoloured state reminded him of being inside a child's unused drawing book, with himself as a cartoon, his own edges sharper than usual. He was silently proud of his work. The paper was hung straight, the overlaps parallel and neatly finished off with a thin layer of filler to help hide the seams. Even Molly was impressed.

She came in that evening, surprised that he was still working. 'I thought you'd forgotten the lights,' she said, standing uncertainly in the doorway, then added, 'You're keeping queer hours.'

O'Grady shrugged and said, 'The window sashes need replacing.'

'You're looking, aren't you?'

For a while now, O'Grady had suspected she had guessed – Molly's antennae were always up – and he was surprised she didn't sound more critical. If anything, she seemed worried.

'Just looking,' he said casually, inspecting the windows, as if to say that he was more concerned about them. Again Molly's response was softer than he would have expected, a sigh of protective concern.

'Well, don't come crying to me when it blows up in your face.'

He wondered about her real feelings, under all the disapproval and resentment. Perhaps the two of them were closer than either would admit.

'Like I said, only looking.' He put the words together carefully, trying to make it clear to her that he wanted only to know where they were, nothing more. 'No harm will come of that.'

'No good, either,' replied Molly tartly, sounding more like her usual self. The speed of her reply took him by surprise and he found himself laughing.

'Ah, Molly. You always did have the last word.'

It wasn't often that he was as quick as her. Molly used words as a block against uncertainty, as a way of cutting out the to-and-fro. The uncharacteristic nature of their exchange had been noted by Molly, too, he saw, because as she left she gave him a rare smile.

The solidness of the empty rooms he was decorating was the only thing he felt secure with. Maybe Molly was right and the looking would turn to temptation. Perhaps his original plan to do nothing had been correct. Nothing came of nothing. As soon as you started asking questions, even if you told yourself you were going to do nothing about it, you were on the lookout and that changed everything. He sensed Shaughnessy waiting for him to make his move. As for Kathleen, he suspected he was making a mistake thinking that whatever was going on between them was only to do with them, rather than part of something else, to do with Shaughnessy, perhaps. In the minicab when she had put her tongue in his mouth, and again when he was worrying about the basin supporting her weight, he had asked himself why she was doing this for him, without finding an answer. Nevertheless, there seemed to be no tricks about her, and her easy accommodation of him suggested that she enjoyed guilt-free pleasure and would take it where she could, and he felt a complicity between them over being the odd ones out in his sister's house. And there was her carnal flesh, the thing of being inside a woman again after so long, and the solid weight of it. He had forgotten about that part. His prison fantasies had all been weightless, he realised. He kept hoping that he would surprise her in his room again, but it didn't happen. He thought of knocking on her door at night but her room was too close to

Molly's. A couple of times during the day they passed on the stairs but said nothing, and O'Grady wondered if there was a part of her that was shy.

In the end, for all the elaborations of his fantasies, the next move was straightforward. Returning one morning from Safeway, which he had started using again, O'Grady noticed that the State was showing the Western Kathleen wanted to see and he asked her if she wanted to go.

'I thought you'd never ask,' she said and in the cinema she looped her arm through his and wouldn't let him talk during the film. Afterwards, without either of them mentioning it, they took a short cut down an alley parallel to the High Road, a lovers' lane from his youth, and she remarked, 'Not much kissing in Westerns.'

He steered her into the shadows and kissed her like he was a teenager again, with a cock full of confidence, leaning against a wall. He felt her breasts and asked if she minded the cold and she laughed and said that was why her nipples were hard, and feeling him through the fabric of his trousers she laughed again and said, 'Aren't you the randy one.'

O'Grady waited for her in his room after making elaborate plans for them to return to the hotel separately. He left his door unlocked and turned the fire on to warm the room. He didn't know what to do with himself, whether to wait up for her or go to bed. Fifteen minutes passed. He started to feel foolish standing there, trying to kindle his lust. In the end, he got into bed, keeping his underwear on. He waited another fifteen minutes, then decided she had played him for a fool and wasn't coming.

He woke up at some point, angry at being stood up. Then he saw her, kneeling before the fire, naked from the waist up, looking at him. His mouth was thick with sleep. 'What time is it?'

'Two o'clock. Your sister had her light on till after one.'

He asked what she was doing sitting there. He had the impression she had been there some time. She told him she had been watching him sleep and hadn't wanted to wake him, which he took to mean that she'd had second thoughts and would have slipped away if he hadn't woken. But he was wrong because she said, 'Budge over. Not much of a bed.'

'Does Shaughnessy have a car?' he asked, his mind still not clear after waking up. The thought had been chasing him as he had surfaced. In his journeys around the city he had seen the same orange Datsun several times.

'Let's not bring Shaughnessy into this.'

He saw the car again in Quex Road, parked and empty. It was orange and pitted with rust. If it was Shaughnessy's, there was no sign of him. There was a crowd on the steps of the church, hanging around after mass. The last couple of Sundays O'Grady had made a point of going to an earlier mass than Molly, as well as the ten thirty with her, in order to scan the congregation for familiar faces. He'd stand a better chance going over to one of the churches in Camden Town, he told himself.

It was a lad of eighteen or so who gave him his first hope. He looked the same as when O'Grady had last seen him as a boy of seven or eight. The father had run a house-clearing business and looked just like the boy, with the same buck teeth and stuck-out ears. He had also had a nervous affliction that took the form of a permanent grin, which got him into trouble. O'Grady remembered being in a pub with him once and a big stereotype Cockney had asked what he thought was so funny, and O'Grady, who didn't like the look of the man, had made an argument of it, as it was clear that the Cockney was all front. Once he had been stood up to, the Cockney went whiny and apologetic, complaining that neither of them could take a joke. 'No offence, mate,' he kept repeating.

O'Grady asked after the lad's father and was told he had fallen off a roof seven years ago.

'Christ, I had no idea,' he said. He felt shaken for the first time in as long as he could remember.

He told the lad what he was looking for. 'Is it Michael?' he asked. He couldn't remember. It wasn't. It was Stephen. Stephen had no idea but said they should ask Theresa. Theresa was found.

She was deathly pale and extremely frail and looked about fourteen, though she carried a babe-in-arms. O'Grady recognised her from mass because the baby had spent most of the service wailing and he had watched her taking it to the back. He wondered if the child was Stephen's. People falling off roofs, babies being born: it was the stuff of newspapers, and he realised how much he had been missing, and missing its messy sprawl.

Theresa had grown up in Camden Town. O'Grady didn't remember her. She said she now lived in Kilburn but since the boom her side of the High Road was calling itself West Hampstead. She and Stephen were saving to buy somewhere. O'Grady was astounded. They looked too young to afford it. Now the baby was quiet she seemed happy to stand and chat all day. With her sense of purpose and talk of different types of mortgage and Stephen's accountancy exams she was like someone from an alien planet. There she was, barely eighteen or whatever, behaving like she had made a deal with life for exactly what she wanted. In O'Grady's day there had been no sense of any of that being available. If you avoided getting exploited you were lucky, and that was about all there was to be said for it. There was no question of marching up to the counter and ordering what you wanted without having to fight for it.

O'Grady said who he was. If Theresa knew anything about him, he figured it probably would be that he'd gone away. Knowing Maggie's social ambitions, prison would not have been mentioned. Theresa, it turned out, had been in the same class as Lily at the primary school. Theresa remembered Lily moving early.

This was what O'Grady wanted to know, where they had gone to.

But Theresa, who until then had been chatting on as though she remembered everything that had ever happened to her, grew vague, then was distracted by the baby starting to bellow. At that point her composure fell apart, leaving O'Grady secretly pleased, because such self-assurance was frightening in one so young.

She thought they had moved to somewhere starting with a 'w'. Wembley or Watford, maybe. She thought Watford, but seemed not at all sure.

'Walthamstow? Willesden?' prompted O'Grady. The baby was sounding like it was recycling the same scream on a loop. Theresa was close to panic and O'Grady could see he was about to lose her.

'Please,' he urged. 'It means a lot to me to know.'

Stephen was frowning at O'Grady, as if he had remembered something unpleasant about him.

'Wembley, I think,' said Theresa, obviously saying the first thing that came into her head. 'We spoke a bit on the phone. They had a phone where they went. But I never saw her.'

Their own phone would have been a big thing. The bane of O'Grady's life had been contacting anyone. The phone in the flat had been taken away and the telephone boxes never worked because they were always vandalised.

'Do you still have the number?' He knew the question was hopeless. The baby was being passed like a parcel between Stephen and Theresa in a futile effort to quieten it.

'It was years ago,' snapped Theresa. 'Try the phone book.'

'I did already.'

The gaps between the baby's whoops got longer and the volume lessened. Theresa and Stephen looked like they'd just gone five rounds with Sonny Liston. Unfortunately at that moment two fire engines decided to turn on their sirens in Quex Road, setting off the baby again.

O'Grady was sure he had glimpsed Shaughnessy standing across the road when he looked towards the fire engines. But when he walked to the spot Shaughnessy was gone and so was the orange car.

O'Grady took a bus in the direction of Wembley, with no hope of finding anything, more as a way of marking out the territory. He ended up in a new development off the North Circular Road consisting of a huge American-style supermarket, with neatly marked spaces for hundreds of cars. He had never seen anything like it. From what he could remember, the area had previously been good for nothing except lorry parks and bulldozed factory sites.

Even though it was a Sunday the store was open and most of the cars outside were shiny and new. O'Grady felt like an impostor without one. He could see Maggie shopping there and forced himself to go through the revolving doors. He could picture her with her shopping trolley, in there early before the crowds, browsing the aisles.

O'Grady realised he was looking at the future. The place was the size of an aircraft hangar and stocked with enough food to survive a nuclear war. Compared to the bad-tempered supermarkets of the Kilburn High Road, which were barely functional, this was something else − as serene as an empty motorway − a brightly lit, shiny space that was an open invitation to spend money. He saw shopping trolleys full to overloading, and stared at the orderly ransacking of the shelves. There was a whole trench devoted to expensive ready-made meals and aisles were given over to bottled water and wine. O'Grady was certain that this was what Maggie would have been imagining for herself all those years ago in Camden Town, and felt equally sure that, if he returned often enough, he would run into her again, looking spruced-up and smelling of expensive perfume.

As he crossed the car park back to the bus stop it started to rain. He stood in the shelter, the only one waiting, the past leaking into his thoughts. Lily would be nearly eighteen, her birthday in a matter of weeks.

O'Grady spotted an orange car approaching and at first thought it had to be coincidence. But, as the noise of the clapped-out engine grew louder, he saw the familiar figure behind the wheel and turned away, praying that he had not been spotted.

He heard the car go past. He was counting himself lucky when he heard a crashing of gears and when he looked up Shaughnessy was inexpertly reversing the car into the bus bay. Shaughnessy got out and stood grinning in the rain.

'I'm surprised you've not noticed me and my Sunny before, as orange as Paisley and just as knackered. We've been on your trail for days. Well, are you getting in?'

'Fuck off, Shaughnessy.'

Shaughnessy rode the insult, absent-mindedly kicking the bald front tyre. He looked at O'Grady and then at the empty road.

'People have died of waiting here for a bus.' He flipped the car keys at O'Grady who instinctively caught them. 'You drive.'

O'Grady had not held a set of car keys in years. Instead of throwing them straight back at Shaughnessy, as he should have done, he fingered them, wondering, all the while vaguely aware of Shaughnessy needling away. 'Isn't that what you used to do? For a living, I mean. Drive. Besides, I've not the faintest idea where the hell we are. Dodge City, for all I know.'

O'Grady was undecided between accepting Shaughnessy's invitation and punching his lights out. In the end he got in the car because by then Shaughnessy was clearly starting to think he would not. He brusquely ordered Shaughnessy to get in the back as he didn't want him sitting next to him in the front. Shaughnessy laughed and rubbed his hands. 'Ah, boys are boys.'

O'Grady adjusted the mirror, ignored the seatbelt, checked the controls and started the engine. The clutch and brake both felt set in sponge. He managed to pull away without stalling, but mangled his gear changes until he got the hang of things again.

It turned out to be surprisingly easy, like riding a bicycle or swimming, once learned never forgotten. In the rear mirror he could see Shaughnessy lolling on the back seat, looking pleased with himself. O'Grady thought of stopping and walking away, just to wipe the smirk off his face, but it was raining harder and he did not fancy getting wet.

They drove down a long, straight road, through an industrial estate, behind which stood the twin towers of the football stadium. They came to a small roundabout, the likes of which O'Grady had not seen before, more like a stud in the middle of the road. He hesitated and Shaughnessy mocked his uncertainty. 'Hands at ten to two. Mirror, signal, manoeuvre. Grand to have a set of wheels responding to your touch again, eh, driver?'

Shaughnessy leaned forward, hunched between the front seats, elbows resting on top. O'Grady could feel his right arm against his back and, when he started to talk, the man's breath on the back of his neck. He had been sucking a mint. O'Grady made a point of not looking in the mirror.

'Now, unlike you, driver, I do not believe that the past is a closed book, not where the balance of accounts is concerned.'

The sentence hung in the air. In spite of himself, O'Grady turned towards Shaughnessy, who said, 'Eyes on the road, remember. That's right. All coming back, eh?'

They drove past the empty stadium and turned right onto a main road. Shaughnessy, still leaning forward, kept up a running commentary in O'Grady's ear. 'Mind the lady and the pram. Slowing down for the zebra crossing, that's what I like to see. Tel's relying on you, you know that. Of course you do, you're just not admitting it.'

O'Grady wasn't, and wasn't going to allow Shaughnessy the satisfaction of hearing him say so. Shaughnessy rummaged for something and there was a flash of silver in the corner of O'Grady's eye and the smell of whiskey. 'You'll not be drinking and driving, of course. You do know what Tel's been saying? Tel was telling me—' Shaughnessy broke off with a wheezy laugh to signal his pun. 'Tel was saying to me that when the big man got back – when *you* got back – it would be like Jack Dempsey and Wyatt Earp all rolled into one and he was offering ringside seats. Fight of the century. And John and Ronnie would be picked up by the heels and shaken till the loot fell out of their pockets. Well, if that's the case, I'm Freddie and the fucking Dreamers, and are you changing into top or what?'

O'Grady was still in third gear. He ignored Shaughnessy and did nothing for several minutes, which passed in silence – amused for Shaughnessy, angry for O'Grady – until they came to an open stretch of road and O'Grady slammed the gear stick into fourth with the heel of his palm. Shaughnessy started whistling flatly, and irritatingly, through his teeth. The speed limit went up to fifty and O'Grady put his foot down. The accelerator responded like blancmange and the needle on the speedometer crawled towards forty. Shaughnessy stopped whistling and placed a hand on O'Grady's shoulder, to show that he was being both serious and sincere. 'Try as I might, I do not see much of the Jack Dempsey in you. A man retired hurt, maybe, and why not? I might not be too keen to look the world in the eye if they had done to me what they did to you. How long was it, Pat?'

O'Grady shrugged. Shaughnessy would know well enough.

'Say it anyway, Pat. Get it off your chest.'

'You know as well as I do.'

'Ten years, wasn't it?'

O'Grady nodded slightly and Shaughnessy slumped back, looking as shocked as if the time had been handed down to him. O'Grady looked in the mirror, saw Shaughnessy massaging his chest, and murmuring like he meant it, 'Ah, what a waste.'

It was the first time O'Grady had seen Shaughnessy anything other than ebullient. Sensing that he was being watched, Shaughnessy rallied, pointing and shouting, 'Look at that! Did you see that? Fucking cyclist. Shoot the lot of them, I say.'

The next time O'Grady looked in the mirror Shaughnessy appeared to be asleep. He drove out in the direction of Stanmore, as far as the A41, then stayed on that, towards Bushey and Watford. The first stretch was level and straight for several miles. It was where bikers had always gone to do the ton, O'Grady remembered, and there was a café where they used to gather called the Busy Bee. He knew that because he had always wanted a motorbike when he was young.

Before Watford he turned off and went back on the motorway. The Datsun was sluggish and barely managed fifty, which left them on the inside lane being overtaken by speeding drivers who passed with impatient confidence. From the feel of the car, O'Grady thought it probably hadn't seen a service in its life.

At the bottom of the motorway, it was a straight line back to Kilburn through Cricklewood, which was jammed with traffic, as always, and most of the drivers were more than usually aggressive because five minutes before they had been cutting down the motorway at ninety.

Traffic was at a standstill when Shaughnessy woke up. He looked around blearily and told O'Grady to take a right and cut through Neasden and down to Brondesbury. The silver hip flask was produced and a nip taken. He carried on from where he had left off. 'Jack Dempsey. Heavyweight champion of the world. Back when it counted. Unstoppable. Till Gene Tunney beat him. Twice. Psyched him out. Did they psych you out, Pat? Of course, Tunney was a college boy with the benefit of an edu–cay–shun that you and me and Dempsey never had. Not that Dempsey lacked manners. You know what he said to Tunney as they climbed in the ring at the second fight?' Shaughnessy prepared the way with a laugh. '"How are you, Gene?" and Tunney replied, "Quite well, Jack. And you?" Now there's class for you. And moments after they're brawling like a pair of stevedores.' Without pausing to draw breath, he started screaming at O'Grady about another cyclist. 'Go on, ram that bloody arse. Did you see that? Straight through a red. They think they're a bloody law unto themselves.'

Shaughnessy was soon laughing at his own apoplexy and encouraging O'Grady to join in, which he didn't. While they waited for the next set of lights, he hunched forward again, his voice confiding as he finally arrived at the kernel of all his blather. This was why they were there, O'Grady realised.

'Go on,' Shaughnessy cajoled, 'we can psych them out. They're just a couple of Cockney wide–boys, and you would only be asking for what's yours by rights. What are you waiting for?'

It took O'Grady a moment to see that Shaughnessy was referring to the lights. 'They're green, for God's sake, man.'

Without thinking, O'Grady grabbed Shaughnessy by the tie and pulled him forward, half throttling him, until his head was comically wedged between the dashboard and windscreen. Shaughnessy yelped and screamed that he had a weak heart, at which point the car behind started hooting for him to get a move on. O'Grady let go of Shaughnessy's tie, took him by the collar and drove his head against the dashboard, hard enough to stun him and shut him up.

Seeing the force with which O'Grady got out of the car, and the look of determination on his face, the driver behind, who had his window down to remonstrate better, quickly rolled it back up and banged the locks shut with his elbow. Faced with O'Grady the man turned rabbity.

O'Grady was close to laughing. The fellow in the car was now the centre of attention, which was the last thing he wanted, and in the Datsun Shaughnessy was flopped over the seat with his arse sticking out, and horns were blaring from the line of waiting traffic.

He thumped on the man's window, hard enough to make him flinch. 'How the hell am I supposed to drive in peace with him jabbering on' – he stuck a thumb in Shaughnessy's direction – 'and you tooting your horn?'

The man stared straight ahead, blinking hard like he was trying to will O'Grady away. O'Grady left him to it, got back in the Datsun and accelerated away through a red light, cutting through the cross-traffic. Shaughnessy was slumped back on the rear seat, looking grey. 'Law unto yourself, eh, Pat? That's a short fuse you've got there.'

'My name is not Pat,' O'Grady replied.

'Pat, Mick, what's the difference?'

They were somewhere round the back of Willesden Green. O'Grady wasn't quite sure where, though it looked vaguely familiar. It turned out to be the road where his mother was, except they were approaching from the opposite direction to the way he normally came.

Eventually O'Grady said, 'I don't care about the money. I don't give a threepenny damn about any of it.'

He was expecting another smart answer, but Shaughnessy took his time and sounded subdued. 'I don't know a man worth his salt who does. I thought we were talking about self-respect.'

O'Grady had no answer to that.

He had to decide between turning back towards Cricklewood or going right and down through Brondesbury. Brondesbury had big houses and wide streets and made no sense in relation to the surrounding areas, which were all much more run-down. Brondesbury was where the Tommy Doyles of this world ended up.

Shaughnessy began coughing and couldn't stop. By the time O'Grady was aware of the seriousness of the situation Shaughnessy looked like he was doing the breaststroke in an effort to cut through to air. O'Grady pulled over, hoping it wasn't the result of his earlier manhandling. He got Shaughnessy out of the car and bent him over, making it easier for him to catch his breath. The fit gradually subsided, and Shaughnessy, between gasps, told O'Grady that his pills were in his jacket pocket.

After he had gulped a couple down his breathing eased. He clutched the roof of the car, steadying himself. He was scared by what had happened, O'Grady could see.

'Thanks, Pat,' he eventually said. 'I'm getting too old for this.'

Shaughnessy's face had gone the colour of beet during his fit but was now ashen. He looked like a man who had just had the stuffing knocked out of him. Even his clothes appeared to have suffered in the attack. The usual dapperness was gone, leaving him looking blown-about, even seedy. O'Grady noticed his shirt cuffs were starting to fray.

The incident had unnerved O'Grady, for its swiftness and for being outside his control. He wanted to be rid of Shaughnessy and to be alone in his room, and was making a move to get back in the car when Shaughnessy grabbed his arm with surprising force.

Much as he wanted to look away from the other man's watery eyes, O'Grady could not. For the first time he felt he was seeing him properly and was being offered honesty in return.

'I'm tired of bluffing on a pair of twos. I'm tired of nudging you in the right direction,' Shaughnessy said. 'I've seen you over in Camden Town, asking around. You're looking for your family, right? And you're owed what by Ronnie and John, twenty?' O'Grady inclined his head. There seemed no point in denying it any longer. 'And Tel's still owed seven.'

Shaughnessy broke off to cough into his fist. The fingers of his other hand pressed into his chest.

'Are you sure you're all right?' asked O'Grady.

'Yes, yes,' said Shaughnessy impatiently, waving his concern away. 'Tel said you were the legend. I believed him. I still do, hard as you make it. And I'll be frank with you. You're my last chance, Pat. I need five grand from this. That's what I want for finding John and Ronnie. That's all. Then I'm gone.'

'Where does five grand get you these days? It's not worth what it was ten years ago.'

'Ah, fuck the cost of living, it'll get me where I'm going, Pat, don't you worry. Deal?'

Shaughnessy held out his hand. After considering, O'Grady took it. Shaughnessy winked, back to his old self, leaving O'Grady wondering if the fit hadn't been play-acting, to make him drop his guard. The feeling was reinforced when Shaughnessy, making a sprightly move towards getting back in the car, announced, 'Now let's go an see a man about your wife.'

Shaughnessy directed O'Grady but refused to say where they were going or who they were seeing. They crossed three of the roads that O'Grady had always thought of as the great divides, the Kilburn High Road, the Finchley Road, then, via the back-streets of Chalk Farm and Kentish Town, the Holloway Road, always to his mind the most sullen of the lot. He knew little or nothing of what lay beyond, and recalled going as a child with his mother to the Jones Brothers department store and her telling him they were on the edge of the land of the darkies, and the frequent threat of punishment of being sent there to live with them.

Once they were in the Seven Sisters Road most of the shops became open-fronted stores with vegetables on display. In

Kilburn a greengrocer was a rarity. Here they were lined up next to one another, all seemingly identical. O'Grady couldn't decide if they were in fierce competition or run by the same people.

Shaughnessy made him turn left up Hornsey Road, which was clogged with traffic. They inched past the baths, with a big painted sign of a diving woman in a bathing suit, which prompted Shaughnessy to ask, 'Did you miss it when you were inside?'

O'Grady didn't bother to answer. He hadn't much, at first. It had felt as though his whole system had shut down. Anyway, a woman was out of the question, so there was no point in getting steamed up about it. The younger ones had spent their time tossing off for want of anything better to do. It had reminded him of hospital terminal wards, the couple of times he had been, full of old men wanking their way to death. He'd heard you had an orgasm when you died, but he wouldn't like to bet on it. It was probably just nurses' propaganda to give you something to look forward to.

Further up the road was a big police station. Shaughnessy kept nervously clearing his throat, and O'Grady wondered if he was wanted or had form. They were still stuck in traffic when two police cars joined the queue, sirens blaring, bullying their way forward. Because of a set of lights and a traffic island O'Grady had to mount the kerb. Shaughnessy hunched down, anxious. O'Grady stalled, trying to get the car up on the pavement, which resulted in an impatient flashing of lights and an angry horn on top of the sirens.

'Fucking peelers,' muttered Shaughnessy.

As the first car pushed past, O'Grady was given a dead-eyed stare by a lad with a cropped haircut, ready to abuse all the power he had. It was a look O'Grady remembered, the one you got just before they made you accidentally fall over.

O'Grady turned away. Part of him badly wanted the satisfaction of seeing the boy's expression wiped off his face. There was a time when he would have had him out of the car and his teeth all over the road before any of them knew what was happening. He glanced up. The young policeman gave him a dismissive glance that said he had his measure. O'Grady hoped Shaughnessy couldn't smell the funk coming off him, and cracked open the window.

Their destination was a large council estate at the top of Hornsey Rise, on a steep hill with views across the city. The two police cars that had passed them were parked carelessly outside the flats, doors open, looking abandoned. The policeman who had given him the stare was the only one still with the cars. He had a two-way radio that was giving off static. A gang of kids, only about five or six, stood watching with a bored air of mild interest. O'Grady wondered if it was the school holidays already. He wondered if the man they were there to see was the same one the police were looking for.

Shaughnessy made it plain that he preferred to wait, but O'Grady wanted to make up for his funk.

'For Christ's sake, man, let them finish their business,' said Shaughnessy. Seeing that O'Grady was not about to relent, he groaned and made extra-heavy weather of getting out. 'Ah, Pat, you'll be the death of me.'

The young policeman gave O'Grady a blank look and showed no sign of remembering him. Just then the other constables came clattering down the outside stairs, laughing and swearing and looking as if they were still turned on by the noise of their sirens. The children applauded ironically and started to chant, 'Please, misters, can you get our ball back?'

The police ignored O'Grady and Shaughnessy in spite of Shaughnessy's furtive hanging back, examining his shoes like he had stepped in something, and carried on behaving as if they'd just won the gunfight at the OK Corral. A big false alarm, thought O'Grady, to need two cars.

Once the police were back in their vehicles, Shaughnessy caught up, telling O'Grady to hurry up, as though he'd been the one delaying.

The stairs smelt of piss and the lights were broken. By the top flight they were both wheezing. It was an estate with covered walkways and an open drop to one side. Most windows were boarded up. O'Grady had deliberately not thought about the implications of their visit. He had no idea who the man might be.

Shaughnessy knew the flat well enough to know the bell was broken, because he banged loudly on the door and kept hammering until O'Grady told him it was obvious nobody was in. O'Grady was secretly relieved. The last thing he wanted was to talk to a man about his wife.

Shaughnessy stood contemplating their next move. Down below, the children were in a scrum, fighting and swearing. O'Grady heard the latch. Someone was in after all. He turned and saw who it was.

The surge of rage O'Grady felt was more towards Shaughnessy, for wasting his time, for even thinking that Tel could have anything useful to say about his wife or anybody else. Tel was in his pyjama trousers and an old vest. His hair was tousled and he reeked of gin.

O'Grady expected Shaughnessy to defer to his anger, and was surprised when he didn't. Stripped of its usual false bonhomie, Shaughnessy's expression confused him. It wasn't hatred exactly, more a look of scientific curiosity, as if O'Grady was an insect there for the man's study. There was something else, too, which eluded him until Shaughnessy opened his mouth, when he saw it for what it was. Superior knowledge, and its benefit about to be given.

'Ask Tel,' said Shaughnessy, with a jerk of the head, 'who was giving your missus the old Swiss roll while you were gone.'

O'Grady was sure that Shaughnessy was lying. The idea of Maggie and Tel was beyond belief. Maggie was fussy and always looked up. Tel, with his boozer's face and burst blood vessels like silvery blue worms burrowing under his skin, would never have stood a chance.

But looking at Tel he knew he was wrong. Tel's panic was a clear sign of guilt. His mouth flapped open and shut and nothing came out until he managed a pathetic bleat to Shaughnessy. 'You promised.'

O'Grady stood with his fists bunched. Everything was starting to move too fast for him. He had a bad urge to see Tel hanging over the balcony, scrabbling on tiptoe from the pain of having his balls squeezed. Then he looked at the pathetic wreck that Tel had become and the thought of manhandling him left him squeamish and disgusted with himself. Shaughnessy's bright eye betrayed his own excitement at the prospect of a bit of violence, but, when it became clear that O'Grady was not going to act, he shrugged and said, 'Nothing outside the normal rules of debate, eh, Pat?'

Shaughnessy shoved Tel into the flat, gave O'Grady a knowing look close to a smirk, and said, 'After you, I insist.'

O'Grady went first. He was distracted by Shaughnessy rubbing his hands and was late seeing Tel's move. Tel was trying to bring an iron down on his head but with such clumsy, drunken deliberation that he easily had time to parry the blow. Tel collapsed in a heap before anyone could hit him and quickly assumed a foetal position on the floor.

O'Grady picked up the iron from where it had dropped. The idea of Tel even having one handy struck him as absurd. Shaughnessy was standing by the door looking like a witness to perfectly normal behaviour.

'There now,' he said. 'You've gone and made him cry.' Tel rolled over, glaring tearfully at Shaughnessy, and said, 'You bastard, you swore you wouldn't.'

Shaughnessy was doing his best to appear casual. 'Somebody had to move the goalposts to get your man geed up. Christ, you've pissed yourself.'

O'Grady turned away out of embarrassment, but Tel seemed not to care. 'Fuck. Christ, give us a drink.' He sounded matter-of-fact.

'Later,' said O'Grady. 'Come on, get up.'

Tel recoiled. O'Grady held out his hand. Tel eventually took it. He looked scared and uncertain as O'Grady pulled him up, as though O'Grady might be about to hit him. Shaughnessy confirmed as much when he said, 'I'd be giving the man a good digging if I were you.'

'Well, you're not,' said O'Grady still more angry with Shaughnessy than Tel.

They went into a room off to the right of the hall, once a sitting room of sorts. The curtains were drawn and the place hadn't been aired for a long time. A broken coffee table, a sofa with its cushions missing and a mattress on the floor were all that remained of the furniture. The carpet was threadbare and large patches had been rubbed shiny black. The room was conspicuous for Tel's empties, dozens, maybe hundreds of clear-glassed cheap gin bottles, with some green Gordon's, and a few beer and wine bottles thrown in. Tel's current bottle of gin was on the window ledge. He headed straight for it, tilted it to his mouth and managed several large swallows before O'Grady took it away.

'Later,' he said.

Shaughnessy glanced around sourly. 'I see you've been decorating.'

Tel gazed mournfully at the bottle. 'I could handle it till she left. I was always a boozer, but you know what I mean?' A thread of spittle was working its way from the corner of his mouth. 'It wasn't like you think.'

'Where did she go?' O'Grady asked, trying to keep his voice level. For the life of him, he could not see Maggie letting Tel on top of her.

Tel behaved as if he hadn't heard. His hands started to shake. O'Grady took a step forward and Tel looked at him from a long way off. 'Wembley,' he eventually said, fumbling his words. 'Opened a shop in Wembley. Beauty parlour.'

'Whereabouts?' asked O'Grady.

'Wembley,' he repeated.

'Where in Wembley?'

Tel stuck out his lower lip. O'Grady watched him pretend to think. He turned to Shaughnessy. 'I'm wasting my time. Is this the best you can do?'

Tel was trying to put his hands in his pockets, unaware that he was still in his pyjamas. When he realised he smiled sheepishly.

'Guess who lent her the money?' he said, back on track. 'I was flush in them days. All she wanted was the money, and when she'd spent it that was . . .' He lost his thread and stared round for help.

'Behind you,' said Shaughnessy smoothly. O'Grady couldn't see what he was on about. Nor could Tel, who turned and stared. 'Swindow,' he said uncomprehendingly.

'Curtains!' said Shaughnessy, pantomiming a teacher with an exceptionally thick pupil.

O'Grady turned to Shaughnessy in exasperation. 'Are we all comedians now?'

'Lighten up, Pat, and let the man tell his story.'

Tel found his loop again. 'I never saw a penny back. The same old story. Beauty parlour. Did I say that? I wouldn't treat a dog the way she treated me.'

'What's its name?'

Tel went blank. 'It's a beauty parlour. Last I heard she was doing all right.'

'What's its name?' repeated Shaughnessy, louder.

'I don't know, man,' whined Tel. 'Go on, give us a drink.'

O'Grady said no. Shaughnessy marched out of the room and could be heard banging cupboard doors while Tel stood pie-eyed, blinking slowly, trying to work out the reason for the noise. Then something flew through the air at him and he waved his arms as though he was warding off an attack. It turned out to be a copy of the Yellow Pages thrown by Shaughnessy. Tel ended up on all fours, saying that he'd thought a bird had got in the room.

Shaughnessy told him to look up beauty parlours and see if he recognised any of the names. Tel stared gloomily at the directory and started going through the pages as if he meant to turn over every one.

'Christ, man, we'll be here all night,' complained Shaughnessy, who had to find the right page for him.

Tel squinted uncomprehendingly at it, then mumbled that he had lost his glasses. There was a long pause. Then O'Grady realised the problem had nothing to do with glasses. Tel couldn't read. O'Grady felt sad for him and took the directory and read aloud the names from the top. Each time Tel shook his head. They had gone through half a dozen when O'Grady saw he was wasting his time.

'None of these is in Wembley,' he said. 'These are the wrong Yellow Pages.'

Tel giggled and said the shop had a Greek name and they went through all the Greek names they could think of, which wasn't many. Then Tel announced it was a name from a Greek myth. Shaughnessy rolled his eyes and said, 'God help us.'

O'Grady knew there were Greek roads in West Hampstead but he couldn't recall any, except Achilles.

'Who's going to call a beauty salon Achilles?' snapped Shaughnessy.

They carried on, until Tel, with a crafty glance, announced, 'It was Troy.'

'Troy's Beauty Parlour?' asked Shaughnessy 'You fucking eejit. You knew all along.'

Tel smirked. 'Helen of Troy.'

'Helen of Troy, my arse,' retorted Shaughnessy. 'Helen of fucking Troy was never a Greek myth, she was Greek fucking history.'

'Yeah, well,' said Tel, with the air of a man who had scored. 'You're not the only one who can bend the goalposts.'

Shaughnessy appeared annoyed out of all proportion to the size of the argument and O'Grady wondered if it was the pills he was on.

'Get up and get dressed,' said Shaughnessy. 'We're going for a drive. And, while you're about it, tell Pat what they used to call you.'

Tel hesitated, then mumbled, 'Kiss and Tel.'

'On account of how he fancied himself with the ladies,' added Shaughnessy.

It was Shaughnessy's way of scoring a cheap point off both of them, O'Grady saw, and he walked out on them, ignoring Shaughnessy calling after him. He would drive off and leave

them, he decided, and he had got as far as switching on the
engine when the pointlessness of any alternative became clear. He
had nowhere to go except back to his room. He could drive till
the petrol ran out and see where he ended up, but there was no
future in that, either.

He turned off the engine. Shaughnessy and Tel were a pair of
jokers, he decided, easily enough handled if watched. The sight of
them approaching confirmed as much. Tel's spindly, pigeon-toed
tottering made the solid Shaughnessy seem so smooth he could
have been on wheels.

There was no Troy Beauty Parlour in Wembley that they could
find. Or in Wembley Park. Everywhere was shut for Sunday,
which meant there was nowhere to ask. The occasional passers-by
they stopped regarded them with a mixture of humour and sus-
picion. Rightly so, thought O'Grady. Three men in a car asking
for a beauty parlour.

Wembley struck O'Grady as one of those places that were too
far from the centre to count and not far enough out to have any
point of their own. But he could see why Maggie might have
aspired to it. Unlike Camden it seemed to offer a choice, and
wasn't the kind of place you had to dig your way out of. The
houses were newer and the streets generally had the safe and
deserted air of a suburb, which would have suited her. She had
never been one for a crowd.

O'Grady tried to remember what being married had been like
and couldn't, any more than he could remember what smoking
had been like. He could not even recall what getting married had
meant to him. He supposed he had been rebelling against his
mother, who had disapproved of Maggie. He hadn't seen that in
reality he was conforming to what everyone else did. He had been
distracted by his own unspoken battle, the one between how he
saw himself, which was never very clearly, in relation to the
words of priests and teachers, like 'duty' and 'honour', which had
never amounted to much in his book.

Tel spent the journey drifting in and out of sleep when he

wasn't being jabbed awake by Shaughnessy, who seemed morose. Phone boxes failed to produce phone books, or the right directory was missing. When at last they found the relevant one there was no Troy Beauty Parlour listed.

When it started getting dark O'Grady began to think in terms of a wasted day. Shaughnessy poked Tel again and said, 'Since you can't remember where she worked, perhaps you might like to tell us where she lived.'

Tel stared at O'Grady with pleading eyes, and said, 'It wasn't what you think.'

Shaughnessy shouted, 'It never is.'

'She conned me. I only went to the house once to ask for my money back. It was out Stanmore way.'

'Old, new?' asked Shaughnessy testily.

'It had a sort of, like a little drive.'

'They've all got drives out there!'

'I don't know, it was a long time ago. Just give us a drink.'

Shaughnessy said to O'Grady, 'You've every right to cut this fellow's balls off.'

Shaughnessy baited Tel, saying there was no drink in the car and, as the pubs and off-licences weren't open until seven, he would have to wait. Eventually O'Grady said, 'Give him your flask and leave the man alone.'

'Find me a toilet, then,' Shaughnessy snapped and they quarrelled about that.

'You'd argue the hind legs off a donkey,' O'Grady said and Shaughnessy gave him a mirthless grin.

'Give the man his drink,' said O'Grady.

'When you find my toilet.'

O'Grady wasn't even sure where they were. Kingsbury or Queensbury, maybe even Canons Park. It no longer felt like the suburbs, more like the suburbs of the suburbs.

He managed to locate a municipal car park near a shopping centre with toilets that turned out to be locked. Shaughnessy announced he was going round the back. First O'Grady made sure he left his flask with Tel.

O'Grady listened to Tel sucking gratefully and was surprised when he spoke. 'You used to be one of the best.'

'You used to be sober. How much are you still owed?'

'About half.'

O'Grady turned round and said mildly, 'I catch you lying I will cut off your balls.'

Tel mumbled, 'Seven grand. How come you're interested all of a sudden?'

'A man can change his mind.'

Things changed, at first without O'Grady noticing. There was a shift in power between him and Shaughnessy, starting with O'Grady taking the Datsun. He took to parking it in the street outside the hotel and kept the only set of keys. On three occasions he drove at night over towards Stanmore looking for where Maggie lived. The first time they all went. O'Grady divided up the streets on the map and drove down each one, hoping to jog Tel's memory. Tel sat in the front, happy with his bottle, shaking his head.

The second time Shaughnessy excused himself. O'Grady drove Tel down another set of streets, then back over some of those from the time before, which Tel failed to notice they had already been down. At that point O'Grady began to realise the futility of their search. Tel wouldn't recognise the house if he walked into it and found Maggie standing there. They drove in silence for the most part. O'Grady's mind was full of unasked questions about Tel and Maggie. Given his own neglect of her, he had no business being jealous, but he was.

From the look of its houses, Stanmore was safe. Stanmore was secure. If Maggie was living there she must have done well. Most places had their own garage and a private driveway so the car could be shown off in relation to the house. The cars were all shiny and definitely not old. Lawns were neat and life was tidy.

To him Stanmore had always been the end of the line. It was where the trains that went through Kilburn stopped. Stanmore held for him a measure of desperation, representing everything he would never be, unlike Maggie, who aspired to such places. It was commuter land, with men in overcoats carrying briefcases. The sight of a briefcase always caused him mild panic, each one a small reminder of an education thrown away or, rather, never offered.

They drove past the same pub twice, a big half-timbered building and ended up having a drink there, to give some point to the evening, and to save themselves from being just stuck in the car. O'Grady wondered if they would get served, as it was clear they did not belong. It was like walking into a private party. The lounge was full of couples and small mixed groups, sitting and murmuring politely and drinking shorts. The landlord was in a jacket and tie, and his up-and-over hairstyle summed up the place's pretensions. O'Grady was tempted to lean forward and blow.

He did his best to engage the landlord, saying he was looking for his long-lost sister and giving a description of Maggie. He couldn't think of any believable way of saying that she had been his wife.

He wasn't hopeful. Maggie had used pubs in her time but he doubted if they went with her new lifestyle. She would be careful of what she drank, on account of her looks. It would be white wine in restaurants now, or a glass or two at home. The landlord pursed his lips, then said he didn't have any Irish women among his customers, which put O'Grady in his place.

Tel wanted to talk about the old days, about John and Ronnie. He was keen to appraise their chances. When O'Grady said he didn't want to, Tel looked hurt.

'It was my time that was taken away,' added O'Grady. 'Not yours or anyone else's.'

When he was ready to talk it would not be to Tel. He went over the whole thing incessantly in his head as it was. If he could have turned back time, even for a second, none of it need have happened. The child would still be here.

Tel, nursing half a lager instead of his usual gin, said, 'I know it's none of my business—'

'Then don't ask,' said O'Grady.

Tel laughed, as if O'Grady had just made a joke. 'Why are you looking for Maggie?'

'I'm not. I'm after the girl.'

'Lily?'

The next time O'Grady drove out on his own, less to look, more to think. The pattern was getting clearer. He wasn't interested in John or Ronnie, or Tel, or any missing money, or Shaughnessy's games. He was only interested in Lily. Eight when he went, almost eighteen now. A young woman. She would be beautiful, he had no doubt.

He didn't even want to talk to her. He didn't see himself as having the right. All he wanted was a look, to see how she had turned out, see her laugh, see that she was happy. He wondered if she was still at school, and if Maggie had sent her to a Roman Catholic one.

The bargain he had agreed to was to go along with Shaughnessy's scheme for finding John and Ronnie in exchange for help locating Maggie. But, given that Tel had a memory like one of those cheeses with holes in, O'Grady decided he would be as well off tracking her down himself. The John and Ronnie business was secondary, if that. They would both be long gone, O'Grady was sure.

He had started to enjoy the driving again. It was what he had done for years, then stopped, after swearing he would not drive again. Now it was as if his body had made the decision for him, and his mind had played no part. His hand had automatically caught the keys Shaughnessy had thrown at him, and his hands and feet were enjoying being reacquainted with the controls.

Driving was one of the few things he did well, that he didn't feel clumsy doing. Even with the violence, when he had done it, he was never good enough in his own mind. He never had the timing. He could give a man a clattering but he was never going to win any prizes.

He remembered an illegal fight years before which had been arranged in an industrial estate in Harlesden. One of the contestants he had vaguely known, a henchman of Tommy Doyle's, and he'd been invited as a result. Doyle's boy was a beefy lad with deceptively lazy eyes whose trick was that the left he led with was also his knock-out punch, so any wary opponent keeping an eye on the right didn't see what was coming. The fight was part of a so-called freestyle evening, which meant that no holds were barred, though opponents were supposed to stop short of spitting, biting and gouging. It was, as Tommy Doyle had said, an excuse for a jar.

The building had a loading bay and the crowd stood on the platform looking down into a makeshift ring. O'Grady had been surprised to see a couple of women there, smartly dressed and scarcely able to contain their excitement.

'My boy's fighting a midget,' said Doyle to O'Grady with a broad smirk which wasn't there after the fight. It lasted about fifteen seconds. Doyle's boy was fighting a slim lad. He was from Nepal, O'Grady learned afterwards, and had been a Gurkha. He stood not much over five foot and next to Doyle's strapping boy looked comic. The fight turned out to be a joke, too, but not in the way everybody was expecting. Doyle's boy took a couple of swings and missed, then was invited to hit his opponent in the stomach, which he did to absolutely no effect. The Gurkha didn't even grunt. He pirouetted on one foot and struck his opponent behind the ear with the other. When Doyle's boy went down and stayed down the crowd at first thought it was part of the act.

Doyle's boy was in tears afterwards and Doyle came looking for O'Grady muttering about the humiliation and asking O'Grady if he would take on the Gurkha. It was like a prediction come true, thought O'Grady, and one partly willed by himself.

Watching the demolition of Doyle's boy O'Grady had known he
was witnessing something extraordinary, a perfect combination of
balance and timing, with mind and body in complete tune. Part
of him wanted to experience that at first hand. He remembered
his early Sunday School and stories of the Apostles and moments
of revelation, and in that instant he wanted his life to change,
completely, and to learn other ways.

He lasted two or three minutes, only because the Gurkha let
him, though afterwards he tried to excuse himself by saying that
he'd been on his way to getting drunk and in no condition for a
proper fight. He tried to think and box clever but it was as
though they were in two different worlds. He was left punching
air. Even with the blows he landed he could have been hitting
wood for all the effect it had. The man didn't look at him so
much as through him. O'Grady became distracted thinking of the
space behind him and knew he was already demolished. His mind
caved in long before his body. There was a confusion in his
head, a terrible sense of hopelessness, and the flickering images
that kept appearing in his mind were all wrong for what he had
to do. He saw Molly dancing and Lily showing him the knee she
had cut in the playground.

Nobody talked about the evening afterwards and he never saw
the Gurkha again. The last thing O'Grady remembered was a terrible pain to the outside of his knee. The crowd watched,
disappointed, and afterwards the Gurkha was blamed for spoiling
the evening's fun. A good, long-drawn-out brawl was what everyone wanted, with a couple of big-hearted lads well matched,
rather than the wily stuff. The sadness O'Grady had felt afterwards he could not define. Now he thought it had to do with
wanting his defeat to have had a more decisive effect. But it had
made no difference and his life had carried on its usual course.

He tried losing himself in Kathleen but there was a sadness in that
too. Her enjoyment seemed real enough but his own felt forced.
The night of his drive alone to Stanmore he had crept past
Molly's room, which still had the light on well past midnight, and

put a note under Kathleen's door saying he was waiting in his room.

He had been wanting her all evening but when she came to him he couldn't get hard. 'Why's your cock bust?' she asked. She seemed amused and took it upon herself to mend matters. 'Lie back and think of Ireland,' she added, 'while I head south.'

Straddling him later, she said, 'Girls on top, and take your time.' She rode him slowly, even pausing for a cigarette. 'It's not the one after that's best, it's the one during. Did you ever smoke?'

'Oh, sure.'

'But you gave up.'

'I gave up.'

'Like you gave up most things?'

The room would smell of tobacco in the morning. O'Grady nodded and said, 'How old would you say I am?'

Kathleen blew smoke out of the side of her mouth. 'Ancient history's not my subject.'

'Why are you here now?'

'For a fag and a fuck, I would have thought that's obvious.'

'But look at me. I've got nothing. I've been nowhere and I'm back where I started.'

'Oh, excuse me. Why am I here with *you*, that's what you mean?' He could not say if her exasperation was put on. 'Shaughnessy said you were about to come into money.'

'Is that what he calls it, and is that why you're here?'

This time her irritation was plain. 'If you think I'm whoring for that old goat you've another think coming. You men, sooner or later the lot of you start feeling sorry for yourselves. Stop looking grim and start paying me some attention.'

'Give me a drag on that cigarette before you put it out.'

'All the old vices coming home to roost?'

Conversations with his mother he might as well not have had for all the response he got. She had taken to her room more and when he visited they sat in front of the television. Because of the variable reception O'Grady spent part of his time trying to get a proper picture, which gave him something to do. Resolution or not, he suspected his visits were increasingly trying for both of them. His mother seemed to have no need for contact with the outside, least of all with him, and he could see why. He had been a poor son, so why should she bother, any more than his own daughter should for all the father he had been to her?

They watched racing when it was on and if not whatever there was, usually a word game. When 'conundrum' came up O'Grady wondered if that was what he was facing.

His mother's room had double glazing and was overheated. It often gave him an image of himself sealed off from the world, and sealed off inside himself from everyone else. His soul, if there was such a thing, resided in one of these tight airless spaces.

'Peace and quiet is all I was after,' he said, to himself as much as to her. 'At least, that's what I told myself and that's what I said to Molly, but what's the point of that now? It all catches up in the end.'

His mother remained as indifferent as a totem pole. He wondered what spaces lay inside her head now, compared to the sharp tongue he remembered and her curiosity and her questioning of everything, and the way she read newspapers and watched the news on television. As a boy he had been embarrassed by her interest in what went on, because it only drew attention to what was missing in their lives, to the gap between their uneventful existence and what happened beyond.

'If I'd had the education I deserved I'd be running this country by now, mark my words' was a remark she had often made. O'Grady reminded her. 'Do you remember saying that? And do you remember Uncle Harry saying, "Get away. They'd never let a woman be in charge?" Do you remember? Look how wrong that turned out. You know she comes from Finchley, just up the road?'

He looked at her. Not a glimmer. 'What happened to us? It seems to me we've all been left to sit around. It all passed Molly by, wouldn't you say? And this, Ma, what's this all about, this room and your saying nothing? The matron says you can talk perfectly well when you want. Is it the old silent disapproval you're giving me? Is that the message I'm supposed to be getting? Women are good at that. Showing how they feel by saying nothing. You taught Molly well enough that she could play for Ireland.'

The television filled in the silence. The contestants sat behind separate cubes and a man in a grey suit, with a well-rehearsed smile, pointed from time to time with great confidence, gently correcting mistakes.

'You could still knock spots off this lot, Ma,' O'Grady said. She had been a subscriber to the *Reader's Digest*. Her favourite section was 'How to Improve Your Word Power'.

No one had said anything funny, yet his mother started laughing. At first he thought it was the beginning of an attack and it took him a while to realise what it was. He smiled cautiously, wondering whether the joke was on him.

'And sure enough,' he said, wanting her to understand, 'it's all starting to get out of hand.' A burst of applause came from the television, which made his mother laugh harder.

'So what should I do?' O'Grady finished lamely.

His mother's laugh stopped like it had been switched off. She was staring hard at him. O'Grady found the experience unnerving. Usually she looked anywhere but at him. She beckoned him to lean closer. Her breath reminded him of dust and old books. He turned his head, like a priest awaiting confession, wondering what sins she had.

When nothing happened he started to feel self-conscious. He went to pull away but was stopped by her grabbing his wrist with a quite unexpected strength. Her nails dug in, sharp, and O'Grady had the sensation of her words coming from somewhere much deeper than her frail body.

'Fuck them all and to hell with the lot of you.'

She pushed him away and fell back laughing again, acting now like some mad old bat in a horror picture. O'Grady was sure it was done to upset him.

There she was, proud and tall, heels at nine in the morning, walking a line, putting one foot directly in front of the other like a model or a dancer, knowing she was being looked at. The expectation of being watched meant that she in turn did not look, which was why O'Grady went unnoticed. Maggie, and not a day older. Time had stood still for her.

She was shopping in the big American-style supermarket, just as O'Grady had known she would. The previous Saturday he had shown the place to Molly, driving her over in Shaughnessy's car, which he'd told her was borrowed. The supermarket had its own road and shrubbery and the feeling was of driving into some private estate that let you take things out. He wasn't sure why he had brought Molly, because she was bound to disapprove, just of the size of the place, being thrifty to the point of meanness. But she had surprised him. Faced with such an abundance of choice she had become an instant convert and translated the episode into some sort of religious experience. 'Look at the aisles – they're wider than a church,' she said in awe. If there were tins in heaven then Molly would be happy, O'Grady thought.

'Look at that,' he said. 'You'd pay more in Safeway.' She filled a trolley and took it through the checkout and over to the car. The trolley wouldn't push straight, which Molly thought was O'Grady's fault until he told her it was the wheels. Otherwise, everything was perfect.

'Is this how they do it in America?' she asked, her tone almost flirtatious. He was slow to realise that the remark was a joke, perhaps even an apology for having made out that he had been there instead of being in prison. They loaded up the car like they were normal people and O'Grady wondered why life couldn't always be pleasant and ordinary like this.

Molly's blessing meant he was free to shop there whenever he wanted. Because the store stayed open, he sometimes went in the evening and sat in the car park watching the late shoppers. Once or twice he'd mistaken the back of a woman for her.

The moment he saw her he knew, from the way she stood and the tilt of her head. His heart started banging like it wanted to be let out and he felt faint enough to fall over. It was like a long-dead connection being made inside him, and his body threatening to shut down.

He followed from a distance, wondering what he would do if she spotted him, and telling himself that he was fretting for nothing. Maggie was, as ever, caught up with herself. Seeing her again O'Grady marvelled at what he had thrown away. She was a fine-looking woman, tall and beautifully boned, and immaculately turned out, her make-up just so. Dressed to kill, he thought. From the sensuousness of her walk he guessed the underwear was silk. She looked dressed for a date, or a play, for something outside the normal scope of things. No tins of baked beans for her. The items she placed in her trolley were carefully middle-class. She loitered in front of fancy olive oils, and in the dairy section took a low-fat spread. Even in his day, he remembered, she had refused to buy margarine like everybody else. 'Too many airs and graces for her own good' had been his mother's verdict.

His own trolley stayed more or less empty as he forgot to fill it. Maggie's purchases seemed idle compared to most shoppers'.

Nothing so vulgar as bulk buying. Her bored saunter announced that she had time and money to spare.

He loitered in the drinks section while she queued and paid and he watched her push her trolley over to a sporty hatchback Golf. He left his own shopping in the aisle and hurried to his car once she was in hers. He saw her leave the car park then lost her. There were no cars on the slip road. He could not understand where she had gone.

Then he saw she had turned off into the filling station and was getting out of the Golf. She seemed to look straight at him as he drove past, which started his heart banging again, but as she showed no surprise he thought he was probably safe. He came to one of the new small roundabouts and looped round the garage and back into the car park. He got out and watched from a distance, using a hedge for a screen. He saw her come back from paying, putting her purse in her handbag.

He was thirty yards behind her by the time she got to the little roundabout and he tried to keep that distance, following her onto the North Circular then off at Wembley. After Wembley he recognised the road as one he had driven down with Shaughnessy on that first day. It was a faster road, straight and with common land on either side and a camp of gypsy caravans he recognised from before. There were a couple of cars between them, which meant less chance of her spotting him. He was probably safe enough, anyway. He doubted if Maggie was one for rearview mirrors. That they had once shared a life now seemed beyond the remotest possibility.

He guessed correctly that she would carry on north to Stanmore. The name of the road after the Kingsbury roundabout was Honeypot Lane. Eventually he recognised streets from his drives with Tel.

Maggie's house was on a modern development in a cul-de-sac. He watched her turn in, then drove past, turned and slowly went back. The hatch of Maggie's car was up and she was unloading her shopping. The house was smart, what Tommy Doyle would have called executive-style. The place was deserted, as empty as a dream. Either it was so new that half the houses were still not bought or the inhabitants were too discreet to let their homes give anything away.

He went back, secretly, three times hoping to see Lily. Each time he restated his promise that he was there only to look. He would make no approach.

His first problem was parking. Because each house had its own space there were no cars in the street and the Sunny's age and condition made it conspicuous. The first night he contented himself with several drive-bys. There were no lights on. He found a pub about a mile away, had a drink and drove by the darkened house one last time.

The second time he parked further away and walked. He found the land behind Maggie's was still being built on, and directly opposite was the shell of a new house whose land backed onto her garden. The roof was on but no doors or windows were in, which left O'Grady free to enter. The stairs weren't built yet but there was a ladder and the upstairs floors at the back were partly boarded. From there O'Grady had a good view of the back of Maggie's house and several others in the cul-de-sac. Maggie's place was still in darkness. The curtains were not drawn and she was clearly out. He wondered where Lily was, whether she was with her mother. He had nothing else to do but wait, all night if he had to.

He watched the people in their houses. Because they were not yet overlooked most of them didn't bother to close their curtains and O'Grady observed the winding down of another day. One lot were eating while another watched television. He could not see what was on, only the light the set threw into the room. Nobody was old and they were all smartly dressed, probably still in the clothes they wore to the office. O'Grady tried to imagine what it would be like leading a regular life.

By one all the lights were out. Maggie still hadn't come back. O'Grady wondered about this, not in relation to her, but Lily. Where was the child? If she was out, it was far too late. Perhaps they were away. A light went on in one of the other houses and someone got up for the toilet. The night was so still that the noise of the flush carried to him.

As he continued his watch he thought of all the hours Molly had put in down at the church. He wondered if she experienced the same sort of expectation and doubt as he did. He worried that he had the wrong house. Perhaps Maggie didn't live there and had been dropping off for someone else.

He had no idea how long he had been waiting. It was still dark and there were probably a couple more hours until daylight. And he was cold. Nobody would be coming back that night.

He was there again the next night. The unreality of the previous night had in the course of the day come to feel more solid than the day itself. His transactions with Molly and Kathleen had felt paper-thin compared to the solid reassurance of the dark.

Maggie returned just before midnight. It was raining hard and O'Grady didn't hear her car arrive. The hall lights being switched on was what alerted him. Then Maggie walked through into the living room with its large picture window. She wore a long coat and heels she kicked off as she went to the window to swish the curtains closed. O'Grady thought there was a man in the background. The downstairs lights went out shortly after and an upstairs one stayed on for about an hour while O'Grady told himself he was not jealous, and worried about Lily.

His uneasy balance held for several days until his dream about Lily. With his waking nights and lack of sleep the days felt increasingly strained. He started to experience a time-lag, between thinking he was doing something and really doing it.

He dreamed of her funeral, which he had been refused permission to attend. The prison governor turned him down in person. As he was being told of Lily's death, O'Grady wondered if he was dreaming, and was on the lookout for unusual details that would alert him. Then he was being driven in a car through the night, and the streets of the town were inexplicably lined with watching children. There were three other men in the car, none of them he recognised. Nobody spoke and O'Grady, when he tried, found he couldn't. The cemetery was behind the pub where he had run into Shaughnessy and Tel. O'Grady knew he hadn't seen Shaughnessy in a while, and the truth of this observation convinced him that he was not dreaming. Although he was at a funeral he did not connect it at first with Lily's because he had been refused permission to attend. As it was night and wet, most of the crowd was lost in darkness and umbrellas. The hole for the coffin was lit by floodlights. O'Grady could not see where the electricity was coming from or how it managed to work in the rain. Tommy Doyle slid in beside him and O'Grady told him there was no such thing as a funeral at night.

'You've been away too long, Pat. Everything is at night now. It started with the football. There isn't enough time to do everything in the day.'

'My name's not Pat.'

He woke in a muck sweat, with the sheets and blankets twisted round him like a winding sheet. For a moment he thought it was his own struggle out of the grave he had been dreaming about, then he remembered the coffin sliding of its own accord over the mud and crashing into the hole and the sight of his daughter failing to claw her way up the side of the hole, screaming that they were trying to bury her alive.

He drove out to the house again the morning after the dream, as soon as he could get away from doing the breakfasts. It was still the end of the rush hour and the traffic going the other way was solid. O'Grady had to remind himself that the dream was not true but only an unconscious scramble of all his anxieties. What he could not understand was why parts of it seemed so real. The exchange with Tommy Doyle had been far more vivid than their real-life meetings. But Lily had blurred. He had no idea what she looked like, yet in the dream he had known her straight away and she had been as sharp as a picture.

The look on Maggie's face when she came to the door was worth the wait. Her mouth dropped.

She was still in a robe and looking good, even wearing yesterday's make-up. Close to he could see the lines around her eyes but they did nothing to take away from her looks. She tried to shut the door in his face but he blocked her and forced his way into the hall, feeling it was his dream controlling him and he was being acted upon by a force beyond his own will. His plan had been a reasonable conversation between two grown-ups. Instead, there she was sprawled on the floor of the hall, her legs showing. He wanted to help her up and say he was sorry. More than that, he wanted to start again by saying, 'I'm not here to make trouble, I'm only here to know how Lily is. Tell me and I'm gone.'

He could see she was frightened of what he might do to her. Her vulnerability distracted him. It made him want her, which confused him. Coming for the daughter and finding himself still wanting the mother was not part of the plan.

'Where is she?' he asked.

Maggie, still on the floor, stared at him with growing rage. 'Out. Out of this house. This is my house.'

'And who did you fuck to get it?'

He hadn't meant to say that. Nevertheless it left him with a mean feeling of satisfaction. He had not been prepared for her resisting, had not taken into account the shock his turning up would cause. His only concern had been Lily.

His cheap crack helped turn her fear to anger. Maggie had never been backwards in standing up for herself. Then the years fell away and they were rowing like he had never been gone. He badly wished they could see the funny side of that.

'Maggie, I didn't come here to fight,' he said, trying a different tack.

'Don't you Maggie me.'

'Where is she?'

He felt he was throwing words into the grave of his dream. It was starting to turn black inside his head. He was calling out Lily's name, and Maggie was pulling him back from going upstairs. He could feel the softness of her breasts beneath her robe. An electric pulse jumped in him, alternating between attraction and repulsion.

He freed himself, knowing things were close to getting out of hand, and hurried upstairs. He saw shame in everything around him. Even the expensive stair carpet mocked him. In its pattern he saw another picture of Maggie, which told of hours of hard work and saving, of an ambition and purpose he had never had, and was quite different from the image of her he carried in his head.

The first room he checked was Maggie's with its unmade double bed, still smelling of sleep.

She was on the landing, arms defensively folded, and sounding composed. 'I told you, I want you out of here.'

He walked past her to the door opposite.

'Where is she?' he asked, going in.

He took in the narrow bed and the posters on the wall, sissy boys in bands, some surly, others with milk-white grins. The room confused him. The smallness of it reminded him of his cell. From its contents he would have guessed it belonged to someone younger than Lily. The house was brand new but this room felt, somehow, it had been there longer. None of it made sense.

There was no clutter. The drawers were empty except for a few bits and pieces. In the bottom one was a doll O'Grady thought he recognised as an early birthday present. An eye was missing. In an image that failed to go away he pictured Lily taking out her anger at him by stabbing the doll's eye.

O'Grady felt coshed. What he wanted most was to curl up and lie on her bed. The energy that had got him into the house and upstairs had gone. He felt ashamed to go downstairs.

He was going to apologise, but down in the hall Maggie was picking up the telephone. When she said she was calling the police he yanked the phone from its socket, more violently than he had intended, and the plate came away from the wall. He tried to offer to mend it but she screamed at him, 'You clumsy great arse. You've not changed.'

And he was yelling back, asking where Lily had gone, unable to stop the rising hysteria, truly scared he would end up hitting her because she was in that moment the embodiment of all the hostility he felt towards himself.

'I'm telling you nothing.' Her accent slipped back into the hard North London she had lost somewhere along the way. He told her he had a right to know where his own daughter was.

'She's my daughter,' he repeated and when Maggie pulled a face that said don't be so sure, his right arm swung back.

'Don't you fucking hit me. Don't you ever fucking hit me again!'

The last word burned into him. He stopped and said, 'I never meant to.'

It was true, he hadn't, but he knew now that was no excuse, drinking or not. He might not have learned much but he thought he had at least learned that, and he was shaken to find himself so close to doing it again, and so soon. Sensing that the fight had gone out of him, Maggie retaliated, slapping him about the face. He stood there, head bowed, letting her until they were interrupted by the postman shoving letters through the door, followed by the bell ringing, which was like the undoing of a spell.

Maggie quickly rearranged herself and answered. O'Grady could hear the postman asking if she was all right. 'Fine, thanks,' said Maggie brightly, adding that the racket was her daughter watching a film.

After she had closed the door O'Grady asked why she hadn't told the truth, that she had been slapping him around the head because he'd marched into the house without asking. A shrug was her only answer, by which O'Grady understood that he was in a neighbourhood where those things were not supposed to happen, and if they did you didn't go telling the postman.

Seeing her standing there, breathless from the effort of hitting him, he knew he was staring at a stranger. The ties that still bound him to her, separated or not, did not exist for her. She was gone, moved on, and he had been painted out of the picture. Everything until that moment had felt like a throwback to the past. Fighting was what they had always done. It was their way of resolving things. Strange, he thought, how after all these years he was still trying to work out what their relationship meant. He felt calm for the first time since being in the house. He could hear the tick of an expensive antique clock and thought he still might be able to explain himself, thought he detected a softening in Maggie. What he wanted most was for them to be able to sit down and talk.

'All I want is to see her, see how she turned out,' he said. 'She'd not even recognise me if I walked up and introduced myself. I'd just be another fellow in the street to her.'

She spat in his eye for an answer, inviting him to hit her. O'Grady had no trouble controlling himself. He felt saddened because he'd had the feeling that in the last few moments they had moved on.

'You dare,' said Maggie, and in that he saw the depth of her hatred, which took him by surprise. Whatever else he had expected he had not been prepared for so much anger.

After Maggie, he sat a long time in the car, chastened. He had left, still needing to ask why Lily was not living there and wanting to apologise, aware of Maggie regarding him stonily as she shut the door on him.

The rage he still felt against himself made him want to go out and do great damage to someone. She was right. He was clumsy. His clumsiness had lost him all chance of finding Lily. He had barged into Maggie's life again and expected her to fall over with delight.

That night he drank in the Black Lion. Shaughnessy came in and O'Grady told him to fuck off.

'Well, if that's how you feel,' said Shaughnessy, trying to make light of it.

'It is,' said O'Grady.

Taking note of his look, Shaughnessy checked as he was about to sit down. 'Suit yourself.'

He left O'Grady to his drink. The drink numbed the buzzing in his head. He wanted to be alone. At the same time he knew he was looking to pick a fight.

With weakening resolve he returned to the drudge of his days. Going back to square one was how he thought of it. He forgot about the big supermarket and went back to the Safeway in the High Street. He bought a second-hand television from a junk shop and in the evenings watched it in his room, using a wire coat-hanger for an aerial. The way people behaved on television, whether they were acting or reading the news, had no bearing on life as he understood it. Too much happened to them. There was always too much news and too much going on in the dramas.

'**A**re you all right?' Kathleen asked one evening after sneaking in to watch one of her favourite shows, which featured two impossibly good-looking men who wore shoulder holsters with floral shirts. O'Grady wasn't sure what she meant. Of course he wasn't all right, but he was certain it did not show.

'I've not been feeling very well the last few days,' he said, hoping that would be the end of the matter. She told him he needed a holiday and started planning one. She wanted somewhere with lots of sunshine. O'Grady decided she was trying to humour him.

'I wouldn't know what to do on holiday,' he said. It was true. He had never been on one even when there had been money. There had been a couple of trips back to Ireland but he didn't count them as holidays. Secretly he liked the idea of sitting in the sun somewhere with Kathleen and neither of them being able to understand a word of what was said around them. But the effort of it all would be too much – the organising, the travel, the going away together and hiding it from Molly, then sitting on a beach in all his clothes because he would be embarrassed by his pallor.

O'Grady sighed. What was the point of pretending?

Although he kept telling himself he was keeping everything normal, he knew he was not. Breaking into his old flat was not normal.

The afternoon had started as a walk, down the High Road and across to Swiss Cottage. There he decided it was the open space of Primrose Hill he was after. From the top of the hill he could see Bethlehem House. It was where he and Maggie had lived after getting married and it was Lily's first home. He remembered the humiliation of his last visit, being told to fuck off by the old woman. He decided to give her another go. But when he got there he did nothing. He got as far as her door but didn't ring her bell. Instead, he went and sat on the back stairs and wondered what he was doing. He must have sat there several hours, listening to the sounds of the building and the noise of the lift going up and down. It hadn't been working the last time. He reckoned on a couple more hours of daylight and he would give it until dark because she wouldn't go out after nightfall.

He had always liked the flat. It had been difficult living there with Maggie because what they each wanted, even on the simplest day-to-day level, clashed. She was always looking ahead and planning while he was happy with the drift. She wanted better and complained all the time about the state of the building. The lifts didn't work, there was shit on the stairs and graffiti everywhere. But O'Grady liked living high up. He had once tried to explain this to Maggie, saying it made him feel he was on top of everything, and she had snorted. It was true, but not in the way that she had understood. Up there nobody could touch them, and he wanted that to be clearer to her. Then maybe in return he would learn to accept the idea of what she meant by a home.

It grew dark and O'Grady took the bus back to Kilburn, telling himself that it wouldn't happen like this on one of those television police shows. He went back the next day, with no expectations. Sometime in the middle of the afternoon he heard the woman's door open and shut, and through the crack in the fire door he watched her take the lift.

He gave her five minutes. He had bought a metal nailfile in Boots, which had earned him an odd look from the sales girl. He tried it on the lock without success. Picking locks had never been a skill of his. He checked the front doors for sounds of life in the other flats, then gave the old woman's door a sharp kick. It flew open and O'Grady felt like he was in a television show of his own. He went back and waited on the back stairs, ready to run if anyone came, but no one did and he walked in, pushing the door to behind him.

It was still recognisably his old flat apart from the furniture. The kitchen cupboards were the same green and the doors to the rooms were blue as they always had been. He sat for a moment in the living room, wanting to stay there for the rest of the afternoon watching the clouds. There was rain over to the east. The television had been left on with the sound up to deter intruders.

There were two bedrooms. The bigger, where he and Maggie had slept, was empty. The old woman had her bed in the narrow room that had been Lily's. It smelled of old age and talcum powder. O'Grady thought of the baby that had been shown round at his mother's home, and how Lily had always smelled so fresh. It used to make him feel sad in a sentimental way. There had been talcum powder in the room then, too, but with none of the sense of collapse that now hung in the air.

He took a chair from the kitchen, placed it in the hall under a trapdoor that led to a small storage area, not big enough to call a loft, and hauled himself up. There was still no proper light and only room enough to crawl. From what he could see, the place had not been disturbed since he had last been there. The old woman had none of her stuff stored and a couple of battered cardboard boxes that had been left up there looked old enough to be theirs. He checked them by the light of the trapdoor. One held children's clothes, the other looked like a mix of his and Maggie's. It made him uncomfortable, thinking of a part of them still accidentally together all those years.

He knew he was taking too long. The woman had probably only gone to the corner store. He thought about why he was there. He knew it had something to do with the confusion in his head after Maggie, and going back to the flat was about touching the past. Whatever guide-rope he was using to lead him through the obscurity and muddle in his head had taken him back to the flat, as if it might be a point from which he could move on.

As to what he did next, he could not tell if it was because he was reminded, by being back in that space again, or if it had been at the back of his mind all along, and was the real, underlying reason for his being there.

He crawled forward to the cistern in the corner. It was too dark to see and he had to work by feel. He pushed up his sleeve to his elbow. The coldness of the water made him gasp and for a second he felt he was deep underground but inside his own head. The tank was bigger than he remembered and he had to put his arm in up to the shoulder.

He walked his fingers along the bottom of the tank, picturing the old woman in the lift. He didn't want her to surprise him and everything to go wrong. He forced himself to keep calm and found the package in the end, up against the side of the tank, not flat on the bottom as he remembered.

It had been carefully waterproofed and he wondered if it had kept out the wet all this time. He squeezed his own clothing dry as best he could, and on his way back collected the boxes.

He closed the hatch after him, returned the chair to the kitchen and left by the stairs.

He saw the old woman getting out of a mini-cab. The boxes helped hide his wet sleeve. He wondered what she would make of her broken lock and nothing missing.

He walked around till he felt normal. He told himself it was still fifteen years ago and he was taking old clothes to the charity shop, which would normally be Maggie's job, but with Lily ill, he was having to do it instead.

O'Grady sat on a bench and inspected the boxes more thoroughly. The smaller was just the child's clothes, tiny brightly coloured cardigans and tee-shirts with pictures on. Maggie had always bought expensively. He remembered asking her what was the point of spending money on Lily's clothes when she grew out of them so fast. The other box was mainly Maggie's, apart from some old shirts and trousers of his. He tried to picture the boxes lying undisturbed in the dark and forgotten all those years, like ghosts of the family he had once belonged to.

The box with his and Maggie's clothes he left in a charity shop on Camden High Street. Lily's he took home, along with the package, which he placed unopened at the back of a drawer, and tried not to think about it, or the implications of what he had done.

Nothing happened to make anything seem out of the ordinary but O'Grady could not shake off the feeling that these were strange days full of unseen consequences. He grew convinced that breaking into the old woman's flat would result in another action, seemingly unconnected, but part of a chain. He told himself it was a guilty conscience he was suffering from.

One afternoon he went with Kathleen to the Welsh Harp, a wind-ripped stretch of water by the North Circular, without understanding why he was taking her there. They sat in the car and kissed, neither of them able to tell if that was what they wanted. O'Grady sensed they were drifting apart – not that they had been close in the first place – and losing whatever desire there had been. He couldn't see what he had to offer. No fun, that was for sure, and he didn't tell stories or make people laugh like Shaughnessy.

They got out of the car and walked to the water's edge.

'What are we doing out here?' Kathleen asked.

'I used to come here. Quite a bit.' He didn't say with Lily. He wondered about the real meaning behind these visits to old places.

Kathleen walked into his room after breakfast the next morning without knocking and announced bluntly, 'There's someone to see you.' She looked hostilely at O'Grady, who said he wasn't expecting anyone.

'A woman,' said Kathleen, sounding extremely cool.

Maggie was the last person he would have expected at the hotel. But there she was standing in his doorway, and he knew then that this was the random consequence he had been waiting for.

She was smartly suited, dressed to make a point. Her outfit made Kathleen look scruffy and humiliated. She stepped into the room, missing the dark look given her by Kathleen, who followed that by saying scornfully to O'Grady, 'I'll not be used.'

Maggie watched Kathleen's departure in a way that reminded O'Grady of a grown-up's pained reaction to a normally obedient child answering back. She looked at him with the same expression, then took in the room with its shabby furniture and bashed-about television which lacked even a proper aerial.

O'Grady said nothing, watching her take her time, treating his pathetic little space to a full inspection. Apart from her clothes, the smell of her perfume was the most expensive thing in the room. O'Grady wondered if her being there was in reply to his visit, a measure of how far she had travelled from him, and to give him the full benefit of her contempt. It wasn't gloating exactly but something more complicated, like a reckoning of accounts. He was reminded of her house full of its smart appliances.

'How did you know where I was?' he asked.

She considered his question from an amused distance, only half listening. 'I phoned your sister. She lied for you, you know, but she did it so badly I knew you had to be here.'

Maggie was poised, totally in control, one high-heeled foot tilted, toe in the air. O'Grady doubted if Molly's establishment had ever seen heels so high. Her jacket gave her square shoulders.

Whatever the reason she was there, it wasn't for talk. 'Have you seen what you came for?' O'Grady asked, shamed by the tattiness of his surroundings and the untouchable woman Maggie had become. He had expected her to sneer, not conduct herself with such armour-plated composure.

'This is the last time you and me see each other,' she said. 'Do you understand?'

She wasn't satisfied until O'Grady answered her.

'Yes,' he said, knowing then what it would feel like to kick away the stool.

'Ever,' said Maggie. 'And this is my farewell gift.'

With that she handed him a folded piece of paper from her bag. For a moment O'Grady thought she was passing him some sort of legal summons. He could smell her perfume even on the paper. It was an address.

'What's this?' he asked.

She watched him, enjoying his bewilderment. 'You deserve each other' was the last thing she said to him.

That night, her parting words still a puzzle, he drove to the address. It was in Totteridge, right on the northern edge of the city, on a hill that looked over it. Totteridge was money. Totteridge was so much money that it barely registered in O'Grady's universe and he could not understand what it had to do with Lily.

He had once met a bent accountant who lived in Totteridge and managed the finances of several pop singers. Associates from the old days had occasionally preached the virtues of legitimising income, or at least appearing to, and it was for this reason that O'Grady had met the man. Nothing had happened because he had grown too used to running his affairs with cash and he could not see the point of putting it through the books.

The address was not easy to find, even with a street map. The road was all big houses. Most were without numbers, hidden behind fences or high hedges and standing so far back that half the time it was hard to tell if there was a house there at all. Even the road stopped being a normal street and became more like a country lane. These were the sort of houses most people weren't meant to find, and you went there only by invitation. The point was proved when O'Grady eventually found it. There was a party going on.

The house was a large half-timbered affair with floodlit grounds. It lay sealed off behind electronic gates wide enough for several cars and about twelve foot high. O'Grady noticed cameras on the gate pillars, monitoring the entrance. Thumping music drifted across the lawn, and cars were parked all up the drive. He wondered who owned the place and what Lily had to do with it.

The music stopped for a moment and he heard the sound of breaking glass and the thin, high peal of female laughter.

When he got back to Kilburn there was an ambulance in the street with its lights flashing and a small crowd of people standing around, several in their night clothes. A blanketed figure was being carried from the hotel on a stretcher, head covered and obviously dead. He spotted Molly following the ambulance men and went over. She looked grim and upset.

'What's going on?' asked O'Grady.

'It's mother.'

Nothing made sense for a moment. His mother was in a home.

But his mother, it turned out, had come home to die. 'She still had her keys,' Molly told him.

O'Grady noticed a police car parked behind the ambulance with a policewoman using her radio. She looked bored. As the ambulance doors shut the crowd started to drift away.

He still could not grasp what had happened. His mother was virtually bedridden yet had somehow managed the journey of a mile or more down to Kilburn. He noticed the woman in charge of the home, looking worried as she talked to one of the ambulance men. She walked over to them and apologised. She said they were still trying to work out how their mother had managed to leave the home unnoticed and what had happened.

'She walked,' said Molly.

'Walked!' echoed O'Grady. 'How could she?'

'She told me she did.'

'But she was a very old woman,' said O'Grady. 'Tell me what's going on.'

He sensed Molly's anger and the pressure building as she addressed him. 'I'll tell you what. Mother managed to get herself dressed, after not bothering for years, and find her coat, her hat and her keys and to walk out of that godforsaken home and somehow, with just the help of her stick, get herself down here from Anson Road. At least that's what she told me, though, who knows, perhaps she was exaggerating for the sake of a bit of a story and she caught the bus or took a taxi.' Molly gave an unexpected high-pitched laugh. 'Either way it was a fucking miracle.'

O'Grady had never heard his sister swear before, beyond the occasional mild expletive. She sounded hysterical. The woman from the home looked shocked. Molly said to O'Grady, 'And where were you, brother of mine?'

O'Grady shook his head. He wasn't sure what she meant. Molly sighed to say he was stupid.

'Mother was asking after you. I found her downstairs in her hat and coat, and she said she had come back to see us. She was fretting about you, saying she thought you were on the end of a raw deal.' Molly shook her head in violent disagreement. 'And she said, "Where is he?" I went and looked in your room and you were out, so I sent that Kathleen to look in the pubs and she couldn't find you, so I told Mother you weren't around and she said, "Typical." And that was the last word she said. I went to phone the home and make her a cup of tea, and when I came back she had gone.'

Everything went on hold while his mother's affairs were sorted out. The days passed in a blur, and were measured in O'Grady's mind by Molly's barely restrained anger. Their mother's death unleashed in her years of held-back resentment. In the kitchen in the morning she snapped relentlessly at Kathleen and bossed O'Grady as if he was a moron. O'Grady was not sure what he was supposed to be feeling. Standing in his room looking out of the window, he felt sad. The rest of the time he was puzzled or confused, reminding him of when he had been a child and could not relate his behaviour or feelings to what he was told was right or wrong. He felt guilty because he did not feel more.

The funeral was on a blustery day with a high blue sky. It affected him less than his funeral dream had done. He spent most of the burial thinking that it was happening too late. Everyone, including his mother, would rather she hadn't hung on. The handsome priest was the star turn, twinkling with grief, hands clasped with a sincerity that came only from years of practice.

Even Molly squeezed out a tear. Unable to connect with anything directly, O'Grady hung on to the details – dandruff on the collar of one of the funeral men, a driver standing in the distance, cigarette cupped in his palm. The home had mislaid his mother's suitcase and he'd had to take her few clothes and possessions away in a black plastic bin liner. There was a photograph of him as a boy, but none of Molly. She must have kept it in a drawer because he had not seen it. The photograph shocked him. He had always thought of Molly as the favoured one.

There was no wake. He and Molly had a glass of sherry with the priest. There had been less than a half a dozen people at the funeral, and at least two of them O'Grady was sure were strangers looking for something to do. Molly's way of coping was to regard the whole business as an unwelcome interruption to her routine. She became frantically busy, sorting out linen cupboards and organising the washing of windows. O'Grady, by contrast, drifted. His days became purposeless. He sat for long periods in his room doing nothing. The thoughts that passed through his head never formed into anything coherent. He watched them slip by like they belonged to someone else. With other people he felt the same, quite unconnected to what was around him. He went for a drink once with Kathleen and Maureen. They were joined by a subdued Shaughnessy who treated O'Grady like a casual acquaintance. It reminded him of being a youngster returning to school after the long holidays and finding boys who had been friends no longer were, for reasons that were never clear.

Sometimes in his room O'Grady held up the clothes that had once been his daughter's but beyond making him feel vaguely sad they failed to jog his memory in the way that he had hoped. Sometimes he thought about the laughter he had heard drifting from the big house and across the lawn, and believed it was Lily's.

The solicitor's office had its name stencilled in faded gold on the window, which looked down on the High Road. The solicitor's parting stood about an inch above his ear so that he could scrape what was left of his hair over the top in an effort that fooled nobody. O'Grady thought solicitors were supposed to be smart enough not to look like idiots. He noted the hat hung on the back of the door, which was just as well because with any hint of a wind the whole ridiculous arrangement of the man's hair would be blown away. His mother's death was introducing him to a world that had passed him by, of offices and arrangements and documents, one that Molly was far more familiar with. She seemed at home sitting in her black clothes opposite the solicitor. O'Grady wore his overcoat. It wasn't black but it was dark enough.

'Mrs O'Grady's will is brief and to the point,' said the solicitor.

Down in the street O'Grady could see Shaughnessy walking on his own, making his way up towards the Black Lion. Again O'Grady was surprised at how down he looked and he wondered whether the high spirits were an act. If Shaughnessy was hanging around to conjure up something out of O'Grady's situation, he was a lot more desperate than he was letting on. O'Grady hadn't thought of it like that before.

The will left everything to Molly.

'Meaning?' said O'Grady, knowing he sounded stupid. It was perfectly clear.

'The hotel passes to your sister. There is nothing else. The home ate up most of your mother's savings and by the time her estate is settled and fees paid the balance is virtually nil.'

O'Grady thought it a waste of time being there. He knew he did not have the right to expect anything, and since he'd had nothing to do with the organisation of his mother's life he felt like an impostor sitting in on the meeting.

Molly regarded him coldly. 'I'll tell you what it means. Twenty-five years of my life is what it means.'

'What would have happened about paying for the home if she hadn't died?' asked O'Grady.

Molly stood up. 'It was taken care of. It has been taken care of for years.'

She walked out without waiting for him, leaving the solicitor to explain that as his mother's money went down the council contributed more to her upkeep. O'Grady felt uncomfortable, left sitting there by Molly. Getting up and excusing himself he felt even more awkward.

That night he was awoken by a banging. At first he thought it was someone trying to smash the front door down, then he realised it was inside the house.

It was coming from Molly's room. He found Kathleen hovering on the landing and told her to go back to bed.

He knocked on Molly's door. The banging carried on and she didn't answer. He tried the handle. It wasn't locked. Kathleen was still standing watching and O'Grady motioned her back to her room. One or two other doors were opening.

'Jesus, Molly,' he blurted out, 'what are you doing?'

His sister was on all fours, banging the floor planks with a hammer. The carpet had been stripped back. He could smell the drink in the room. He tried to avoid looking at Molly. She was wearing a candlewick dressing gown which was undone and beneath that a slip. He was embarrassed by the white flesh of her legs.

Seeing him, she checked. He watched the confusion and guilt on her face. Then she grew brazen and snarled at him with undisguised hostility until drool came from her mouth. 'You great pig-arsed cunt. You feckless backslider, creeping back to where you're not wanted to parade your mean little prison sentence like you were one of the Forty Holy Martyrs. Dispensation! Dispensation!'

She waved the hammer at him. O'Grady was distracted by her slip, which looked expensive, silk even. More alarming was that Molly had a body any woman would be proud of. He wondered how she had managed to hide it away so successfully.

'Cut it out, Molly,' he said, shocked by his reaction and feeling out of his depth.

'Smell the gin on me? Well, can you?'

She started banging the floorboards again. O'Grady moved to stop her and she swung at him with the hammer, glancing him on the forearm.

'Come on now, Molly,' he said, trying to sound calmer than he felt. 'You're waking people up.'

'You're pathetic.' She stood up. O'Grady held out his hand for the hammer and she tried to hit him again, until he managed to grab her wrist and twisted so she dropped it. He wanted that to be the end of the matter but she launched herself at him, beating his head and chest with her fists, reminding him of Maggie.

The only way to stop her was to pick her up. She struggled and the pair of them lurched awkwardly round the room in a parody of a drunken dance.

'Get your filthy hands off me!' Molly shouted. 'And all the time you were away in your holiday camp feeling sorry for yourself, did you ever think what I got? I got life. Think about that.'

Sensing the struggle going out of her, O'Grady let go, catching her as she fell. He shook her by the shoulders until the hysteria had gone, then sat her down and closed her dressing gown.

'Plain at best,' she said, 'that was me. So holy she should have been a nun. That's what they said.'

She cried, not bothering to hide it. O'Grady took her hands awkwardly. She flinched but did not resist, and he stayed with her a long time while she sat silently weeping, until she said she wanted to go to sleep.

Back in his own room O'Grady kept himself awake with the memory of the peal of a girl's laughter drifting across the darkened lawn of the big house.

Others were making their moves. The next morning O'Grady saw Shaughnessy hanging around outside the hotel. He made him wait.

When he went to the car that afternoon Shaughnessy was sitting in the passenger seat reading a newspaper. 'You took your time' was all he said.

O'Grady got behind the wheel. He knew why Shaughnessy was there. Everything was getting bound up together and he could no longer keep the strands separate the way he wanted to.

'Awful, terrible news about your mother. Not meaning to intrude on your grief and all that,' said Shaughnessy with a stab at moderate sincerity.

'Cut the crap,' said O'Grady, turning on the engine.

'We need to talk,' said Shaughnessy. 'I've found one of your erstwhile double-crossing partners.'

'Ronnie?'

'The other one. John.'

O'Grady shrugged. 'John was a nobody.'

'Tel's scared enough of him.'

'Tel lost his nerve years ago.'

'How's yours?'

'I've no problem. Now, if you don't mind, I have business of my own.'

'I'll come for the ride if you like.'

'Private business.'

Shaughnessy shrugged and said, 'I'll leave you the paper. I've read it twice. I hear your sister was making a racket last night.'

Shaughnessy as usual seemed very well informed. O'Grady dropped him outside the Black Lion. Finding John would not get them very far, he was sure of that.

He sat in the car a long time, watching the house. The Datsun was pulled in to the side of the road about thirty yards from the open gate. A couple of builder's vans had gone in and out but nothing said what sort of people lived there.

O'Grady found a less conspicuous spot to park the car, about quarter of a mile away, and walked back. Faced by the imposing size of the house and its air of rich calm, he saw how flimsy his plan was and nearly turned back. He felt exposed walking in the gates. The drive was made of asphalt with white flecks to show how expensive it was. The house was covered with greenery and looked as if it had about sixteen bedrooms. A red Mercedes sports car and a black Range Rover stood by the front door. The idea of owning anything like this, of claiming so much space, left him even more nervous. He tried to picture himself moving through so many rooms, and finding a reason for each one. He wondered for a moment if the address had been given to him as a cruel joke and had nothing to do with Lily.

There was a builder's van parked round the side of the house, carefully out of the way. O'Grady tried hard to look as though he was meant to be there. The builders were plastering in an outbuilding that was being turned into some sort of proper space, as though the house itself was not large enough.

Putting his head round the door and trying to sound as casual as possible, O'Grady said, 'The fellow asking for an estimate, who would that be?'

The first builder shrugged and said, 'The kid who owns the place, whatisname.' Without turning round, his mate added, 'Keith.'

He was told that Keith would be somewhere in the house and that the front door was open. It was. O'Grady hesitated and thought of ringing the bell. Had the door been properly shut he probably would have done, but it was temptingly ajar. He pushed it open and stood on the threshold looking into the cool, dark hall. Over the stairs was a large stained-glass window which spangled the light, making it look expensive.

Though it was well into the afternoon the remains of the night before's party were still in evidence. O'Grady wondered if there was a party every night. Empty glasses stood waiting to be tidied away. Full ashtrays lay on the floor. Nobody was around. From somewhere in the distance came the sound of a vacuum cleaner.

O'Grady stood there a long time, hoping someone would turn up. He was aware of his own awkwardness, with his sleeves too short and his clothes grubby. His paralysis ended when a sleepy-looking girl came out of one of the rooms off the hall, still in her rumpled party clothes. She walked with a bad limp. O'Grady was embarrassed, thinking she had a deformity that would make it harder for him to sound normal, until he saw all she was missing was a high-heeled shoe.

She asked if he had seen it. Her make-up was smudged and he could see the acne beneath.

'Are you Lily?' he asked, without meaning to, hoping it wasn't.

She shook her head vaguely, and winced. She looked badly hung over. O'Grady wondered again what sort of house this was.

'Do you know where Keith is?' he asked. Hung over or not, the girl was starting to give him strange looks. She shrugged and said, 'Upstairs, maybe.'

The staircase was wide, with shallow treads, and turned round a well. O'Grady felt better for having talked to someone, but upstairs he became nervous again, confronted by a long corridor of closed doors. Only one was open. He glanced inside but it was empty. What he was doing felt close to snooping and would be hard to explain if he was found. He decided to go back downstairs.

He was not aware of being watched so he could not say what made him turn and look back as he reached the top of the stairs.

There she was. He was sure of it. Standing in the doorway at the far end of the corridor with the light behind her. He could not see her properly, only her silhouette, but he knew it was her.

'I was told to look for Keith,' he said.

'Told to look up here?' She sounded sharp, clearly used to telling people what to do. When he heard her voice he was disappointed. She sounded too old for Lily and he was making a fool of himself. Why should it be her? She walked impatiently towards him, saying, 'Who told you to look up here?'

She had long blonde hair. She was wearing tight dark blue jeans and a white shirt. O'Grady was not sure any more if she was his daughter. In a way, she no longer was, even if she once had been. If this young woman, with her confident swing of the hips, was Lily, she had nothing to do with the little girl he had known. He had always told himself that when the moment came he would know, from first sight, but now he felt only doubt. In his memory Lily had been gently fair, not a bright blonde. He tried to match the young woman approaching to the Lily in his dream, but the dream had faded. He was desperate to ask but his nerve failed. He felt crushed and let down by his uncertainty.

She walked past with barely a glance and paused on the stairs to make sure he was following. He tried not to stare too hard.

They crossed the hall and went down a long corridor. She talked to him over her shoulder. 'He's probably in the studio. Who are you, anyway?'

Her tone was cool. O'Grady's heart nevertheless did a flip. 'Just your Daddy-oh,' he wanted to say, though he knew already that the likes of him didn't register in her world.

They arrived at a door with a red light and waited. Puzzled by the delay, he was about to say something, but she motioned him to be quiet. She stood half turned away, which prevented him getting a proper look. When the light went off they were allowed in.

The door was so thick he thought he was entering a bank vault. He stepped into a darkened space, lit at the far end. The young woman pointed to a spot by the door, making it clear that he was to wait.

As his eyes grew accustomed to the dark O'Grady saw several nonchalant-looking young men sat behind a large raised electronic desk. Nobody paid him any attention or even glanced at him. He might as well have been invisible. A young woman at the far end of the room was sitting in a glass booth wearing headphones. She was not Lily. She was a mixture of Caribbean and Asian. Apart from her and the young woman who had brought him there, the rest were men. O'Grady decided Keith was the one sitting furthest away doing the talking, while his hands slid different knobs up and down the desk. He called the singer Cherry. His dominating tone made it plain she was only there because of him, because he had seen something in her nobody else had, yet, which allowed him to treat her as his property. The other young men were arguing about something technical.

The young woman who had brought him lit a cigarette, using a book of matches. O'Grady watched her striking the flimsy match clumsily several times before getting a flame. He felt a wave of tenderness for her for the way she was trying to be so grown-up while being so obviously jealous that the other woman was getting all the attention.

She threw the book of matches at a standing ashtray by O'Grady and missed. He picked it up. On the cover was a design and a name. Seeing her watching, he asked, 'Restaurant?'

She blew out smoke, not interested. 'Club,' she said, implying he was a fool for having to ask.

O'Grady was about to say that he would come back later as everyone was busy when the man who had been talking to the singer said offhandedly, 'Fix us a coffee, babe.'

He didn't even look at her as he ordered it. O'Grady wanted to teach him some manners. He realised then, in that gesture of wanting to protect her, that this was the moment he knew it was her.

'And Lil?' the man asked. He turned and leaned forward and O'Grady saw him properly for the first time. He was shocked.

The man wasn't young at all. His hair was greased back flat to his skull in a way that O'Grady hadn't seen since old films. Because everyone else in the room was young O'Grady had assumed that he would be, too. He wasn't old, he certainly didn't look old enough to own the house they were in, but he was a lot older than his daughter, and O'Grady was in no doubt from the way he addressed her that he was fucking her too. The crudity of his observation shocked him. He was jealous. Not, he quickly told himself, because the man was with his daughter, but because he knew her better than he did.

O'Grady watched her go over to the man, who whispered something in her ear, and noted his possessive look. His heart cracked at the sound of her uncertain laugh, which told him she knew she was being used and was in pain. The look on her face as she passed him on her way out revealed a transparent unhappiness which made him want even more to protect her.

He followed her, saying he would come back later. She shrugged. She had barely given him a glance since he had first seen her. He let her walk away down the corridor. Then, as if hit by a delayed reaction, she turned and asked sharply, 'Who are you? What do you want?'

'Nothing,' he said, which was the truth.

She turned and walked away again. O'Grady made his way slowly back to the car. He sat behind the wheel, half in, the door still open, and watched the wind skim a puddle, followed by the first drops of rain. She was seventeen, he thought, for only another few days. He wondered when Maggie had let her go. He didn't like the set-up in the house, nor did he like the man, but there was nothing he could do. He had promised himself that, and now he had said the same to her.

After Lily, O'Grady's moods swung violently. He'd seen her but the gulf between their worlds was so great that it left him feeling worse than helpless. Since Maggie's inspection of his pathetic world, his room seemed even more of a shabby embarrassment, and the box of child's clothes struck him as a hopelessly sentimental gesture. He had lost her years ago. The clothes should have told him as much. Instead, he had taken their discovery as a sign of good luck. He had always read the world in superstitious terms, even in his hard days. The long years in prison had taught him that the hardness went with the sentiment which he tried so hard to deny, and both were false: they acted as a cover.

Molly was conspicuous by her absence at breakfast and Kathleen appeared in a bad mood and O'Grady was left wondering if he had offended her. He had not had a chance to explain Maggie's appearance. Apart from a curt 'Good morning' they served breakfast in silence and it wasn't until they sat down to eat themselves that she spoke.

'What do you think of the news?'

O'Grady had no idea what she was talking about. When she saw he wasn't joking she produced a folded note and passed it over. O'Grady read it slowly and wondered in turn if it wasn't a joke.

'She's giving you notice,' he said, puzzled.

'Out by the end of the week.'

His first thought was that Molly was getting rid of her because Kathleen had seen her drunk.

'It's not just me, mister. It's the lot of us, guests and all.' Seeing his confusion, she added, 'You mean you don't know? She's selling up.'

He confronted Molly immediately, without waiting to finish his breakfast. He found her in her room. She was wearing a new outfit, something much less dowdy than usual, and faced him with the determination of someone who had made up her mind.

'Did you expect me to keep the place for sentimental reasons?'

O'Grady had never considered Molly doing anything else except the hotel.

'So I was decorating the place just to help you sell it.'

'Not necessarily. It was only after Mother died I realised what I wanted.'

'Don't you think I had a right to know before the others?'

'Why?'

'I am your brother.'

'It's a bit late in the day to start playing that card.'

From the way she began fussing about, moving things around, he could see he had embarrassed her.

'Why are you selling?'

'Because it's worth it.'

O'Grady was puzzled. He couldn't see how. Kilburn was Kilburn. A house in West End Lane had changed hands for twenty pounds before the war.

'What's worth it?' he asked awkwardly, thinking she meant something other than money.

'Half a million pounds, or thereabouts.'

'It never is. This isn't Mayfair.'

Molly, it turned out, was talking about five houses. Over the years she had acquired the ones on either side and added them to the hotel. O'Grady knew about those. He didn't know about the two more beyond which she had bought cheap the year before and let stand empty.

'Five houses in a row,' he said, shaking his head in disbelief. 'How does it feel to have the last laugh?'

'I'll be going away for a week or so,' she said briskly, ignoring his question. 'There's a set of keys at the agents. I've told them you'll be here so they'll telephone first. You can stay here until the place is sold, which will take a month or two, I'm told.'

'If that's what you want,' said O'Grady lamely. He had taken the place for granted and never thought he would have to move.

Molly said nothing. O'Grady sensed she was putting distance between them after the other night.

'What do you want?' he persisted.

Molly busied herself with putting on gloves. She was a rich woman now, he realised with a shock, and could live the rest of her life off the interest from her capital.

'I want what you had,' she said slowly, 'and threw away. That's what I want. Except it's too late now for that.'

However hard O'Grady tried to ignore them, Shaughnessy's plans slid into the frame.

He was still coming to terms with Molly's unexpected move, wondering where that left him. Her place wasn't home exactly but it was familiar, and with his mother gone too it was starting to look as if all his props were being taken away. Even his room provided him with a refuge of sorts – regardless of Maggie's estimation of it – and he was afraid of any alternative. For the moment his life had enough order for him to pretend he was still putting it back together again by tracing Lily. He kept telling himself that, regardless of the feeling that he might crack at any moment like an old plate.

He even thought of throwing in his lot with Shaughnessy, who at least offered some plan, until one wet afternoon he was picked up and told he was driving them to west London to see John. Tel sat in the back of the car looking even more wrecked than usual. It was impossible to believe he had once been an operator, thought O'Grady as he got in.

He also wondered what Tel had been saying to Shaughnessy, who had got it into his head that John and Ronnie had been life-long buddies of his. That was not so. O'Grady had driven them and otherwise avoided them, especially John, who was nasty and unpredictable and saw an insult where no one else did.

Shaughnessy had also heard of Molly's plans. 'Half a million pounds, and here are we scratching around after what? For that kind of money I'd consider marrying her myself.'

When Shaughnessy gave directions that took them over the Harrow Road and across the top of North Kensington, O'Grady grew concerned about their destination. When they drove down North Pole Road and Shaughnessy told him to turn left at the junction of Scrubs Lane, O'Grady knew for sure where John was. He made the right into Du Cane Road without being told, with a look at Shaughnessy, who half-shrugged an apology.

O'Grady pulled up past the prison. It was a big old Victorian building pretending to be a castle or an army barracks rather than a civilian prison. The cheap box-housing around it suggested that the standard of living for the prison staff wasn't great, either.

O'Grady made no move to get out.

'Giddy-up, Pat, visiting time.'

He felt a dull stubbornness in the pit of his stomach which translated into nausea. He sat there in angry silence, not budging, thinking he'd not go back to prison for any man, even as a visitor.

'Ah, quatsch, Pat, stop being paranoid.'

'Qvatch?' said Tel from the back.

'German for balls,' said Shaughnessy testily. 'John's expecting us. It would be a shame to let him down.'

O'Grady nodded, only because he needed to get out of the car.

'Good man. I knew you wouldn't let me down. I don't have to tell you the routine,' said Shaughnessy, trying to make light of O'Grady's nerves.

O'Grady was next aware of standing in the middle of the road still not knowing what to do. He hated his indecision and his inability to speak up for himself. He hated himself for not telling

Lily who he was. He turned and looked back at the car. Shaughnessy made a shooing gesture, motioning him forward.

He looked up the street. For once in his life there was a bus coming and the stop opposite. He waited in the road until it drew up, walked round the back and swung himself onto the platform as it pulled away, feeling good about his escape. He didn't look back.

Shaughnessy tracked him down in the Black Lion that evening. O'Grady was sitting in a corner on his own. He had come in earlier and seen Kathleen drinking with a young man. She had her back to him but he knew she had seen him in the mirror and was ignoring him.

By the time Shaughnessy arrived O'Grady was feeling sorry for himself. By running off he was sure he had lost the use of Shaughnessy's car. No more trips to Totteridge without time-consuming journeys on public transport and a long walk at the other end because he didn't have the money for taxis.

Shaughnessy seemed to sense his mood because when he sat down he made no mention of O'Grady's disappearance. 'Keeping a low profile?' was all he said.

They drank without talking and Shaughnessy fetched fresh drinks without asking. The silence threatened to become comical and in the end Shaughnessy couldn't resist a joke. 'That's what I like about you, Pat. A real touch of the blarney. Never knew a silent type that had an easy shit. They always end up with haemorrhoids.'

O'Grady regarded his glass stonily.

'Forget about it,' said Shaughnessy airily. 'Water under the bridge.'

They ended up in Totteridge. O'Grady wondered if Shaughnessy hadn't picked him like a lock, opening him up to say what was on his mind.

'Ah, so you've found her,' Shaughnessy had said with an air of wonder.

In the end, chasing the stout with Jameson's, O'Grady had told him everything, about the house and the man Lily was with. He could not help it, even knowing that Shaughnessy was not to be trusted. He knew that at some time in the future what he was saying would be used against him. Shaughnessy went out of his way to flatter him, complimenting him on the presence of mind he'd shown getting into the house, and O'Grady was pleased, however insincerely it was meant. He knew Shaughnessy was encouraging him to talk for reasons that weren't clear to him, but he did not care. The man was trying a different tack, that was obvious, but O'Grady had only one immediate aim, and Shaughnessy duly obliged by dangling the Datsun's keys and saying, 'Jesus, Pat, let's go and chase up that girl of yours and do something useful instead of moping.'

Part of the price was that Shaughnessy went with him. Whatever had happened after O'Grady jumped on the bus Shaughnessy was not saying, which was clever of him, O'Grady thought, because he was starting to get curious. He wondered what John was inside for. Assault or grievous bodily harm, no doubt. As for himself, he was liable for a drink–driving charge but that didn't bother him. His driving had been alert and steady all the way there.

They sat in the car for an hour or more. Being high up Shaughnessy tried the radio, which didn't normally work, and managed to pick up a late-night phone-in with bad reception that sounded as if everyone was trying to talk and gargle at the same time. Shaughnessy made him laugh imitating it and O'Grady felt comfortably drunk, waiting there in the warmth of the car. They might be wasting their time, but he pushed the thought from his mind. The night still held promise.

'Look,' said Shaughnessy.

Someone was leaving the house in the red sports car O'Grady had seen in the drive. It paused briefly for the automatic gates, too far away for him to tell who was inside. But as it drove past he saw a splash of blonde and glimpsed Lily in the passenger seat.

'Pretty girl. Likes the good life,' said Shaughnessy. Seeing

O'Grady transfixed, he dug him with his elbow. 'Are we following or what?'

The Datsun was facing the wrong way. By the time O'Grady had turned, the Mercedes was out of sight and Shaughnessy fretting.

'And you were the getaway driver.'

O'Grady wasn't worried. He had a good idea of their route. The road they were on ran down to a big roundabout and from there he guessed the Mercedes would head along the A41 towards town. Shaughnessy was less confident and grumbled, 'You haven't got a clue where they are.'

They were on the Barnet by-pass when O'Grady spotted the Mercedes again, cruising in the inside lane, in no particular hurry. It had a soft top, which made it easier to spot.

'There it is!' shouted Shaughnessy after O'Grady had already tucked in behind. The rest was easy. The Mercedes signalled its directions and kept to the speed limit. At a set of red lights O'Grady eased the Datsun alongside and out of the corner of his eye saw Lily in animated conversation. She looked angry. The man glanced across at their car, dismissing them. Shaughnessy tapped his teeth with his fingers. When the Mercedes sped away from the lights O'Grady was confident enough to let it get ahead.

'Hurry, man!' said Shaughnessy. 'They're getting away.'

'We'll pick them up on the North Circular.'

'How do you know?'

'Because they're going to Harlesden.'

'What the fuck's in Harlesden for the likes of them? Harlesden's a ditch.'

They caught up on the Staples Corner flyover and Shaughnessy said, 'Well, Pat, the angels are with you tonight.'

After that O'Grady stuck close. He wasn't worried about being spotted, even if the boyfriend saw the Datsun again. O'Grady was willing to bet he was so wrapped up in Lily that they wouldn't register.

He followed the Mercedes to a turning off Old Oak Lane

close to the railway sidings, not far from the prison where they had been earlier that day. Their destination was not at all what O'Grady had been expecting, and the place was not at all what he had imagined. He associated nightclubs with puffy awnings over the door and populated areas, shops at least, but this looked like an industrial shed stuck on a trading estate. Nevertheless, there were cars all over the place, half up on the kerb, and a large open piece of wasteland was also being used for parking.

'You could make enough noise here to raise the dead and nobody'd complain,' said Shaughnessy.

The Mercedes pulled in to the open space. O'Grady chose not to follow but drove on, turned and pulled up short, and switched off the engine and lights.

Lily and the man took their time. O'Grady wondered why they were being so long. Shaughnessy sat with his eyebrows raised, fighting the temptation to say something funny.

Other cars drove into the car park while they waited. 'Busy place,' said Shaughnessy. 'Do you know about them?'

O'Grady shook his head. He wondered what was going on.

'Thousands cram into them and they all take a happy pill and jig up and down to loud music. Sounds like hell to me. There they are.'

O'Grady caught sight of Lily and watched greedily but his view was partly blocked by the man catching up and putting his arm round her. He wished he did not have to endure Shaughnessy's running commentary: 'Is that really your girl? Well, I take my hat off to you. Her mother must have been a good-looking woman. I don't like the cut of the boyfriend's jib. Cocky little sod with his ponytail. He could do with being brought down a peg or two.'

When O'Grady made no move, Shaughnessy looked at him in exasperation. 'Look, Pat, do you mind my asking, if you have no intention of talking to her, what are we doing here?'

'Seeing she's all right.'

'Pretty girls usually are.' Shaughnessy yawned. 'You'd not

have a hope in hell of getting in there. We're a hundred years too old for a start. Ronnie's in Spain, by the way.'

The remark was met with a long silence.

'On the Costa del Crime,' he added.

'I know,' replied O'Grady.

'Wait a minute, are you telling me you knew all along, after it has taken me all this time to find out?'

O'Grady smiled, pleased to have the upper hand.

'You've an odd fucking sense of humour if that's your idea of a joke,' said Shaughnessy, riled.

'I'm not interested. I don't care about any of it,' he said.

'Do you remember any of your Latin from your church days? Quid pro quo, for instance?'

'I decided I don't want to die of cancer.'

'What the hell's cancer got to do with it?'

O'Grady shook his head slowly from side to side.

'What the fuck have you been reading? "A Doctor Writes"?' Shaughnessy was near to losing his temper. 'You won't catch cancer from wanting to get even with Ronnie.'

O'Grady was tired to death of feeling tested by the man's words. He did his best to cut out the slow drip and needle of his voice, at first cajoling, then threatening. He thought of all the people he had wanted to hit since Shaughnessy had wheedled his way into his life. Tel. The boy copper with the crew-cut. Maggie. Even the handsome priest who had done his mother's funeral — more than once he had wondered what he would look like yelping as the blood leaped from his nose. And the man who was using his daughter, for the way he had treated her like dirt when asking for his coffee.

'And all you care about is sitting here making goo-goo eyes at your little girl,' Shaughnessy said.

O'Grady thought of the pleasure belting Shaughnessy would give him, but was afflicted by his usual paralysis. There were too many equations in his head distracting him, to do with things being taken away, to do with what the priests of his childhood had called 'limbo'. It didn't take much of a brain to work out that he had deliberately sought out that state – which was only a continuation of his sentence – going back to Molly's, until he started chasing the ghosts of the past, thanks to Shaughnessy.

'Well, I've had enough of sitting around waiting for you to make up your mind,' said Shaughnessy.

O'Grady wanted Shaughnessy out of his life, not looking over his shoulder. He sat there, bunching his fists in his pockets, refusing to speak, wishing him gone.

'Is that your final answer?' Shaughnessy eventually said. 'Well, so be it. You may be refusing to dance but plenty of others will.'

They sat a long time in stubborn silence, O'Grady watching the main door of the club for any sign of Lily, until Shaughnessy cracked and lost his temper, and loudly cursed him for sitting there like a useless cunt and refusing to do anything. O'Grady could almost smell the man's bile coming off him and wondered where all his rage was coming from.

His own indifference frightened him even more. It was sick, wanting Shaughnessy to turn against him because he was too feeble to act for himself.

'This is what you want, isn't it?' Shaughnessy concluded, reading his thoughts. 'What you've wanted all along. Someone to come and put you out of your misery. Well, let's hope you don't live to regret it. You're on your own now, and don't come crying to me saying I didn't warn you.'

Shaughnessy got out, leaning down through the open door to deliver his parting words. 'You should get one of those cripple stickers for the car because that's what you are. I'm walking.'

The next morning a minicab came for Molly. O'Grady helped load her suitcases. He could not remember his sister ever having taken a taxi before. He ended up standing awkwardly by the boot of the car, with one foot in the road, while Molly gave the hotel a parting glance.

'Good riddance?' said O'Grady, in an effort to make her smile. 'Well, goodbye, Molly. Have a good time in the old country.'

She gave him a queer look and hurriedly said, 'I'll be back next week.'

On impulse she kissed him on the cheek, followed by a terse smile, before getting in the back of the cab. O'Grady leaned down and said, 'It's a minicab so you don't have to tip.' He couldn't think of anything better or more encouraging to say.

He stood in the street a long time after Molly had gone.

There was nothing left to do. The rest of the guests were leaving that day. With Kathleen, O'Grady had served his last breakfast. Soon he would have the place to himself – empty heart, empty house, unless he persuaded Kathleen to stay on. They could move into one of the rooms with a big bed and make as much of a racket as they liked.

Shaughnessy would be dealing with Ronnie now, O'Grady was certain of it, pushed by his own indecision into selling him out. Something was making Shaughnessy desperate enough to cut a deal in any direction. Remembering his fit in the car, O'Grady wondered if Shaughnessy wasn't a well man, and what price he would settle with Ronnie, a cheap deal, no doubt. He could hear Shaughnessy saying to Tel, 'I've been on the blower long-distance to Ronnie. Ronnie's been putting a very interesting proposition.'

O'Grady had the feeling events were starting to move beyond his control. He had heard the going rate for breaking an arm was less than he'd won on Shaughnessy's horse. Unless he was very much mistaken, guns or the like would come into it soon.

When Kathleen came it was to say goodbye. He was sitting half watching television in one of the larger rooms at the front, for no real reason except that it overlooked the street.

'Well, see you around, mister.'

O'Grady stood up. She remained in the doorway. Whatever had been there between them had been spoiled since Maggie's invasion of his room. For the hundredth time he asked himself why Maggie had come and given him Lily's address, and still he had no answer.

He meant to ask Kathleen to stay on till Molly got back and didn't, thinking he was probably too late. He thought about what would have happened if they had got off on the right foot, whether they might have made something of each other. He wished he had the words to talk to her properly, not fancy ones, enough to make sense of the skim of his ragged thoughts. In the end, he decided it was easier to let her go and keep her alive in his head.

The two of them were stood like they were posing for a picture. O'Grady had once seen a photograph of an old painting of a young couple with a dog and floor tiles which had reminded him of another floor, he had never managed to remember where. The painting was hundreds of years old and after seeing it he had spent a long time thinking about what it must have been like to live so long ago. He wished there could be a picture of him and Kathleen at that moment, which someone would look at in five hundred years' time, and wonder about them.

'Well, take care of yourself now, Kathleen,' he said awkwardly, grimly thinking that he must sound like her father. Saying good-bye was bad enough. He wished the moment over so he could go back to the safety of the television.

'Don't worry about me, mister. It's you you should be worrying about.' She took a step in from the doorway. 'This empty house suits you.'

A car went by in the street below. He was aware of Kathleen sidling up to him, part of Shaughnessy's set-up all along, no doubt, being used to make him drop his guard. More likely, he thought angrily, he was too scared to be seen asking anything of her. What he would do, to be on the safe side, was let her go now but arrange to meet later in the Black Lion. Then he could still ask her to stay.

Kathleen was talking to him. He sensed she had been for some time.

'Something moved out of your house a long time ago, didn't it, mister?' she said. 'You know who you remind me of? That fellow in the Bible the nuns clapped their hands over, the one Jesus brought back to life. "It was a holy miracle, to be sure, a dead man returned by Our Lord to the land of the living. And what was his name, Kathleen?" "Lazarus, Sister." What we're not told, because I looked it up, is how Lazarus felt about the whole business. But seeing you, mister, I'd say he would have been none too grateful and the second time around was no fun.'

The next thing he knew it was much later and getting dark, and he had been asleep. The television was still on. O'Grady looked round, expecting to see Kathleen. He had no recollection of her leaving, or if they had made a date for later. The street lamps were coming on. O'Grady thought it strange. He knew he would remember that moment long after forgetting the more important business with Kathleen.

He went to his room. He got the box of Lily's clothes from under the bed and laid them out.

The package he had retrieved from the water tank at the old flat lay still wrapped up in the drawer. He opened it knowing he had reached, one way or another, a point of no return. Layers of polythene had kept everything dry. He oiled the mechanism with a can from a cupboard in the kitchen. There was no rust. Everything was in working order.

He put it on the bed, reminding himself to remember to hide it when the estate agents came round. Molly sitting on half a million pounds: who would have thought it? He hoped she would give up the religious mumbo-jumbo, throw over the traces and find a man to appreciate that surprising body of hers.

The telephone downstairs went several times. O'Grady ignored it. There would be time enough later. If not, none of it mattered anyway.

He didn't know what to do. He was no longer sure what he was waiting for. Someone would come sooner or later. If nobody had come by the evening he would go out again looking for Lily. He sat in the empty front room, indulging himself in the sentimental idea of them all having rooms of their own, one for Lily, one for his mother, and Molly, and himself with Kathleen. He pictured them all in the dining room in the morning. Everyone would know Kathleen was sharing with him and no one would mind. He felt sad because he knew there would be no room for him in anyone else's version of the game.

The next morning the telephone rang in the empty hall, stopped and went again immediately. Thinking it was Molly, O'Grady answered.

'Jesus, Pat, where have you been?' It was Shaughnessy, sounding dangerously friendly, like nothing had happened. From where he was standing, O'Grady could see the top of the stairs where he had first seen Shaughnessy what felt like a long time ago.

'Listen,' said Shaughnessy, 'I want to talk to you. You know there's a Mrs Ronnie, a different one from in your day, and a daughter and a big spread out in Essex.' He said it like he was just chatting. 'They use it sometimes. The girl goes to one of those posh boarding schools.'

'Boarding school?'

'Times have changed. There's stuff to talk about. We need to meet.'

O'Grady sensed the trap being sprung. He had been expecting to be offered an out by way of a lure. He thought of what might be waiting, of the tiny gains of his life unravelling, of the security of the hotel being taken from him and familiar figures like Molly and Kathleen leaving, of his return to emptiness, of losing the present and the hopelessness of trying to return to the past. He was afraid of the future, was afraid he had no future, the stubborn resistance of the daily round nearly done.

O'Grady had the impression of watching and listening to himself from a great height, and recalled a favourite saying of his mother's: 'I'm not feeling myself today.' Great shifts were taking place in short spaces of time, he thought, as opposed to the endless drudgery he had sought for himself by coming back to Molly.

Shaughnessy wanted to meet in the Black Lion before closing time. O'Grady took his time agreeing, seeing how he was a man who was supposed to have trouble making up his mind.

'Ten thirty, then?' Shaughnessy finally said, his temper barely under control.

'The funny thing is, I've been as good as dead for years,' said O'Grady mildly. 'You'd be doing me a favour.'

'Ah come on now, Pat, there's no sense in talking like that,' replied Shaughnessy, refusing to let himself be tripped up. 'We're all in the same boat more or less, facing the big maw.'

'I'll see you there,' said O'Grady ambiguously, certain someone would be waiting on Shaughnessy's say-so to put his lights out afterwards. He would not be there for them.

In the afternoon he took the bus up to Colindale to the newspaper library. He remembered the date well enough. It was the first time he had seen the story written down in black and white. If the facts had dimmed in his head with the passing years, what remained inescapable was the crushed feeling it had left in him, which could still bring on a cold sweat of panic. Not that the newspaper showed any great care for the facts. It was more concerned with depicting him as a monster.

O'Grady read that three masked men had held up a building society in an armed raid. As they left a member of staff pressed the alarm. A driver was waiting in a getaway car. The raiders escaped at speed, but soon afterwards the driver ran down a child on a pedestrian crossing. The driver stopped, forcing the others to escape on foot, and waited with the dying child for the police.

The newspaper started at the end of the story, with the child, and ran it backwards. A large picture showed a little girl under a shock headline. O'Grady read his name. The article made a big thing of the child being on the crossing and having right of way, which made the crime worse. But the scene that replayed in O'Grady's head always showed the girl running out between two cars, some way from the crossing. There had been no time to react, and the force of the impact had thrown her onto the crossing.

It took less than a minute to read the story. The accident itself had taken a fraction of that, though he had been aware of time stretching horribly, as they always said it did in a crash. One of the police officers said to him afterwards, sounding formal as if he, rather than the judge, was passing O'Grady's real sentence. 'You will live with the consequences of this for the rest of your life.'

It was true. He had come to realise that he had no way of coming to terms with what he had done. Nor was he any longer sure if the version carried in his head was the truth, or a modified one that helped him to live with what he had done.

There was always the recurring flash in his mind's eye of a blue coat with a hood and an upside-down look of surprise on her little face as she flew in the air. The worst of it was that he had felt sorriest for himself in that moment, cursing his luck.

He knew he should have done more to make amends, apart from not running away, but he never had. He had tried writing to the parents and failed. Now it would only upset them, getting in touch after all this time. He could find out where the grave was and leave flowers, he supposed.

He dressed smartly, putting on a tie and a jacket to hide the gun tucked in the back of his waistband, then, not trusting himself, replaced the gun in the drawer.

The bell rang as he was about to leave, and rather than answering he stuck his head out of the window and called down. Shaughnessy stepped back from the porch and stood in the path, looking up at him.

'Do you fancy that drink now?'

'What's the time?'

'Just gone nine. Leave it till later if you want.'

'Are you on your own?'

Shaughnessy made a show of looking around. From the way they were conducting themselves it could have been any other Saturday night. O'Grady wondered at the extent of Shaughnessy's thick skin. The man was as relentless as the slow drip of a Chinese water torture.

He left the house in a hurry and hustled Shaughnessy down the path, giving him no time to think. Shaughnessy asked in some confusion, 'What's going on?'

'Where's your car?'

'Round the corner.'

'Show me.' He was half expecting someone to be waiting in it but it was empty. 'You drive' was all he said.

'Where to?' Shaughnessy asked.

O'Grady told him to go up Willesden Lane and over to Queen's Park. Shaughnessy's driving was worse than usual. They drove in silence. The car was full of unspoken tensions. It was one of those nights that might end up anywhere, O'Grady thought. The uncertainty only made him sharper.

'You seem worried,' said O'Grady.

'Me, worried?'

O'Grady could feel himself feeding off Shaughnessy's nerves.

'You know I killed a little girl?' he said, as if it was everyday conversation.

Shaughnessy, thinking he was sitting next to a child-killer, looked horrified until he remembered. 'Tel said you panicked.'

'It's the first time I've told anybody.'

'Tel said it was all over the papers.'

'But it's the first time I've talked about it.'

'What made you panic?'

'I'd been having the feeling for days. Like getting on an aeroplane you know is going to crash.'

'Premonition,' said Shaughnessy.

'Premonition,' repeated O'Grady, wondering why he had kept it bottled up till now.

'You know there's a Mrs Ronnie and a girl at boarding school,' said Shaughnessy.

'We had this conversation before.'

Shaughnessy grunted. 'And the one about you being a dead man. Excuse me for repeating myself.'

'Is that why we're being followed?'

'Nobody's following, Pat.'

He had spotted the car in Queen's Park and after directing Shaughnessy down a couple of side streets it was still there when they turned onto the Harrow Road by the cemetery.

'Does Ronnie think I'm so dangerous, then?'

'How would I know?' Shaughnessy lied badly. He said it again with no more conviction.

'Premonition,' said O'Grady.

It was the first time he had seen Shaughnessy having trouble with his words.

They drove to the club. The spot on the wasteland where the Mercedes had parked was free and O'Grady told Shaughnessy to take it. The car behind seemed uncertain what to do. In the end it pulled up around where O'Grady had waited before. He hoped that this reverse repeat of their previous positions was a good sign.

'No red sports car,' said Shaughnessy.

'She'll be here.'

Shaughnessy continued to look uncomfortable and kept massaging his gut. O'Grady had not seen it until then, that Shaughnessy was afraid.

Eventually Shaughnessy said, 'Jesus, Pat. I thought we had shaken on it.'

O'Grady shrugged and said, 'There's a full moon tonight.'

'What's that got to do with anything?' Shaughnessy briefly sounded more like his usual self.

'It's not me dealing with anyone else,' O'Grady said slowly, with a look towards the other car.

Shaughnessy appeared puzzled as he realised that there was no ulterior motive to O'Grady bringing him there. 'I don't understand you, Pat. Are you still saying all deals are off? Is that what you are saying?'

'That's what it looks like.'

'So be it. Don't say I didn't give you your opportunity. You're on your own now.'

'I'll take my chances.' He reached over and took the car keys from the ignition, saying he still needed a ride home. 'Get your pal to take you back.'

O'Grady saw the red sports car pull into the car park and watched Lily and the boyfriend get out. They were in the middle of a row and stood angrily mouthing at each other. When Lily turned back to the car the boyfriend went after her and pulled her, resisting, into the club.

When O'Grady got out Shaughnessy did as well, which surprised him. He had imagined Shaughnessy waiting in the car till he was gone. O'Grady kept a careful eye on the other car. It was too dark to see inside.

'Like I said,' Shaughnessy said, 'you're on your own now. So long, Pat.'

Funny how they seemed to be having a perfectly normal exchange when the situation was anything but, thought O'Grady. 'Be seeing you,' he said casually, wondering why he didn't feel more scared; quite the opposite.

Through the main entrance was a large, crowded lobby full of people. There was no sign of Lily or her man. From what O'Grady could see, entry was by pre-arranged ticketing rather than payment on the door, with access to the interior controlled by a security team of oversized bouncers with necks far too big for the dinner suits they were improbably squeezed into. Everyone else seemed very young and informal, hopping up and down and looking like they were going on safari, with their flimsy clothes and bottles of water. O'Grady could not figure what the water was about at all.

He asked what looked like a couple of rich ex-hippies, older than the rest and dressed like a pair of South American gauchos, what it cost to get in and was amazed at the price. It took all the money he had for one of the bouncers to let him through.

Inside was huge, the size of a football pitch, and dark and heaving. A pounding din reverberated right through him. Spotlights played randomly over the crowd, making it hard to pick anyone out. O'Grady had thought getting in would be the problem. Now he saw how hard it would be spotting anyone in a space that size with several thousand people milling about. He had had no idea such places existed. He didn't know what he had been expecting, something more old-fashioned, he supposed, with people conveniently sat at tables.

He spotted a couple of men his age, grey hair pulled back in ponytails and dressed casually in the style of the crowd, in what he would have called Hawaiian shirts. From what he could tell there were two types of dancing, a kind of swooning which involved waving the arms around and a stomping war dance like Apaches in old Westerns. He thought it unlikely, from the way they had been fighting outside, that Lily and her man would have headed straight for the dance floor.

O'Grady was starting to feel panicked by the noise and the crowd – he had not been among so many people for as long as he could remember – and the possibility that Lily, along with everyone else in the room, might be on drugs. The way the lights kept flicking over his face started to annoy him. They came from a gantry next to a suspended platform where the music was being played by a prancing young man who twitched as if he was plugged into the same socket as his equipment. It was a long way from the National.

Next to the gantry he spotted a room high up in the roof, with a big window like an aquarium, and inside was what looked like a private party. He was sure he could see Lily up there standing by the glass in a crowd with the boyfriend.

He went looking for a way up there and found a set of stairs past the toilets and a corridor full of people hanging about, wet with sweat and in a state of docile semi-exhaustion. Bottles of water were being passed around. O'Grady caught a whiff of reefer.

At the top of the stairs there was a room with people trying to get into another room beyond, which O'Grady reckoned was what he had seen from below. The mood was more hostile than downstairs. It was also much hotter, with the rising body heat from the dance floor making the place as steamed-up as a sauna. O'Grady felt the sweat running into his jacket. After watching a while he understood that the room beyond was for famous and well-connected people only. He also realised that everyone in the first room had no hope of getting into the second and were only there to stare at the ones who could, their task made easier by the door being kept open on account of the heat.

There were two security men, top-heavy like the ones downstairs from too much weight training, guarding the door. They told O'Grady no admission without a pass.

He hung around with the other rubberneckers. It was less crowded in the room beyond, but not much. That still left an awful lot of famous people, O'Grady thought. The whole thing was starting to feel like a bad dream following the one he'd had of Lily's funeral, perhaps, where they all wake up and find they have gone to hell.

He spotted the boyfriend first, in a gap in the crowd, the centre of attention in a tight little group, behaving as though he owned the place, laughing haw! haw! He was with the singer from the recording studio, and had his hand up her dress, his tongue in her mouth. O'Grady burned with anger for Lily. He could not see her. He wanted to drag the boyfriend away from the girl – enjoying her look of surprise at finding her kiss gone – and smash him in the face.

A sexy girl with practically nothing on was throwing herself around in another part of the room, rubbing herself up against the man she was dancing with in an ecstasy of abandon. O'Grady watched for some time before her face caught the light.

After that he could no longer tell what he felt, apart from the shame of catching himself lusting after his own daughter. He wanted to turn away but couldn't. The pounding music held him to the spot. He watched Lily leave the man she was with and dance over to the boyfriend, knocking into people on the way. The ones who weren't annoyed laughed at her. O'Grady thought she looked drunk, as well as on drugs. He didn't know if he should be feeling protective or angry, or if he should be chastising himself. Whatever was going on was beyond his understanding. (His mother ironing in the kitchen, complaining, 'It was worse than a Roman orgy!')

People in the room were starting to block his view but he could still just make out Lily shimmying and showing off in front of the boyfriend, making an exhibition of herself. The boyfriend said something to make his friends laugh, then, with one arm still round the singer, he leaned forward and took Lily by the hair and mashed his mouth against hers. O'Grady watched her struggle to break free. When the boyfriend finally let go he laughed, throwing his head back and showing his teeth, while Lily turned away and, rubbing her mouth with the back of her hand, fled from the room, bumping into him, even, but too upset to notice. In the background the boyfriend said something to make the others laugh again and went back to kissing the singer.

The crowd had closed around Lily and O'Grady could not see her. He searched the room in vain. The stairs outside were busy. He cursed himself for not following sooner. The corridor outside the toilets was even more crowded than before, with a commotion going on. O'Grady could feel the thumping beat of the music turning into a pulsing headache. He pushed his way deeper into the crowd. The commotion was about a boy who had fainted. O'Grady saw Lily watching, a picture of misery, to use another expression of his mother's, so forlorn he wondered if it was the same girl.

He even questioned if she was real at all and not just a projection of his anxiety, brought on by the flashing lights and deafening music.

He followed her into the big room, watched her dancing, swaying from side to side, saw her embrace two complete strangers in exchange for a swallow of their water. She looked switched off, away on her own and quite oblivious of her previous upset. Once or twice he thought she was looking at him but it was hard to tell from the dreamy way she was rolling her head, quite at odds with the rat-a-tat of the music, almost as though she was tuned into a different sound entirely.

O'Grady didn't know how long he stood watching, not thinking anything except for timing his move so as not to frighten her. When he eventually trusted himself to take her arm – he had, after all, seen her walk up and touch strangers – he realised immediately he had done it wrong. Her eyes started open and flashed at him angrily. 'Get away from me,' she said, then with dim recognition, 'Who are you?'

Because of the noise, her words sounded like they were on a delay. She looked panicky when he said her name and he saw the slow bewilderment on her face, then her embarrassment as she realised who he was. In the changing registers of her expression O'Grady read his miscalculation. His own emotions since seeing her upstairs had gone through many changes. But she, of course, had no knowledge of him, or his whereabouts. He could see that all he was succeeding in doing was shocking and frightening her. The reality of her standing before him, skimpily dressed, eyes glazed, mocked the absurdity of his fantasy, that she had been waiting for him, when it was obvious she hadn't given him a thought in years. And now he was confronting her in a place where he had no business to be, embarrassing her on a night out with her smart friends, when all he'd had in mind was quietly surprising her when no one was looking and passing her the note he had carefully written out, in capital letters for easier reading, with his name and telephone number, asking her to call.

He was hurt rather than surprised when she ran away from him, her hand to her mouth like she was about to be sick. He saw her go back the way they had come and caught up with her past the toilets as she reached the bottom of the stairs, taking her arm to stop her running off again.

'I know this isn't the time and I'll not keep you,' he said. 'I know I'm just another fellow in the street to you.'

It came out sounding wrong, too apologetic and whiny. Shouting over the music made his voice too thin. Lily looked like she was about to burst into tears.

'I never meant to frighten you, I only wanted to give you this,' he said, opening her clenched hand, putting his note in and closing it again. He didn't manage to finish what he was saying because she started crying and O'Grady had no way of dealing with that except telling her to stop and apologising uselessly for upsetting her.

She bowed her head, hiding her tears, while O'Grady stood there inadequate, wishing he had a fraction of Shaughnessy's gab. Then, reminded of Shaughnessy, he had his moment of inspiration.

'Listen. I want to say,' he said, tripping over his words in his excitement. 'I know money can't buy back the past and I'm not asking anything in return, but I've money coming, and you should have it. I want you to.'

It was strange, he thought, how the two things he had denied most – the money and his daughter – perhaps went together in the end. He was thrilled by his discovery and studied Lily for some reaction, but she kept her head bowed. Then he heard a voice say, 'What's going on here?' and Lily glanced up and O'Grady saw the gleam in her eye and turned and saw the boyfriend, who asked again what was going on, with a hostile look at O'Grady.

O'Grady read many things into that gleam. He saw her sly triumph on seeing the boyfriend and the fact that he had come looking for her. He saw the emotional ties between them and the way she was bound to the boyfriend, and not at all to him. His first impression was right. He meant nothing to her. His pathetic attempt to rescue the situation a moment earlier lay in ruins. Lily was looking at the boyfriend like he was her white knight come to her rescue.

'This man has been pestering me,' she said.

'Who the fuck do you think you are?' asked the boyfriend.

Not wanting to embarrass her, O'Grady held his palms up in surrender.

'Go on, fuck off!' said the boyfriend.

Lily ignored him as she turned away, putting a possessive arm round the boyfriend, leaning her head against his and talking in his ear as she led him back upstairs, her trophy regained, leaving O'Grady with the feeling that the bridge he had been trying to build had just collapsed on top of him. She had done the obvious thing, done all she could do, really. She had denied his existence.

O'Grady didn't even have the strength left to blame her. Instead he saw himself as she would see him: as a clumsy Mick no middle-class girl – for that was what she was now – would own up to. She would have cut him out of her life early, encouraged no doubt by Maggie, who would have spelled out all the implications of his running down a little girl the same age as her, which would have left Lily identifying with the dead girl. He saw in her gleam the ruinous effect of her mother's influence, the same material ambition and snobbery, which had rebounded on Maggie already because Lily had in turn rejected her and was aiming higher, and not even eighteen yet.

O'Grady staggered slightly, as if he had received a blow to the heart. He understood now why Maggie had come to him with Lily's address. She knew Lily had rejected him years ago, knew it because she had taught her to, knew that if confronted Lily would deny him. And all he had wanted, in his foolishness, was for them to be friends, sitting in a café somewhere smart like England's Lane, discussing her plans and her life. It was as simple as that. He wanted nothing more than some sense of her future.

Everything fell in on itself to the point where O'Grady was barely aware of his surroundings, more conscious of the throbbing in his head and a dry-mouthed dizziness. For the first time since prison he saw his life for what it was, a long, slow suicide note. There was nothing left. Not only had he turned into a ghost to his own daughter, but he had become a ghost of himself. As he now understood Maggie's motive, he also understood what fetching the gun from the old flat had been about. It was meant for him to use on himself. Unconsciously he must have known then that whatever fantasies he was using to sustain himself would in the end prove a snare and delusion. The gun was waiting. All he had to do was go back and use it. He didn't think it would be hard.

As he reached the car O'Grady was aware of a coughing sound and a burning pain in his side. He knew the two were connected but it took him what felt like an eternity to understand what had happened.

He turned round and saw a scared-looking kid in a long coat, a couple of yards away, standing there goofily, apparently in more of a state of shock than himself, with a silly expression on his face, like he couldn't figure out where the gun in his hand had come from. O'Grady thought of the Western he had seen with Kathleen and all its easy action, in contrast to the poor fist the boy was making of it. The gun was shaking so hard that O'Grady decided he was bound to miss if he fired again. The boy tried, snatching at the trigger, but the gun jammed and he was still staring at it in disbelief when O'Grady barged him over and kicked him once in the head, hard, his main feeling one of anger – in the light of what he had been going home to do – that the boy could not have finished the job properly.

It was dark in that corner of the car park and O'Grady had trouble making out the face. It was nobody he knew. He looked very young. Then the moon came out and O'Grady saw the boy's eyelids fluttering like he was dreaming of something very fast. O'Grady knew he had been standing there only a few seconds, but it felt an age, and even longer since Lily was with him, like another time and space altogether.

O'Grady left the boy on the ground and drove off in the Datsun, surprised that he was still moving without too much difficulty. Shaughnessy appeared briefly out of nowhere, filling his windscreen, flapping his arms and calling his name. O'Grady accelerated away, trying to pretend to himself that the last couple of minutes hadn't happened, which was almost possible because the bullet didn't hurt to speak of.

He rested a long time in the hall, propped against the wall, remembering Molly's charmless welcome, telling him there was no red carpet. There would be if he was bleeding, he thought. In his light-headed state the observation reduced him to weak laughter.

When he could stand no longer he sat on the floor. There was a hole in the front of his shirt and he berated himself for entertaining the ridiculous notion of what excuse he would use to the menders.

His mind kept drifting to Lily, regretting what he had done. It had been no business of his to interfere.

At some point he must have hauled himself upstairs because he was next aware of lying on the floor of his room, on his back, trying to feed the gas meter upside-down. He was wrapped in blankets and still shaking, and scared as well, his adrenalin surge having worn off. Once or twice he heard the telephone ring but didn't have the strength to get up.

The situation looked bad. Now everyone had got themselves into a mess and it was too late to back down. Shaughnessy had sold him out to Ronnie, who would have paid for the job, which had been botched, which would mean loss of face all round, and somebody coming back to finish him off. Getting himself shot had rather taken the edge off his own plans for shooting himself. Shooting himself was the last thing he felt like doing. O'Grady succumbed to another bout of weak laughter. Really, when all was said and done, what he wanted was what he had wanted all along – to be left in peace to do nothing.

He thought of the slug inside him. He had no idea if he could live with it, or for how long, or whether he was bleeding inside and in a matter of hours would be gone. He could phone the hospital and find out, he supposed, but he didn't want the fuss of ambulances and doctors, and most of all didn't want to end up in another institution with all the familiar smells of massed humanity. As he had told Shaughnessy, he would take his chances.

After

O'Grady woke up, not dead, as he had half expected, but caught in the familiar limbo of the empty hotel. He found the morning light very harsh and white. It made his skin look bluish. He lifted his shirt and looked at the hole. There was a neat pucker and no exit, meaning, as he had thought, the slug was still inside. In Molly's room he found a bottle of gin hidden and sloshed some into the hole by way of an antiseptic. The sting of it made him cry out.

He was running a temperature. What he had felt so like the 'flu that he wondered if he hadn't caught something as well as getting shot. The bouts of feeble laughter that constantly affected him always ended up close to tears.

He pictured himself a man alone on an island where no one could come until he wanted them to. Outside was the Kilburn Ocean, he told himself. Kilburn, Cricklewood, Willesden Green – and Harlesden, come to that – would all be better for being at the bottom of the sea. When the telephone rang he let it, telling himself it was in his head.

He sat by one of the front first-floor windows, using a hard chair because it was easier to stay awake. Even so, he drifted in and out of consciousness. Outside it was raining.

O'Grady was startled awake by the front door opening. Three men by the sound of it and none of them talking. From the way they moved around they seemed to know where they were going. He pictured Shaughnessy letting them in, using a key given to him by Kathleen, who had not returned hers, imagined him saying to her right at the beginning, 'Let him give you a bit of the old Swiss roll and I'll make it worth your while.'

O'Grady had no plan and no hiding place. He couldn't get into the loft without leaving the ladder down, and all the nooks and crannies had been knocked out to make more rooms. All he could think of was the flat roof above the back extension which could be got at through a small window in the linen room.

He eased himself up and tiptoed to the landing. He wasn't sure where the men were. Everything had gone quiet.

O'Grady moved carefully upstairs, using the outside of the treads to reduce the chance of noise, and moved onto the landing as a door opened downstairs.

The linen-room key was in the door, but the linen-room window had deadlocks. O'Grady searched in vain for the key. He could hear the men on their way up. The best he could do was shut himself in and hope.

The men were a long time coming. Surrounded by the reassuring smell of fresh sheets, O'Grady almost managed to convince himself he was alone. It was in this very room that he'd had a rare glimpse of Molly's private parts, playing doctors and nurses when they were kids. Tommy Doyle had been with them. Tommy had found a real doctor's stethoscope somewhere and they used it to explore Molly naked.

The memory, and the ridiculousness of his present situation – a grown man hiding in what amounted to a cupboard – made him see that his dealings had on one level always remained childish, even when criminal. Living outside the law had been seen as glamorous, setting him apart, when all it had really meant was that he had not adjusted. The criminal violence never failed to remind him of playing with guns as a boy. He wished he'd carried on with the doctors-and-nurses games instead. He remembered Molly telling Tommy that you had babies by two of you pissing in a pot and stirring it together and drinking it. It was the only time he had seen Tommy gullible.

The men were outside. O'Grady started shaking so much he was sure they would hear his teeth chattering. He tried squeezing into a corner behind one of the shelves.

'Well?' a man said.

'I've seen enough,' a second man said.

A third voice joined in. 'I think you'll find her open to offers. She seems to want to sell pretty quickly, and cash would be an incentive.'

'Pretty typical. Gas and heating all on slot meters. And the decor, well—' said the second man, but was interrupted by the first saying that he didn't have all day.

O'Grady knew he would have to get a better grip. Yet part of him didn't care, he knew. The drift of his thoughts and the raft of memories seemed as important as anything else. He thought back to Tommy as a boy in this room, Tommy who had grown up to be a big man, tough and clever, both inside the law and beyond it. They'd had little to do with each other since, yet O'Grady had continued to carry Tommy in his head, and in some way that he didn't understand he regretted not remaining close. O'Grady had always thought of the past as something to be got rid of. Life was about moving on.

Night felt longer than day. O'Grady tired of his isolation and wanted someone to come. In spite of having taught himself to live a life of no expectations, he still found the waiting hard.

Molly's gin store ran to a fair supply. The booze kept him from feeling more scared. He tried to keep to a limit where his body was still alert, and his mind could float above everything. He moved from room to room – gun and bottle, bottle and gun – giving himself an hour's watch in each. Sometimes he thought he heard voices – Molly's, his mother's, Lily's and Kathleen's – at other times he heard only his own.

He was thinking about Molly when she called. He was downstairs, patrolling the back of the house. Molly phoning to check up on him – she sounded concerned, bordering on angry, because he had not answered when she had called before.

'Where are you?' he asked.

She was in a phone box, she said.

Talking to someone real, after all the voices in his head, O'Grady wasn't sure where to begin. He heard himself gabbling, not letting her get a word in, over-explaining.

'I'm fine now,' he said. 'Thanks for asking. I was sick for a bit with the 'flu and couldn't get to the phone. And the estate agent, I'll talk to him. I think he was here. I expect he was. Right as rain now. I'm sorry to put you to the trouble. Do you remember when—' He had to stop himself bringing up Tommy and his stethoscope.

Molly asked sharply if he was all right.

'Right as rain now,' he repeated. 'I'm sorry to put you to the trouble. Don't worry about a thing, it's all taken care of. Molly?'

The pips went and they were cut off. He waited in vain for her to call back. He wanted to apologise for hogging the call and to ask how she was. He was sure she wasn't visiting anyone and he hoped she wasn't as lonely as him.

He heated a can of soup and ate it watching television with the sound down. It was the news, followed by the weather and local news. It took him a while to recognise the club in Harlesden because the item had been filmed by day. He turned the volume up. The knob was faulty and the sound blared out and he missed the next part of the story trying to get the level under control. There was an artist's drawing of the man being sought and O'Grady was relieved to see that it bore no resemblance to himself. If anything, it looked more like Shaughnessy, but not much. He got the volume back to normal as the report was ending with a statement from a senior police officer looking self-conscious as he announced that the shooting bore the marks of a professional killing.

O'Grady could make no sense of it. His first thought was that they must be talking about another, unrelated, incident. He was sure he hadn't hit the boy that hard.

He needed to talk to Ronnie.

He knew Ronnie was in Marbella, and if he wasn't there he would be in Fuengerola. There had always been a bolt-hole in Marbella, though Ronnie preferred Fuengerola, which was where he had told O'Grady he wanted to end up, running a nice little curry place. In spite of hating Indians for invading his old patch in the East End, and regarding them as useless except as a docile source of protection money, Ronnie had developed a passion for Indian cuisine.

O'Grady was pretty certain Ronnie would be in the international phone book. Ronnie was more illiterate than Tel and took an unreasonable pride in seeing his various names in print, which were among the few things he could recognise. Ronnie had previously been listed in the London phone book under the several aliases he used. Sure enough, Ronnie was down as being in Fuengerola, under the name he used most after his real one. O'Grady wrote down the number and thanked the operator. He wasn't sure if Spain was the same time as London. He decided to leave it until later, when he could be more certain that Ronnie would be in.

Ronnie was a talker mainly, a pub man. Pubs were one of the few places O'Grady could think of where there was absolutely no need to read, which always made Ronnie's jukebox selections interesting. Ronnie talked all the time. It was his way of keeping control. He liked to see himself as an entertainer, even in the administering of violence – 'What's the point if you can't have a good laugh?' – and numbered several television comedians and chat-show hosts among his friends. Thanks to them, he prided himself on his timing and his charity work. As a result of his show-business connections, Ronnie had always overplayed the Cockney.

O'Grady drank more than he meant and fell apart a little, thinking about the dead boy he hadn't killed. He needed the gin to help put the stopper back on his fear of what the slug might be doing to his insides, but it made everything worse.

He tried distracting himself by replaying his meeting with Lily, running it endlessly back and forwards, torturing himself trying to work out what he could have done differently to have made it better.

The telephone rang. At first O'Grady could not make out who it was, even when she repeated her name. Lily was the last person he would have expected to call.

'Lily!' he said. 'Is that really you?'

She hadn't thrown away his note after all.

O'Grady wasn't used to the telephone and didn't know what to say. As it turned out, he wasn't required to say anything because Lily was very precise about what she wanted, to the point of sounding rehearsed.

'I'm splitting up with my boyfriend,' she said, 'and I need a flat and you said you had some money.'

There was no apology, just the bald statement regarding what she thought was her due. O'Grady knew she was using him, but in exchange for any contact he was glad to let her.

'Well, I have to get the money first. It's still owing,' he said, wondering if there was any way he could still get it.

'When can you have it by?' She sounded disappointed. 'I can't stay here much longer.'

'It might take a week,' said O'Grady. That meant getting Ronnie over after all. He hoped Lily could not tell that he had been drinking. 'It's twenty thousand pounds. Would that be enough?'

If that was the cost of buying her, so be it.

'Twenty thousand pounds,' she repeated. She didn't sound curious or grateful. O'Grady supposed it wouldn't buy much in Totteridge, not if a house in Kilburn was fetching a hundred these days. He had no idea what she was thinking or if the conversation was going the way she wanted.

'Is that enough?' he asked again, feeling helpless.

She didn't answer him and said, 'I have to go.'

It left him thinking he had said the wrong thing. 'Will you call me in the morning?' he asked. He had no idea what time it was.

'I don't know what to do,' she blurted, sounding desperate. O'Grady knew he was failing her again.

'Tell me. If it's money . . . ?'

'It isn't. I can't talk now,' she said and hung up.

By the time he had sobered up enough to call Ronnie it was first light. Ronnie answered quickly and without fuss. O'Grady remembered Ronnie saying he always had been a light sleeper.

The first surprise was that the Cockney act had been dropped. There was no banter, no surprise, real or faked, just a couple of yeses. O'Grady felt he was not talking to Ronnie at all. Ronnie was noncommittal when he asked what was going on.

'Are you paying to have me shot?'

'No reason to,' replied Ronnie, sounding reasonable.

'There is. You cheated me, remember, and you still owe me. It would be a lot cheaper to have me taken care of than pay me what I'm owed.'

'The rules have changed. Let's say the business we're talking about went belly up. All debts are off. We're trading under a different name now, different sort of business altogether.'

'That doesn't answer my question.'

'I don't pay to have people shot and it doesn't pay to have people shot. What you're talking about is another era.'

Ronnie sounded so different and so bored that O'Grady thought he might be telling the truth. But if Ronnie wasn't responsible, who was? Perhaps Ronnie, like Lily, had not given him a second thought in all those years. That was what it sounded like.

'Did Shaughnessy tell you I was coming to Spain? Is that why this is going on?'

'You can ask till you're blue in the face, the answer's going to be the same. Nothing to do with me.'

Ronnie hung up without saying goodbye, leaving O'Grady

confused. The only way he could see the story straight was through a connection between Shaughnessy and Ronnie. Shaughnessy was, for reasons he could not fathom, the only active figure in the whole business.

Shaughnessy had not meant to shoot the fellow in the car park. His excuse was that in picking up the gun he had ducked to avoid a car's lights and it had gone off. The fat silencer resulted in almost no noise, apart from a crude smack of lead on bone. In reality, he thought the shot was more likely the result of a spasm in his finger, caused by his infuriation at seeing his plans close to ruined. Nevertheless, he had been surprised at how easily the thing had fired.

He'd then had to grope in the lad's pockets for his car keys, squeamish at the thought of so much cooling flesh, before walking away with as much nonchalance as his leaky bowels would permit.

The stiff was named Brendan. In happier days he had hinted that he was a member of a nameless paramilitary organisation, kicking his heels on the mainland after several shootings, and keen for a little side action. The Belfast accent was real enough but Shaughnessy was left wondering about the rest.

Two wild brothers from Sligo, who ran a heavy-plant hire company in Upper Holloway, had been his first call. When he had first known the Fitzgerald boys they had been rustling cattle out of Galway and driving them straight to an abattoir run by their in-laws, which, so the story went, had a sideline in the disposal of unwanted bodies.

When Shaughnessy told them he needed someone for a free-lance job at a cheap rate he had been referred to Brendan via the landlord of a pub in Highbury. Though Brendan was polite to the point of calling him 'sir', he seemed profoundly disconnected and Shaughnessy was sure he'd found his man. More to the point, Brendan was agreeable to Shaughnessy's fee, with an advance of only a couple of hundred.

'Do you come with your own equipment?' Shaughnessy had asked, hoping the lad would not think he was trying to pick him up.

Shaughnessy had found the two hundred still in Brendan's back trouser pocket, where he had watched him put it. On the night, Brendan – whether he came with his own equipment or not – turned out not to be quite the Johnny Cool he had made out. Watching him dither around the car park, Shaughnessy realised that what he had taken for a pro's detachment was in reality plain thickness.

The Fitzgerald brothers found the story highly amusing when Shaughnessy complained to them, and it didn't take long to find out why. It was already going the rounds that Brendan had been hanging out in hardline bars, making a nuisance of himself and shooting his mouth off so much that Special Branch was on to him. One conclusion was that Brendan was a fantasist. The only mystery was where he had got the gun he produced for inspection in the bars where he drank, given that it was a model favoured by the British security forces. A counter-rumour was that he was a clumsy attempt at a plant by military intelligence. Shaughnessy hoped to Christ he wasn't, because the last thing he needed was a posse chasing him down the Kilburn High Road.

He lay low for a couple of days, camping out at Tel's place on Hornsey Rise, because the phone by some miracle had not been cut off. He set himself up in a room which showed big skies that made him think of holidays. He was tempted to cut his losses and fuck off to the Balearic Islands and live well off what he had for a couple of months, and hang the consequences.

He made a couple of calls, including one to the Black Lion, and was told that O'Grady had been asking for him. That settled it, Shaughnessy thought, it was the Balearics. He was still entertaining the idea when the telephone rang and everything changed again.

The whole thing had turned into an unholy mess, his plan ruined because of O'Grady's shrivelled *cojones*, his back-up scheme even more of a balls-up because Brendan had turned out to be such a clot. Worse, it had already got back that the job wasn't finished. That was the trouble with playing both ends against the middle, thought Shaughnessy: if you weren't careful you were the one who ended up being squeezed, which was exactly what was happening to him. Now he was being threatened because he had taken a down payment, which to the maniac he was dealing with was the equivalent of a blood oath, the job had been botched and, unless the contract was satisfactorily and instantly completed, old favours would be called in, meaning that Shaughnessy would find himself with his head in a bucket of wet cement. The extent of the threat had been spelled out at length and in great detail, and Shaughnessy had been left in no doubt that it was meant, and he could not think of any more horrible way to die.

The pity of it was that he had since come up with an even better plan, and no one left to help him execute it. He tried calling O'Grady but there was never any answer, which meant that, however reluctant he was, they would have to go in. He would need Tel as back-up. While Tel was worse than useless, the fact was Shaughnessy was too scared to go alone.

They drank away the afternoon and on the way from Hornsey Rise to Kilburn Shaughnessy's driving was so erratic that even the normally unobservant Tel remarked on it. Shaughnessy was secretly hoping to get pulled over and breathalysed, bringing their outing to a premature conclusion.

Molly's place had none of its lights on. Shaughnessy prayed that it was empty.

'Are we really going to kill him?' asked Tel with an air of drunken amazement, staring at the carving knife in his hands. They had only the one gun between them.

'That's the general idea, before he can do the same to us.'

Tel looked miserable and Shaughnessy had to force him out the car. Shaughnessy wasn't cut out for action, either, and his legs were shaky. Tel lagged behind and swigged a large pull of vodka from the half-bottle in his jacket pocket. He still had a full half in reserve in the other pocket.

'For God's sake, lay off that stuff a minute,' said Shaughnessy. He took out a big ring of keys. He had forgotten what most of them were for. Some fitted lock-ups still in use around Queen's Park and Willesden. The keys to the hotel dated from his stay there.

Shaughnessy checked through the letter box. The hall was dark and empty. He unlocked the door and pushed Tel inside. Tel was staggering. Shaughnessy wondered how much he'd had on top of what they had drunk together.

He was aware of a television on in the sitting room to their left. With luck, he told himself, O'Grady would be asleep in front of it. Tel had started to twitch like a patient in a hospital for tropical diseases. Shaughnessy was trying to relieve him of the carving knife, because of the noise it would make on the tiles, when he dropped it anyway, but on the mat.

The noise of the television barely masked Shaughnessy's clattering heart. It sounded like a film from the way people were talking. 'You know I will never forget you, Marianne,' a man said, and an orchestra pitched in to underline the point. Shaughnessy wondered about his nerve when it came to going through the door. The heavy cylinder of the silencer made the gun awkward to hold. He had spent some time acquainting himself with its mechanism, but looking at himself with it in the mirror he had not been convinced.

At least the door was ajar, which meant he didn't have to push much to get his head round. He could see the flicker of the picture reflected on the wall. Otherwise the room was dark and it appeared empty, unless O'Grady was hiding. Shaughnessy held the gun in both hands, like he had seen TV cops do, which helped steady the tremor. Once safely inside and seeing the room really was empty he willingly let himself be distracted by the television. A pretty girl was smiling into the sun.

Something moved behind him. Shaughnessy swung round and pulled the trigger, congratulating himself on the speed of his reaction. But nothing happened, which was just as well because it was Tel standing in the doorway, desperately waving his arms, and if Shaughnessy hadn't forgotten the safety catch they would have been looking at Tel's brains all over the wall. He angrily motioned Tel into the room and told him to keep quiet.

He wondered if they should just sit and wait. O'Grady was bound to come down sooner or later. Shaughnessy glumly thumbed the safety off: who was he kidding he was some Deadeye Dick? The film looked quite new, but the girl's dress was old-fashioned. She had coppery hair.

When he next looked round, Tel was even more pie-eyed, swaying and unfocused on the edge of his chair. Shaughnessy took away his bottle but it was empty. Tel giggled. He knew he was going nowhere. He had drunk himself into a complete slobbering funk. Shaughnessy had done it too often himself to be surprised – the prospect of action leading to drink being taken, blundering incompetence the result.

Shaughnessy regretted not bringing something to steady his own nerve, which was not holding. On the screen the girl was kissing a boy in uniform on a station platform full of soldiers carrying rifles. The girl and the boy looked scrubbed and unreal. Shaughnessy badly wanted to believe in them and their story, wanted them and their uniforms and guns to be real, and the pistol he was holding to be a toy. He told himself it wouldn't be him going upstairs but someone playing a part, and if he didn't get it right he would be allowed to go down and do it again.

He hissed at Tel, 'Stay there and don't move.'

Tel immediately looked more cheerful. 'I'll be covering the door,' he answered in a stage whisper and Shaughnessy said, louder than he had meant, 'Ah, God help us all.'

He tiptoed down the hall and started up the stairs towards the darkness at the top of the flight where he had first seen O'Grady.

He wondered if there was a sorrier sight than a man with a vacuum cleaner.

One of the treads creaked, catching him in mid-step, like a cartoon in an exaggerated freeze. Very slowly he shifted his weight towards the edge, testing. The moment he put his foot down there was a loud burst of gunfire. Shaughnessy clutched the rail and waited for the bullets.

It took several heart-stopping moments to work out he wasn't hit and what was going on. The racket was Tel messing around with the television and he had managed to turn the volume up to ear-splitting level. If Shaughnessy needed further proof that life was a hollow joke, this was it. Another loud exchange of gunfire followed before Tel got the set back under control.

Shaughnessy stood a long time in the dark, talking himself into carrying on, half expecting to find himself flying backwards at any moment as O'Grady materialised and booted him down into the hall. He could now hear a second television playing somewhere above him.

The noise of this second television came from Molly's room down at the end of the landing. Before that there were a lot of empty rooms for him to check, including his own old one and those O'Grady had been decorating, with their paint cans stacked neatly in the corner. The process of going through each door, in the expectation of being attacked at any moment, only to find it safe, and the prospect of having to do it over again with the next room, played havoc with Shaughnessy's nerves and left his stomach cramping with fear, as did Tel who had taken to stumbling around downstairs, drunk in the dark.

His first attempt at opening Molly's door failed because his hand was so sweaty he had to dry it on his jacket. He pushed the door slowly to start with, but his patience was frayed and he ended up throwing it open and jumping into the darkened room. He had a split second to react to the dark figure opposite him that he could just make out by the glow of the television. Shaughnessy raised his arm, saw the white flash, and the return, and wondered how on earth they had both missed.

Some sixth sense, then something vaguely familiar about the outline of his opponent, stopped him from blazing away. As his eyes adjusted, he saw what he had done. Saw that he was looking at himself. A large glass spider lay where his heart should be. He had shot himself. Drilled himself in Molly's wardrobe mirror.

He wondered at the significance of shooting his own reflection, and whether he had done a terrible thing to what little luck he had left. Contemplating his starred silhouette, he saw that all his courage had been used up getting that far.

Retracing his steps down the corridor, he had no idea what to do. He thought of the warm fug of the Black Lion round the corner and wished he were in it. He saw himself standing at the bar, jingling the change in his pocket, working on the story of shooting himself, telling his audience. 'There was that big fellow used to drink in here sometimes, you'd not think to look at him but he robbed banks once, and you'd not think to look at me that I once had the job of shooting that fellow, on account of an unholy mess he had got himself into with one of those Cockney gangsters that sit around in Spain watching too many spaghetti Westerns, thinking they can put a price on a man's head, and I was the mug that fell for it, except I was reckoning I could sub-contract the job cheap to this eejit bounty hunter Brendan and still walk off with a profit, except it didn't happen like that. I have to add I was a desperate man at the time, and going round pointing six-shooters at people is not my style at all. I prefer the stiletto of the spoken word. All that bollocks about sticks and stones. In my experience it's words that do the real harm.'

Shaughnessy's thoughts were interrupted by an almighty splashing. He stood there, incredulous, as he recognised the unmistakable sound of a bladder being discharged into a full pan. He wondered if Tel was making so much noise deliberately or if he was trying to piss down the side of the bowl and reeling too much. The splashing stopped, only to start again, followed by the rush of a toilet flush, then carried on a while longer before dribbling to a stop.

'For fuck's sake, man!' Shaughnessy yelled, and felt much better for it. He couldn't remember when he had last kept quiet for so long.

'Pat!' he called, reassured by the sound of his own voice. 'Are you listening?' There was no answer. 'Ah, don't make me go up another flight of those stairs, my heart won't take it.'

He hummed a shaky refrain from 'Mack the Knife'. Bobby Darin, dead in the bath at thirty-eight, or was that the Doors fellow? He had always liked the snap and swing of Darin. A dodgy ticker, he was pretty sure.

He called again. 'Pat? We need to talk. Straight up. We shouldn't be having to do this.'

He tried switching the lights on but they didn't work. He wondered whether the electricity had been cut off.

'I'm coming up, so don't go doing anything rash. Pat?' Everywhere had gone suspiciously quiet. Shaughnessy decided his best line was to carry on talking. 'I'm climbing the stairs now, and I'm trying to think of the name of that black Irish singer who died – not the Band Aid fellow. He was with the daughter of the quiz-show man who shouts, "Come on down!"'

At the top of the stairs there was a lozenge of pale light on the floor, cast by the moon. The corridor beyond looked awfully dark. Shaughnessy could just make out what looked like a bloody hand-print on the wall. He looked closer, wondering if he was staring at Brendan's legacy. For the first time it occurred to him that O'Grady might be dead, and he thought of the starred spider where his heart had been.

A burst of sound from downstairs rattled him. Tel was back to changing channels and had the volume distorting all over the place again. Shaughnessy shouted for him to turn it down but nothing happened.

'I can't hear myself think!' he added in exasperation, then addressed himself to O'Grady's door again, wondering what lay beyond. It made him think of Egyptian tombs.

'Pat, I'm coming in your room now. The door handle's got something on it. Christ, it's on my hand too. I'm hoping it's not

blood.' He pushed open the door. 'Easy does it, boys. I'm standing here in the room and I'm reaching for the light.'

He clicked the light on and stood blinking in the brightness.
Nothing moved. Everything was quiet apart from the rasp of his
own breathing. There was a figure under the blankets on the bed.

'Christ, Pat. That's not you is it?'

He looked at the smear on his hand from the door. There were
a couple more hand-prints on the carpet. The colour struck him
as suspicious. It seemed to relate to the strange smell in the
room. He put his hand to his nose, remembering the cans he had
seen in the rooms O'Grady had been decorating. It smelled of
paint. Shaughnessy yanked back the blankets. Before he could see
what was under them the light went out.

Shaughnessy froze, waiting for something to happen. He
wasn't sure if the meter had run out or if O'Grady was in the
room with him. From downstairs came the noise of a car chase
and squealing tyres.

'Pat?' he asked slowly. 'I'm putting my hands in the air before
one of us does something stupid. My heart can't stand the strain
any more. Pat? Are you there? Pat? Have you any booze in the
house?'

There was still no answer.

'Do you know what I did?' Shaughnessy said, thinking that
O'Grady had every right to put a bullet in the back of his head.
'Fucking shot myself in the mirror. If that don't beat all. I'm
throwing in the towel, Pat. I'm going to the door and turning on
the light, so we can discuss this face to face.'

He inched his way backwards, preferring not to know if
O'Grady was in the room, moving carefully over to the switch.
When he flicked it the room stayed dark.

'The meter needs feeding,' said O'Grady. 'It takes a ten or a
fifty.'

'God help us, Pat, I'm clean out of change.'

The crack made Shaughnessy feel better and he laughed at his
own joke in the hope that O'Grady wouldn't do anything to a
man who was laughing. 'Where are you, Pat?'

'Behind the door.'

'And what do you figure on doing now?'

O'Grady said nothing.

'I wasn't cut out for this stuff, I have to say,' Shaughnessy went on nervously. 'And I couldn't half do with a drink.'

He could hear O'Grady moving behind him and tensed in spite of himself and shut his eyes. There was a click. Shaughnessy waited, then slowly opened his eyes. The light was on.

'There's drink in Molly's room,' said O'Grady.

'My heart was never in it, Pat, you know that and were it not for the fact that I was desperate—'

'And bought off cheap.'

'Below the belt, Pat. But that's my point. We've all been bought cheap by the fellows with the big spreads.' Shaughnessy was aware of babbling with the release of tension. He was also starting to feel stupid standing there with his hands still in the air, which he hoped was a sign that everything was returning to normal. When Tel called uncertainly from downstairs Shaughnessy laughed weakly. 'What a fucking liability. You didn't think I'd come in without back-up? That thing with the light going out, was that deliberate?'

'The meter ran out.'

Shaughnessy suddenly felt emotional. 'Take this fucking gun away from me and give me your hand, Pat. Let's make up.'

O'Grady took his time accepting Shaughnessy's offer. When he eventually did, he ended up being embraced.

'I always said you were my last chance, Pat. I should have listened to myself.'

Shaughnessy was embarrassed to find he had tears in his eyes. He coughed and said, 'I have to clean up, then we'll take that drink.'

As they made their way downstairs there was a loud knocking at the front door.

'Christ!' said Shaughnessy, strangely buoyed by this interruption from the outside world. 'Shooters away! That'll be the police.'

Tel appeared in the hall, looking puddled. The television was so loud the sound was distorting.

'Answer the door,' Shaughnessy called down.

Tel looked around wildly, hoping Shaughnessy was talking to someone else.

'Do something for once, and go and answer before they send in a SWAT team.'

The banging carried on. Shaughnessy had to go down and push Tel into answering, telling him to let nobody in until he got there, while he went and turned off the television.

He found Tel effectively doing his job by being sick on the step.

'Evening, officers,' said Shaughnessy as smoothly as he could. The two policemen looked about twelve. 'Our friend here is feeling indisposed,' he added, believing that when dealing with the police it was always best to point out the obvious.

There had been complaints about noise, one of them said from a safe distance, while Tel groaned that he must have eaten something.

'Our friend got a bit carried away watching the film,' said Shaughnessy. 'He's hard of hearing. The party's over.'

The two policemen looked uncertainly at each other. Tel's puddle of vomit seemed to act as sufficient deterrent to further investigation.

'You better get him to bed,' one said.

'He certainly shan't be sleeping with me tonight, ha ha,' said Shaughnessy, happy to play the idiot now they were on their way. He hauled Tel inside. Tel, eyes still rolling, and stinking of booze and vomit, asked, sounding confused, 'What's that smell of shit?'

O'Grady stood in the kitchen, drinking a glass of water from the tap, and thinking about still being alive when Shaughnessy walked in with a bottle of Molly's gin, and Tel behind him, looking bashful.

Shaughnessy was already carrying on like they'd never left off, ready to turn anything into a story. 'Tel here threw up all over the stoop and I coughed in my rompers, so all we need for a full house is discovering you wet yourself.'

Seeing O'Grady was in no mood for jokes, he added, 'Don't be sore, now. We're supposed to be friends again.'

Not long afterwards, O'Grady and Shaughnessy were drunk at the kitchen table, and Tel was even further gone. They inspected O'Grady's wound. Shaughnessy was all for him going to hospital.

'No doctors,' said O'Grady.

'I know what you mean,' said Shaughnessy gloomily. 'I suppose if you're still standing it's lodged somewhere safe enough.'

Tel looked bleary-eyed at O'Grady, pointed to Shaughnessy and said, 'Ronnie had him barking down the phone.'

'I was improvising,' said Shaughnessy, glaring.

'Woof! Woof!' said Tel. 'Doing his animal impersonations.'

'Tell me about Ronnie,' said O'Grady, watching Shaughnessy squirm, while Tel answered for him, saying Ronnie had heard O'Grady was coming after him.

Shaughnessy stared hard at the ceiling. 'It was all a big mistake. I never should have got us into it. And I swear after the fiasco over the lad Brendan I was going to tell Ronnie the job was done, except you talked to him first. So he knew it wasn't.'

'And he gave you the old good dog, bad dog routine?' asked O'Grady.

Shaughnessy sighed. 'How serious is Ronnie about his dog routine?'

O'Grady looked grave. Tel giggled and slurred, 'And none have lived to wag their tail.'

Shaughnessy sighed again. 'I don't know which is worse in all this. Me desperate or Tel a wreck.'

'Desperate about what?' asked O'Grady.

Shaughnessy took his time answering. 'I've a medical condition. The only cure's in Canada.'

'Get away,' said Tel.

'It's true!' protested Shaughnessy.

'What's its name?' asked Tel.

'There's no point in telling you because you'd not have heard of it.'

'Cancer,' volunteered Tel.

'Not cancer. It's to do with the blood.'

'Septicaemia.'

'Since when were you reading the *Medical Journal*?'

'So you're wanting this money to get to Canada?' asked O'Grady. Shaughnessy nodded. 'And what are your plans now?'

'Well, that rather depends.'

'On what?'

'On you. Ronnie sounds interestingly worked up. He's insisting on seeing you. Your body, at any rate.'

'We're supposed to take you to his place in Essex. There's an airfield he flies in to nearby,' said Tel.

O'Grady wondered if he should tell Shaughnessy about changing his mind over the money. It occurred to him that they still might try and cross him. After more gin he told them anyway that he wanted Ronnie's money. That way, he reckoned, they all knew where they stood.

'Which is where we all came in!' said Shaughnessy, thumping the table. 'What took you so long?'

O'Grady shrugged. He didn't want to mention Lily, but Shaughnessy guessed and asked if it was about her. Tel was so drunk he had to prop up his head with his hand. When it slipped he crashed to the table and stayed there.

'How old is she now?' asked Shaughnessy.

'Eighteen next week.'

'Get her a nice birthday present.'

From not wanting to talk about Lily at all, O'Grady ended up caught in a loop, stumbling over his words in an effort to voice his concern that he was too late to become a father to her again.

'I'd like to be able to feel sentimental about her, not like I'm buying her affection.'

'There's nothing wrong with feeling sentimental about the right things,' said Shaughnessy, nodding as if they were turning over a nugget of profound truth. 'And how old, if you don't mind my asking, was your little girl when you went away?'

'Eight.'

'And how old, if you don't mind my asking again, was the other, you know . . . ?' Out of a rare tact he left the sentence unfinished.

'The same.'

Shaughnessy thumped the table again, loud enough to make Tel sit up with a jump. 'Don't you see, man? Your whole life has been at a standstill. It's time to come back. What happened was an awful, terrible thing, but it was an accident and you weren't drunk at the time.'

Tel slumped forward again. Shaughnessy said, 'He could always get the part of the Dormouse.'

'It's not easy as that,' said O'Grady. 'You can't just come back. Anyway, Ronnie'll not be coming back.'

'He's in and out all the time. Mind you, we could borrow the lot off your sister and she'd not even notice. Wasn't she the dark horse?'

In spite of his exhaustion O'Grady couldn't sleep and spent most of the night trying to believe it might be possible to square everything so the past matched up with the present. Shaughnessy was wrong about one thing. You could not just come back. He saw himself as an agent in a process, rather than playing an active part, now that he regarded the money as his legacy, so long as it went to Lily. He knew the sentimental side of his feelings for her was a false emotion, but it was better than nothing. It was an Irish thing, that kind of sentiment, to do with being away, or drunk, which was another kind of being away.

He slept for a couple of hours and woke with a headache, his first thought being that Lily had not called either yesterday or the day before. Maybe she would before they set off for Essex. Ronnie was due in that evening. The plan was to get there early. O'Grady had not yet got to the bottom of Shaughnessy's dealings with Ronnie. Shaughnessy became vague when it came to specifics, other than volunteering that Ronnie moved his money around through a travel agent in Hackney.

Before they left, O'Grady neatly copied out the letter he'd written the night before in a drunken scrawl.

Dear Lily,

In case I don't speak to you this is to say I'm thinking of you and am taking care of the money we talked about – am about to take care of it. It should be enough to get you a flat and when you are settled in nicely maybe you will invite me over. I'm feeling cheerful as I write this and hope it finds you the same. I was never so great at putting things down on paper, but I'll be seeing you very soon, before your birthday, to give you your present. I hope we can mend the past. This is being sent with all my love.

Your Dad

PS. If you call and I'm not answering it's because I have to go away, but not for long, and it doesn't mean you are not in my thoughts anyway, all the time.

He could not remember when he had last written a personal letter. He read it over a couple of times for spelling and the rest, and decided he was pleased. It described more of what he felt than he had first thought. He wasn't sure if she would be embarrassed by him signing himself like that, but he could not think of any other way of ending, and it was what he was, after all.

O'Grady found getting in and out of the car difficult. Sometimes he thought he could feel the slug eating away like it was alive inside him, feeding off him. He insisted they drove to Essex via Totteridge and was disappointed to find the gates of the house shut and no cars in the drive. He rang the intercom on the gate but no one answered. He posted his letter in the slot set into one of the gateposts. He was sorry not to see her – especially as he had the feeling they were all on the point of something momentous. Thanks to their plan he felt connected to something beyond himself, felt as though it was at least his life at last, whatever was left of it.

After Totteridge they went north as far as the new motorway, then east, along the top of Epping Forest, before dropping down back along the M11 towards Loughton and Chigwell.

Ronnie had covered a lot of ground in the time they had known each other, O'Grady thought, buying his way out here. They were right on the edge of the city, at the start of the rich countryside, where footballers and pop stars ended up marrying air hostesses. It was where the new money came, the sort of money that could afford to keep an empty house while its owner lived in Spain.

In the time O'Grady had been away something had happened to money that he didn't understand. What he was owed had been a small fortune at the time. Now it seemed almost of no consequence and hardly worth the fuss that had gone on over it. Yet clearly Ronnie had managed to turn it into something far more substantial. O'Grady had always thought of money as something on its own, there for the spending. You had it or you didn't, and when you did you lived well. But both Ronnie and Maggie seemed to understand that it could be used for something else, to connect things up, so that it became about something else. It could be used to buy a future, dreams even. He'd been slow to catch on, but he hoped that helping Lily would be a step in the right direction. Maybe he could have himself a slice of the boom everyone was talking about.

Ronnie's place, when they eventually found it, did indeed look like a dream home.

They had driven around beyond Lambourne End down lanes so narrow it was hard to believe the city started only a few miles to the west. Whose directions they were following O'Grady was not sure. Between them Tel and Shaughnessy made a muddle of them but after several wrong turnings they found the place by chance, standing new and alone and surrounded by countryside, which prompted Shaughnessy to ask, 'How the hell did he get planning permission for that? This must be in the middle of the green belt.'

There were stables and outbuildings from a much earlier time, with half-timbering and faded little roof-tiles, quite at odds with the new monstrosity that had been put up.

'Ronnie's built himself a fucking Greek temple with ranch fencing,' said Shaughnessy. 'He must think a lot of himself putting up a monument like that. Look at those colonnades.'

They parked out of sight down a muddy lane in a landscape consisting of nothing but wet fields, skeleton trees and a terrible noise of crows.

According to Shaughnessy they had a couple hours. Ronnie was coming in just before dark. O'Grady checked the place over while Tel and Shaughnessy loitered unconvincingly in the lane. The rooms he could see into belonged in a furniture catalogue and looked brand new and unlived-in, with none of the usual signs of life, like the *TV Times* lying around, or washing-up on the draining board.

Shaughnessy seemed curiously uncertain, and O'Grady found himself taking charge. He told them to stay out of sight while he looked for somewhere for them to wait. The best place was an open barn which was being used to house a car covered with a frost sheet. There was a ladder up to a loft space with windows in the roof. It looked as if it had once been used as a summer playroom. The floor was covered with chipboard, and several dusty dolls' houses stood in the corner. It was cold but would do for a couple of hours.

He went to fetch Shaughnessy and Tel but they bumped into him first and Shaughnessy said, 'Tel's found a pony!'

Sure enough, there was a dividing stable door, bolted but not locked, and inside a pony, which expressed no curiosity on seeing him. Above there was a hayloft reached by a metal ladder.

'How much does it cost to keep one of those?' asked Shaughnessy.

O'Grady didn't know. He was puzzled by the horse.

They went and waited in the barn, where Tel was soon grumbling about the cold.

'Here's the plan,' said Shaughnessy. 'Tel and I will deal with Ronnie. Once we see the colour of his money, we'll take him to the car to show him the goods, so to speak, and there you are waiting in the boot to pop up like a jack-in-the-box.'

'And how long am I supposed to lie in the boot, may I ask?'

'Well, you should be in position by six.'

'And what if he's late, or early?'

'Well, I'm sure he won't be,' said Shaughnessy with a briskness that suggested he could vouch for Ronnie.

'Who's feeding the pony?' asked Tel and they all looked at each other.

Before anyone could speak, O'Grady became aware of the sound of an approaching car. Several had gone by already but this one was turning.

O'Grady heard the tyres on the gravel in front of the house, then the engine idling until it was switched off. A door slammed.

Shaughnessy whispered, 'It's probably just the housekeeper. Stay here while we have a look-see. If it's nothing we'll be back in a minute.'

'Don't let Tel walk on the gravel,' said O'Grady.

Shaughnessy shrugged. O'Grady thought he seemed remarkably nonchalant.

'And if it's Ronnie?'

'If it's Ronnie we'll get him up here, so let's have you waiting.' He pointed to the corner in which O'Grady would be hidden longest from anyone coming up. He winked and gave O'Grady a playful punch on the shoulder and Tel raised his eyebrows in a lazy goodbye. They both seemed so cool all of a sudden that O'Grady wondered if they hadn't slipped themselves a couple of tranquillisers.

He went and waited in the corner behind the steps, sitting on the floor with the gun ready beside him. Left alone, he started to feel very unsure about everything.

He heard a single set of footsteps on the gravel. Something happened away in the distance to set the birds squawking, and a car went by. Then he lost track of time, apart from the impression of sitting for an age listening to nothing, until someone entered the barn. One person it sounded like, which told him that Shaughnessy and Tel were not taking care of things the way they were supposed to. When the footsteps started up they were no more than a whisper on the tread. Someone was being very light on their feet. O'Grady picked up the gun.

The back of a head appeared through the trapdoor. It was small, with ghostly pale hair. O'Grady spent several seconds wondering if he was dreaming before he realised that he was looking at a little girl, which made sense of the pony.

She appeared very still and sure of herself, even when she turned and saw O'Grady. He expected her to scream and run away, but she stared at him solemnly for a long time, to the point of unnerving him, before asking, 'Who are you?'

'A friend of your dad's.'

'Oh.' She sounded put out.

Even her brightly coloured coat failed to detract from her air of seriousness, and her glasses added to the effect. Because of the gloom, O'Grady didn't notice at first that one lens was covered with a patch. It seemed rude to ask about it.

'Is your dad here?'

'Of course not!'

The mention of Ronnie seemed to irritate her.

'Is the pony yours?'

'Her name's Willow.'

From the sound of her, O'Grady had a right bossy little madam on his hands. She walked up the last steps into the loft and looked around, paying him no attention, which at least let O'Grady get the gun into his pocket.

'What's your name?' he asked.

'I thought you were a friend of my dad.'

'Not recently.'

'It's Lee,' she said.

'That's nice,' he replied automatically.

'I'm glad you think so,' she said, sounding grown-up and sarcastic.

'Don't you like it?'

She rolled her eyes. He asked if the dolls' houses were hers. It was a stupid question and she did not bother to answer.

'I don't usually like my father's friends,' she announced. O'Grady wondered where one so young had learned such assurance.

'Nor me,' he said, which earned him a keen look. 'Who did you come with?'

'Trevor.' She sounded bored now.

'Maybe we should see where he is.'

'Trevor can look after himself.'

O'Grady heard footsteps on the gravel. It was Tel and Shaughnessy returning. They were with a third man, presumably Trevor, with a crew-cut and a lot of bulk that his dark-blue chauffeur's suit failed to hide. O'Grady knew the look: polite to a point, then savage.

Shaughnessy said to the girl, 'We've been looking all over for you. Where have you been?'

Lee asked O'Grady sharply, 'Are they friends of yours?'

O'Grady was not at all sure. Trevor didn't seem as put out as he should have done, O'Grady thought, wondering if Trevor was in on whatever was going on. Shaughnessy asked again where Lee had been.

'Seeing Willow.' She looked annoyed by the sight of so many men.

'The pony,' explained O'Grady.

'What's wrong with your eye?' asked Shaughnessy.

'Nothing,' she replied curtly.

'What's going on?' O'Grady asked Shaughnessy.

'There's been a balls-up. Our pal here says Ronnie's not coming.'

'Why not?'

'Changed his mind, he says.'

O'Grady wondered whether he was in the same picture as the rest of them. Lee gave an exaggerated sigh and marched over to the steps.

'And where do you think you're going, Missy?' asked Shaughnessy.

'I've got better things to do than stand around talking all day. I'm going for a ride.'

Tel sniggered.

'Tel, go with her,' ordered Shaughnessy.

'I will,' said O'Grady quickly. He wanted time to think.

Lee said, 'I don't need anyone to come.'

'I'm coming anyway,' O'Grady said and followed her downstairs to the stables. She sulked and he could see she was boiling about something as he watched her saddle up. All he could think about was the unpleasant raw wind blowing the little remaining warmth out of him. When Lee asked him for a hand onto the pony he didn't know what to do and tried to pick her up by the waist, which hurt his side.

'Not like that!' she snapped and showed him how to make a stirrup of his hands.

The metal of the pony's shoes rang out on the concrete, the first reassuring sound O'Grady had heard all day. He tagged along, wondering if she was the only one of the lot of them who was sure what she was doing.

'Don't walk behind her or she'll kick,' she warned.

Lee took the pony to a field at the back of the house, with several jumps. O'Grady stood there, feeling his shoes leak while the girl put the pony through its paces. The damp field was enough to make him hanker after Kilburn, that was how miserable he found it.

The girl thrashed up and down the field at a frightening pace and O'Grady wanted to call out for her to be careful.

Ronnie's money looked further away than ever and if he didn't get it he would be letting down Lily, again. The girl had started over the jumps. O'Grady supposed he could always try borrowing the money. People borrowed all the time these days. If he threw himself at Molly's mercy she might even lend it him. Twenty thousand would hardly make a dent in her savings and he would pay it back with interest. She would need some persuading, which he had never found easy. He could hear her saying in that tone of hers, 'And where's the money coming from to pay me back? It doesn't grow on trees.'

He grew increasingly worried about the girl jumping. Several times she had nearly unseated herself and was attacking the jumps with a fury and concentration that matched the anger he'd seen earlier. She jumped again and O'Grady heard a hollow thud as she clipped a pole. She sprawled forward in the saddle and clung to the pony's neck before losing her stirrups and falling off. She lay quite still, flat on her front in the mud, and O'Grady ran over, worried that she had broken a bone or worse.

'Are you all right?' he asked breathlessly. He could hear the fuss in his voice. He didn't know if he should turn the child on her back or check her breathing, but before he could she raised her head and said, 'Shit!'

Once it was clear she was all right O'Grady grew annoyed. He'd not come all that way to end up acting as a nursemaid. Fields and ponies and riding accidents were not his thing at all, and he was not grateful for being stuck with any of them.

She looked around, irritated. 'Where are my glasses?'

They had come off in the fall, and the reason for the patch, O'Grady saw, was to correct a squint. She quickly turned away and asked him to fetch her glasses and told him not to look until she had them on again.

She insisted on getting back on the pony and jumping some more. By the time she was finished O'Grady had lost all feeling in his feet and was not grateful for having to spend half-an-hour watching a spoiled brat doing gymkhana practice. When she was done she rode over to him. In the saddle she was taller than him and it disconcerted O'Grady having to look up to her.

'What are you doing here?' she asked.

'We're supposed to see your dad.' He told her they had some business to discuss, which she took to mean money.

'It's all he ever talks about. Selling pesetas and buying yen and converting into sterling, then into marks.'

It was a long way from sticking a gun over the counter. Again O'Grady was reminded that it had always been beyond him, this idea of shifting money around so that it grew, perhaps not on trees but worked for itself.

'Well, he won't come here.' She sounded quite sure about it. A strange child, O'Grady thought, not at all put out by their arrival. Perhaps strangers turned up in her life all the time and she dealt with them by ignoring them. Maybe all children were more grown-up these days. O'Grady had no idea.

'So are you staying here the whole holidays?' he asked.

'Of course not. Trevor's taking me to the airport tomorrow.'

'I've never flown anywhere in my life,' he said, making an effort to be friendly.

'You must have. Everyone's flown somewhere unless they're really poor.'

'I took the boat to Ireland a few times. So who's meeting you at the airport?'

'Must you start every sentence with "So"?'

'I'll start my sentences however I want,' he answered sharply enough to put an end to their conversation, and was glad to see it left the child biting her lip.

At the stable she ignored him apart from telling him to take the saddle off after she had undone the girth. He was nervous of the pony, and her easy familiarity with it undermined his confidence further. He was left holding the saddle, hanging around in the damp and gathering darkness, while she groomed the pony. The saddle was heavy and he wasn't sure what to do with it.

He saw Shaughnessy coming from the direction of the house. From the way he was strolling, hands in pockets, O'Grady thought he looked disconcertingly at ease.

'Ah, there you are Pat,' he said cheerfully and motioned O'Grady out of earshot of the stable. 'We put Trevor in the boot of the Granada for the time being.'

'What Granada?'

'The car in the garage.'

O'Grady remembered the silver frost sheet. 'You were supposed to be just doing a recce,' he said.

'I know, I know, until Tel tripped over,' Shaughnessy said, then called out over his shoulder, 'It looks like your dad's let us down.'

O'Grady turned and saw Lee watching by the stable door and wondered how much she had heard.

'Now our friend here can't afford to buy his little girl a birthday present,' said Shaughnessy loudly.

'Cut it out,' said O'Grady.

'How old is your little girl?' asked Lee.

'Eighteen.'

'That's not little. I wish I was eighteen.'

'Don't worry,' said Shaughnessy. 'You soon will be.'

'What's her name?'

'Lily.'

'That's nicer than Lee. Lee's a make of jeans.'

Shaughnessy said out of the side of his mouth, 'Maybe Ronnie'd come for . . .' He left the sentence unfinished.

'Why should he?' asked O'Grady.

'If we said—'

O'Grady interrupted. 'This is not a conversation we should be having.' He asked the girl, 'Can I put this saddle down?'

She showed him where it went in the stable. As he joined Shaughnessy outside she followed him and asked, 'Are you planning to kidnap me?'

Shaughnessy's eyes popped but he managed to sound smooth enough as he said, 'Of course not, dear child.'

Lee looked at him, unimpressed, and asked O'Grady, 'Is it true you can't afford a birthday present?'

O'Grady was irritated when Shaughnessy spoke for him. 'He was planning to give her a big present with the money of his your dad still has.'

'Forget it,' said O'Grady.

'Your friend's right,' Lee said to him. 'He'd come for me.'

'What are you saying?' asked O'Grady though it was obvious.

'She's as bright as a button,' said Shaughnessy with a laugh of encouragement.

'We can't do that,' said O'Grady. 'That would be kidnapping.'

'Not if we stay here,' said Lee smugly.

'She's got the mind of a Jesuit,' said Shaughnessy.

'I can't believe what I'm hearing,' said O'Grady.

'She's right. I think kidnapping involves a removal,' answered Shaughnessy, bright-eyed with the enjoyment of it all. He addressed the girl directly, as if they were making up a game. 'Let me get this straight. Is what you're suggesting to a couple of thicko Paddies that we stay here and avail ourselves of your kind hospitality –' He pronounced it horsepitality and left a pause for the girl to laugh, which she didn't. 'Well, I dare say the pony found it funny. The idea is we put our feet up for a couple of days and in exchange for your dad coming and collecting you he'll give us the money?'

'We can't do this,' protested O'Grady.

Shaughnessy leaned forward and asked with a confiding air, 'Can I ask what you'd be getting out of it?'

She regarded him solemnly, not buying his beaming approval.

'They don't teach manipulation classes at that fancy school of yours by any chance?' he asked, and O'Grady asked Lee to excuse them a minute and pulled Shaughnessy out of earshot.

'For God's sake, man.'

'You heard her. She's smart enough to know that Ronnie'll come for her.' Shaughnessy smirked. Seeing O'Grady's doubtful expression, he said, 'Stop being such an old maid, Pat. It's called cutting your cloth.'

'And when something goes wrong?'

'Nothing will. It's between us and Ronaldo.'

'And if he doesn't like it or sends someone in, or Trevor starts cutting up rough?'

'There won't be any funny business if we've got the girl, and Trevor goes in the stable with the pony.'

'You're serious about this.'

'That fucker Ronnie had me barking down the phone, so any

way I can inconvenience him I will. When the time comes Ronnie'll have to do his share of barking to get Missy back.'

Shaughnessy stuck his hands in his pockets, making it clear he was going nowhere. O'Grady saw that for the moment the issue was nothing to do with Ronnie or money. He was stuck with his usual problem of how to read Shaughnessy.

'Let me talk to her,' he said.

'She seems quite clear about what she wants,' said Shaughnessy, turning back towards the house and whistling.

All the girl would tell him was that she was hungry.

O'Grady had to drive to the nearest village for provisions. He felt uncomfortable leaving the girl but went on his own in order not to attract attention.

The store was a sub-post office with a couple of aisles of tins and a freezer. It felt like Bangladesh after the big place where he'd first spotted Maggie. He got there as it was closing and bought enough provisions for that night, rather than buying up half the store. Tomorrow he'd go somewhere bigger like Chelmsford, where there would be less chance of being remembered.

It occurred to him that the girl might be having them all on, doing what she was doing for the mischief of it, and as soon as their backs were turned would be on the phone to the police station. In some ways he found her the hardest of the lot when it came to working out what she was thinking.

Back at the house he found her watching television in the big sitting room with Tel, who was dozing on the sofa. She had a control that let her change channels without getting up, and flicked idly between them.

He wondered where Shaughnessy was but didn't know how to ask because he wasn't sure if he should be giving away names. She read his mind anyway, saying without looking up, 'He's upstairs resting.'

'What do you want to eat?' he asked.

'I'm not hungry any more,' she said. 'What have you got to drink?'

'Coca-Cola and orange juice.'

She screwed up her face, shoving her tongue in a gap that was waiting for a new tooth. 'I put the old one in a glass of Coca-Cola and it was gone in the morning.'

'That's just an old wives' tale.'

'Completely gone. Orange juice or squash?'

'Juice. The ones in the little cartons.'

'I'll have one of those.'

O'Grady dutifully fetched it. He was about to stick in the straw that came with the carton but she insisted on doing it herself. Juice spurted out of the top of the straw, reminding him of a nurse testing a syringe.

'This thing of talking to your dad,' he said as casually as he could, still thinking it was an idea best forgotten.

'I talked to him already.' She looked at him with a smirk of triumph. 'He's coming over. He's cool.'

O'Grady felt as though a heavy weight was pressing down on him. 'Did he talk to anyone else?' he asked, not wanting to know the answer.

'The man upstairs. He wasn't so cool with him.'

'What did you tell your dad?'

'There were these men to see him, and he'd have to come and fetch me. That's all.'

'When's he coming?'

'Not tomorrow, but the night after.' She looked disappointed. 'It seems like a long time to wait.'

O'Grady found Shaughnessy upstairs, sprawled on his back asleep in the master bedroom. Neither he nor Tel seemed to have any problem making themselves at home.

As well as the main bedroom O'Grady found five others, all as lavishly done out as a smart hotel. There were two bathrooms in addition to the one in Ronnie's room, all fitted out in gold and marble. The larger had a fancy round bath of a kind he had not seen before, with lots of jets and nozzles. The showers were twice the size of a telephone box and there were squat basins for washing your parts. O'Grady thought of Ronnie putting talcum powder on his dick all those years he had been slopping out.

The bathroom had mirrors on all the walls and from certain angles he could see the back of his head. He shut the door and reluctantly unbandaged himself. The hole had started to weep and looked livid. He dabbed it dry, using a tissue from a leather dispenser. His breathing had grown more shallow over the last couple of days, and with it had come a sense of everything slowing down but hardly so he noticed, and not enough for him to worry about, he hoped.

He found Lee hanging around in the corridor, bored. She complained there was nothing on television. She told him the bath was called a jacuzzi and showed him her room. O'Grady had not been able to tell because each one was as impersonal as the next.

'Rusty won't let me put any posters up. All the walls are lined with silk. Isn't that stupid? Can we go to the seaside tomorrow?'

'Who's Rusty?'

The question earned him a curious look. 'You do know my dad?'

O'Grady ducked back to her previous question. 'It's a bit difficult going out for the day if we're waiting on him.'

'He's not coming tomorrow.'

'We'll see what the weather's like,' O'Grady said, stalling.

'It's going to be fine. It said so.'

'Isn't there anything you don't know?'

'You're changing the subject.'

'I said we'd see.' The girl really was exhausting. As they went downstairs he was reassured to see that she was still enough of a child to go down one step at a time.

In the kitchen she followed him around while he cooked, giving him the impression he was under her inspection. She asked him where he had learned.

'This is not really cooking, it's just putting stuff in the oven.'

'Use the microwave,' she said. 'It's faster.'

He looked at it uncertainly. Molly had mentioned getting one for the hotel. 'It's too small.'

'It only takes a minute. Do the chips, then keep them warm in the oven and do the pies.'

There was a complicated-looking set of dials which he studied helplessly until Lee said, 'Let me do it.'

She told him to put the chips in and then set the knobs and said, 'Easy.'

They were joined by Shaughnessy, yawning from his sleep. 'What about Trevor?' he asked.

O'Grady glanced at Lee, who seemed unconcerned.

'Trevor's looking after her pony,' Shaughnessy said, sounding amused. 'We'll take him a tray, if we can find one.'

When it came to unbolting the stable door Shaughnessy covered O'Grady with his gun. O'Grady heard the pony shift. He balanced the tray on the top of the bottom half of the door and waited for Trevor to take it.

'All right in there?' asked Shaughnessy casually, as though the arrangement was perfectly normal. Trevor grunted and Shaughnessy added, for O'Grady's benefit, 'He's got a television in there. We found one of those battery-operated ones.'

On the way back to the house, Shaughnessy said airily, 'I think things have turned out pretty well, considering. It's lucky for us the girl can't stand her father.'

'How was Ronnie?' O'Grady wasn't sure what he felt about Shaughnessy dealing with Ronnie.

'Ronnie's fine. He huffed and puffed, but he can read the situation. He spoke to the girl first, and she bossed him around, saying, "You have to come and fetch me." Then, just so he was sure to get her drift, "Like you always promised." So Ronnie got the hint, and is now revising the situation in terms of her being a chip off the old block.'

After eating they all sat and watched a wildlife programme on television. Shaughnessy kept up a running commentary until he was told by Lee to shut up. Tel, back on the sofa, arms folded and legs crossed, snorted with amusement though to all appearances he was asleep.

Shaughnessy went to bed first, complaining of being tired. Nobody seemed to know quite how to behave. O'Grady and the girl stayed up till just after ten, then left Tel to it.

Upstairs O'Grady was overcome with uncertainty, sure the girl would be on the phone to the police or her father once they were all asleep. That, or Ronnie would be arriving early to take them all by surprise.

He waited for Lee to finish in the bathroom. He decided he didn't have the heart to lock her in her room after all. She came out, changed into pyjamas, and told him to leave the landing light on. 'Seaside tomorrow' was all she said.

O'Grady gave it half an hour then crept downstairs. Tel was stretched out on the sofa, snoring. There were three socket phones he collected from different rooms and a wall-mounted one in the kitchen whose wire he cut. Upstairs he had noticed only the one in the room Shaughnessy was in. There was nothing he could do about that. Having taken the precaution of removing the others he went back upstairs feeling a little easier. He put the gun under his pillow and slept badly, disturbed at first by the stillness and furtive rustlings of the countryside, then frequently starting awake, imagining footsteps on the gravel outside.

The following day the weather was fine, as Lee had predicted, and they drove to the sea as she had wanted. O'Grady opposed the idea on the grounds of organisation and was surprised by Shaughnessy's relaxed attitude.

'I wouldn't mind a day at the seaside myself' was all he said.

In the end O'Grady went along with them because it gave them something to do besides waiting, and if Ronnie was planning anything unexpected they were better off being away from the house. When he agreed, Lee dangled a set of keys in front of them and said, 'Good. We can all stay here.'

Ronnie, it turned out, owned a seaside house in Jaywick, a place Tel knew from when he was a boy. According to Lee, it was where Ronnie's family had spent their summer holidays, and Ronnie had since bought the house. O'Grady was surprised. He had never thought of Ronnie as sentimental.

They took the car that Lee had arrived in, a large Mercedes sedan. 'Glad to see the back of Jap motors for a while,' said Shaughnessy. 'Look at this beast. If we traded it in we'd be well over halfway to what Ronnie owes.'

The only outstanding matter was what to do with Trevor, and after some discussion they left him where he was. 'He can bunk up in the hay. We'll leave him enough provisions and if he gets bored he can sit on the pony,' said Shaughnessy.

The car had automatic gears and power steering and made little more than a whisper. The radio had four speakers and there were leather seats, and O'Grady couldn't remember ever being in such luxury. 'Three swells and a duchess,' said Shaughnessy, who had taken it upon himself to make Lee laugh, a challenge she resisted with ease. She told Shaughnessy where to find Capital, which they listened to until the signal faded, then switched to Radio One.

They joined the A12, which was slow with lorries. O'Grady didn't mind. They were in no hurry and the solid comfort of the car was a pleasure in itself. At Chelmsford they turned off to a supermarket, where they left Tel in the car and went to buy supplies after Shaughnessy had got money from one of the new cash machines. He told Lee there was a gang going round digging them out of walls and carrying them away on forklift trucks. She asked to feel one of the notes, which were sharp and brand new. He told her to keep it as there were plenty more coming, and she solemnly thanked him before carefully folding it.

In the supermarket they filled the trolley with the sort of frivolous things Molly would disapprove of. O'Grady had expected Lee to be self-conscious about her patch in public but she gave no sign of it. He wondered how long it would take to correct her squint.

Standing in the queue, with bright sunshine outside and people drifting by, enjoying the first good weather of the year, O'Grady felt a rare contentment, as if he was meant to be there in that moment. There were sweets on a rack by the checkout desk and he asked Lee if she wanted some. She looked uncertain for a moment and he supposed she went to the sort of school that disapproved of sweets.

'Go on,' he said. 'Help yourself.'

Back in the car, Lee refused Shaughnessy's offer of a Coca-Cola.

'I hate Coca-Cola,' she said.

'I thought everyone liked Coca-Cola. What would you rather?' Lee shrugged.

'I might have known it. One of the bloody Pepsi generation.' He pointed at Tel. 'He shares your dislike of Coca-Cola so you should get along fine. What do we have to do to get you to laugh?'

Lee looked at him impassively and Shaughnessy turned to O'Grady. 'Were you that serious as a child? Here's the bet. Fifty pound I make her laugh before you do.'

Shaughnessy started humming and watched the flat countryside passing by. The sun flashed through a row of poplars. The flicker effect reminded O'Grady of the lights in the club where he'd met Lily. The car smelled of warm leather and he wished that they could drive on for ever.

A Golden Oldie came on the radio and Shaughnessy said, 'I remember this.' It was 'Rock-a-hula Baby' and he started humming along, then, as the words came to him, he began singing and mugging it up for the girl. She remained stony-faced, which led Shaughnessy to declare that she would give Buster Keaton a run for his money.

They left the main road and drove through the flattest of landscapes with fields of turf and several acres of shimmering water which turned out to be long sheets of protective plastic.

Jaywick had sand blowing down the main street, a long strip which reminded O'Grady of a Wild West town. It was too early for the holiday season and most of the arcades and cafés were shut. There was a sea wall and a long row of bungalows built up behind it, facing the sea, most of them still closed for the winter.

The girl missed Ronnie's place on the first drive-by. The town was empty apart from the odd dog-walker. Ronnie's house turned out to be a tatty bungalow up a set of steps and not at all in the grand manner O'Grady had been expecting. A stiff breeze was blowing and through the glass front door O'Grady could see the sea beyond, the waves flecked with white crests.

'Do you come here much?' he asked Lee.

She shook her head. 'It's not the sort of place that Rusty likes. The girls at school would say it's common.'

'What's it like, that snooty school of yours?' asked Shaughnessy.

Lee pulled a face that didn't require any explanation.

The rooms smelled like they had been closed up a long time.

'Who uses it if your dad doesn't come here?' asked O'Grady.

'It gets rented in the holidays.'

'Does he own a lot of places, your dad?' asked Shaughnessy.

'I don't know. There's here, and the house and the place in Spain, and he goes to Florida but I don't know if it's his house there.'

'It looks like I left it a bit late to be getting on the old property ladder,' said Shaughnessy.

With its old candlewick bedspreads, faded wallpaper and parchment-coloured lampshades with tassels, the bungalow appeared not to have been touched since Ronnie was there as a boy. The damp salt air clung to everything, leaving it with a distinctive musty smell and surfaces that were sticky to the touch. Facing the sea was a glassed-in room, with windows frosted at the edges with dried salt. The house itself seemed to moan in the wind. A blue sky and choppy sea made them all look pasty.

Shaughnessy stuck his hands in his pockets and said, 'What we did on our holidays.' Turning to Tel, he asked, 'Did you know Ronnie when you used to come here?'

'It's where we met,' said Tel. 'Ronnie came first in a Cliff Richard competition.'

'Get away,' said Shaughnessy.

'"Livin' Doll",' confirmed Tel.

O'Grady went through to the glassed-in room, where Lee was sitting in a lounger.

'She's as common as muck,' Lee announced as he sat down.

'Who's that?'

'That's what I overheard one of the girls say about me.'

'Girls at school?'

'As common as muck.'

'That's better than as thick as shit.'

To judge by her straight face, he was no good at trying to be funny.

'Who's as thick as shit?'

'It's what I heard a boy saying. "Those Paddies are all as thick as shit."'

'Was he talking about you?'

'In a manner of speaking.'

'What did you do?'

'Beat the shit out of him, in a manner of speaking.'

She continued to look serious. Whatever O'Grady said seemed not to have the slightest effect on her and only reduced him to wondering about the point of conversation.

They were joined by Shaughnessy, who said, 'Ah, this is the life. Blue sky, picture-book sea, little white sails and a good breeze.'

Lee seemed content enough watching the view until they were joined by Shaughnessy and Tel. After that she and O'Grady walked along the beach, leaving the other two stretched out on the loungers. A stiff wind was cutting down the beach, which made walking hard work. Soon O'Grady could feel the stitch in his side, the slug protesting. The girl walked ahead of him in silence. She had put herself in charge of collecting change for the electricity, which was on a meter, which they got from the couple of shops that weren't shut. Most of it went again in the one arcade that was open, a gallery of blinking lights and useless little spirals of noise which had them throwing away their money. They had the place to themselves apart from a trio of leather-jacketed youths with cupped cigarettes and acne who slammed

themselves against the pinball machines as though their lives
depended on it.

They walked back through the town which was less windy.
Again she walked ahead of him, sturdily, in a way that left him
thinking that most of his life he had been out of step.

On their return to the bungalow O'Grady could see Tel in the
kitchen.

'Do you believe in miracles?' he asked.

'What are you talking about?'

He pointed at Tel. 'You're looking at one now. Him in the
kitchen.'

He was growing familiar with the expression of mild exasperation that crossed her face whenever he spoke to her. Her general
manner towards him amounted to one of embarrassed tolerance.

As they came in Tel said to Lee, 'Any good at cooking,
duchess?'

Lee ignored him and went to watch a black-and-white television in the main room, even though the picture was mainly a
snowstorm.

O'Grady found Shaughnessy still on his lounger, coughing
badly. The fit left him breathless, and looking melancholy. The
sun was going down to their right, flaring briefly and bathing the
glassed-in room with pink light.

'Ah, the gathering darkness,' said Shaughnessy, coughing
again.

'Shouldn't you be seeing someone about that?' said O'Grady.

'Quatsch. I'm not going near another quack as long as I live.
It's the Canadian cure or nothing. The last quack gave me six
months and that was over a year ago. I'm running on empty and
have been since I knew you.'

O'Grady stared at the sea.

'Don't worry about me,' Shaughnessy went on. 'Give me a
couple of months and I'll be strolling around with one of those
Toronto dames on my arm. Look, there's Tel with the dinner.
Menu Master. I had to read the instructions to him: "Place the
bag in the boiling water."'

There was rice in one dish and something dark brown in the other, and Tel looked pleased with himself. Inspecting the contents, Shaughnessy murmured, 'Tricky pulling that off, I would imagine.'

He winked at Lee who was sitting waiting at the table. 'After this I'll teach you patience taught me by my Polish grandmother. You'd not think to look at me that I had Polish blood in my veins. Shaughnitski was her name.'

'You'll have to do a lot better than that to amuse me,' said Lee.

'You're a snotty brat, aren't you?' said Shaughnessy affably, taking a pull of scotch from his flask. O'Grady had noticed him taking nips all afternoon, and sensed he was troubled.

Tel served up proudly, encouraged by Shaughnessy, who said, 'A deft hand. Not exactly the Clint Eastwood role you have assumed so effortlessly till now, more the Walter Brennan part, but Stumpy's contribution should never be underestimated. For what we are about to receive . . .'

He took another swallow from his flask, and watched with approval as Lee ate. 'Nothing like sea air for an appetite,' he said, but when Tel passed him his plate he held his hand out. 'Not for me thanks.'

O'Grady said, 'Now you've gone and hurt the man's feelings, as well as the girl's.'

Shaughnessy took the plate. 'No reflection on his cooking.'

He picked up his fork but only toyed with the food and ended up giving it to Lee, who was still hungry.

O'Grady did the washing up. Through a hatch into the main room he could see Shaughnessy and Lee together, having made it up. He was teaching her the German words of 'Wooden Heart', with her following haltingly and him stopping occasionally to correct her. Framed by the hatch, they looked like a picture and O'Grady felt sad for no reason.

Lee went to bed early, tired out. Coming out of the bathroom, O'Grady found Tel standing by her open door, watching her. On seeing him Tel mumbled, 'Night, Pat,' leaving O'Grady wondering how much he was choosing to ignore.

He paused in the doorway to check on Lee, who said, 'What do you want?'

'I thought you were supposed to be asleep,' he said, feeling caught out.

'Nearly,' she said.

'I'm in the glassed-in room, if you need anything.'

There weren't enough bedrooms and O'Grady had opted for a lounger. He lay awake listening to the waves sucking back the stones, trying not to think of the slug.

At some point he was woken up by the girl coming through, complaining she couldn't sleep. She was wrapped in her blankets and sat on the second lounger. O'Grady could see her eyes in the dark. She wasn't wearing her glasses.

'Who's Rusty?' he eventually asked, made awkward by her silence

'Dad's wife.'

'Not your mum.'

'Ugh! No thanks. She pretends to be, and makes me call her that.'

'Where's your mum?'

'She died when I was little.'

O'Grady was surprised by her sudden willingness to talk.

'Do you remember her?'

'Not really. I think she was unhappy.'

'What makes you say that?'

'She always looks sad in photographs.'

'I think I danced with her once.'

'You knew my mum!'

In the time he had known Ronnie there had been a wife kept indoors in the East End and numerous girlfriends. Towards the end he had been seeing a Kilburn girl O'Grady knew slightly and had danced with once, in the days before Ronnie, at the National. Later he had heard, but forgotten, that the first wife had been ditched for the girl from Kilburn. Now that he thought about it, there was a resemblance. He had not made the connection before

and wondered about chance in all their lives, and the strange loop
that had led to his sitting with the daughter all these years later.

Lee kept asking O'Grady about her mother and O'Grady
realised he was raising the child's hopes over what was little
more than a blurred memory of a young woman who had come
alive on the dance floor, a dancing queen. What he remembered
most was his own embarrassment at his clumsy shuffling. Seeing
the child was hungry for information he could not provide, he
changed the subject.

'Do you get on with your dad?'

Her silence told him he was prying too much. 'I'm going to
sleep now,' she eventually said and turned over.

O'Grady lay listening to the girl's breathing, sure that she was
awake. He wondered about her and her holidays in Spain. There
would be a swimming pool and not much else. He pictured her
counting off the laps. Ronnie would discourage her from becoming friendly with any Spanish girls. His days would be spent on
the phone, shifting his money around, and his evenings in the
curry house where he would play the patron without ever getting
off his arse. As for Rusty, he was willing to bet that she was all
hair and nails.

When he woke, Lee was already up. It was another fine day with tall clouds and a sun already high and so pale it was almost white. The light in the glassed-in room made everything look extra-sharp. O'Grady wondered what time it was.

He could see Shaughnessy walking towards the bungalow along the beach, seeming to totter under the burden of some enormous weight. O'Grady experienced the same foreboding he'd had on finding Tel watching the girl, and could not decide if it was his own nerves that were the problem. It was just as likely that Tel was sentimental and Shaughnessy had trouble walking on anything but concrete.

O'Grady went down the steps from the glassed-in room to the beach. It was the sort of day, he realised, when it was impossible not to be hopeful. His bright new mood was endorsed by Shaughnessy's cheerful wave. 'Christ, Pat! Too much fresh air's not good for a fellow. I'm knackered and I slept like a top, the kind of night that's given only to the just. And today's the day that'll see us all clear.'

They were interrupted by Tel calling from the steps, urgently waving them over.

'She's gone!'

'You were supposed to be looking after her,' said Shaughnessy.

'I only went to the bog.'

O'Grady never asked the reason for Tel's smirk. He just hit him. He was surprised by the speed with which he snapped, which he knew was also the start of his final undoing. He hit Tel low in the gut with a clumsy punch and when Shaughnessy got between them he hit Shaughnessy a blow above the ear that left him with a hurting hand and a mean high buzzing in him.

'What have you done with her?' he shouted as Tel tried to squeeze himself under the settee.

He knew the first punch had been caused by a detonation inside his own head more than by Tel. He knew, too, that Shaughnessy was not the real enemy, but that didn't stop him going for him – in spite of Shaughnessy pleading with him not to – puzzling all the while about where the rage in him was coming from, knowing it made no sense on any level, but no more able to stop himself than if he had been trying to empty himself into Kathleen. When in all the history of hard men had anyone done it blubbing like he was?

The beating was not a fluent thing. Furniture got in the way and Shaughnessy was bulky and awkward, as padded as a second-row forward, and used to staying out of trouble. He kept his distance, using a chair like a circus lion-tamer, making it harder for O'Grady, trying all the while to negotiate. O'Grady barely heard him above the roaring in his head. Most of his anger ended up directed towards his own failing strength. Soon all he was aware of was his ragged breathing, mocking his exhausted body. He could hear Molly saying, 'You've hands for nothing,' and saw the broken eggs on faded red linoleum, dropped on his first day in the kitchen, and imagined yellow runny yolk coming from Shaughnessy's nose instead of blood. The once or twice his fist connected with bone, it left O'Grady more aware of his own pain than any real damage to Shaughnessy, who started bleating about his heart.

It stopped as suddenly as it had started, as if a switch had been thrown in him. Tel's arse was sticking out from under the sofa and Shaughnessy, white-faced and trembling, had for the moment had all the wisecracks knocked out of him. He looked at O'Grady with great sadness, as though something had been broken between them.

'She can't have gone far,' he said.

O'Grady drove in vain up and down the main street half a dozen times, telling himself that she would not have run away. After that he went further out of town, though there wasn't any way she could have walked that far. He was panicking. He held himself responsible for her safety.

He stopped the car and got out and stood in a deserted road running straight to the horizon, calling Lee's name until he got a grip and realised where she would be.

He found her playing the machines in the arcade, looking as grave and self-contained as ever. He could see she was upset but thought better of asking. She was at the pinball table, imitating the way the boys had done it, using their bodies. O'Grady felt saddened by her efforts, flipping too early or too late and with increasing frustration as the ball dribbled down the board. She had neither the height nor the reach and O'Grady wanted to help but could see she would not let him. There was such an intensity to the child that he didn't have the heart to interrupt, and he stood watching her working through whatever it was that was in her head.

'There,' she said at last. 'I'm finished.'

Outside the arcade there was a bubble-gum machine and she bought herself a stick, and offered to buy O'Grady one. Out of politeness he accepted, thinking that the act of putting the stuff in his mouth might have a calming effect on his outburst, which was still fizzing inside him.

They stood working over the gum until it became soft enough to blow. O'Grady had forgotten about the extra sweetness compared to chewing gum and the rubberiness of it. Lee told him she wanted to walk, rather than take the car, and he said he would collect it later. They strolled back, saying nothing and blowing bubbles.

When they passed a phone box Lee told him she wanted to call her father.

'You'll see him tonight,' O'Grady said and sensed he had let her down with the remark.

'I need to speak to him now.'

That meant returning to the arcade for change. O'Grady watched her take the gum out of her mouth and carefully put it back in its wrapper, then in her pocket.

She let the phone ring a long time before hanging up, then dialled again and hung on.

'There's no answer,' she said.

'He probably left already,' said O'Grady.

'I want to go along the beach.'

They walked to the sea wall. The beach was almost deserted. O'Grady had to help her down off the wall, asking as he did, 'What did you want to talk to him about?'

She looked at him sharply. 'None of your business.'

She was right, but he could not work out why she was angry with him.

'You should have let me help you back there with the pinball,' he said.

'People only let you down in the end.' It sounded as though she was quoting from something.

'Who says?'

'So it's better not to ask.'

'That's what you believe?'

'I'm not telling you what I believe.'

They continued in silence until she said, 'I don't want my dad to come.'

'I thought that's what this was all about.'

'Well, I've changed my mind.'

He saw he'd not get any more out of her. She got out her gum again and put it back in her mouth and blew. When the bubble burst the wind threw it back in her face and she started laughing. O'Grady joined in uncertainly, but grew alarmed when she would not stop. She was also pointing. O'Grady turned to see Shaughnessy walking towards them, weaving like a drunk. Lee continued to laugh, thinking Shaughnessy was playing the clown for her.

'Hurry inside and wait there,' O'Grady said, pushing her towards the house.

He saw her hesitate, the laughter going out of her as Shaughnessy lurched, fell and rolled over.

'Go on now,' shouted O'Grady, setting off at a run.

He found Shaughnessy struggling for breath, trying to prop himself on one elbow, reaching for his pills and pretending hard that everything was all right.

'Ah, Pat. I think you overdid it back there.'

'Come on,' said O'Grady. 'You're not missing Ronnie's party, and I owe you fifty pounds. You just made the girl laugh.'

'And nearly killed myself doing it.' Shaughnessy's breathlessness folded into another coughing fit, which turned his face beet and had him waving O'Grady away with the hand not clutching his chest. 'Leave me be and don't say anything, Pat. This is my party.'

O'Grady stood back and watched him struggle to suck in air.

'Ah, Christ, my fucking bellows,' said Shaughnessy. 'I hope you can think of some famous last words because I'm damned if I can.'

He coughed again and then fell into a state of weak relief at seeing off the attack. 'Help me up, Pat. I was nearly a gonner for a moment there.'

Shaughnessy retired to the lounger and remained there, looking like a man waiting for an ambush.

'What about later?' asked O'Grady, thinking they should be getting him to hospital.

'Don't you worry about me. Once I'm rested up a bit I'll be as fit as a fiddle.'

Lee, apparently sensing that she was in the presence of something more than a regular sickness, became withdrawn. They left Shaughnessy sleeping and went with Tel to eat in a café in town where they were the only customers. The place was done out in red and green Formica and the ketchup came in a tomato-shaped container.

O'Grady and Tel behaved as though that morning had never happened, and O'Grady made polite conversation with the girl, as a way of keeping his mind off what was coming later. He was certain Ronnie would have retaliation in mind.

'It should be sunny in Spain, this time of year,' he said.

Lee pulled a face. So much for his diplomatic skills, he thought.

'What's wrong with your friend?' she asked.

'There's something the matter with his blood,' said O'Grady.

'He thinks he's got this Aids thing,' said Tel.

'He never has,' said O'Grady.

'Is that the thing men get?' asked Lee.

'They're now saying all of us can get it,' said Tel. 'Not just men.'

O'Grady shook his head. 'He'd be a lot skinnier. People were starting to get it in prison.'

Lee stared at him for a long time. 'Have you been in prison?'

'I have.'

'What for?' she whispered, after checking the waitress wasn't listening.

'It's a long story. I'll tell you later.'

'Did you do something very bad?'

'I did something wrong, which was why I went to prison. And at the same time something bad did happen.'

Lee frowned in an effort to separate the two things O'Grady was saying.

'He'd not get Aids,' O'Grady said to Tel. 'He's having you on.'

'I don't think he is. Whatever it is that keeps you healthy, he says he hasn't got enough of them. Antibodies, I think they call them. When that happens you catch lots of different diseases and can't get rid of them.'

'Christ,' said O'Grady. 'We don't want Lee catching anything.'

'It's not like a cold,' said Tel, embarrassed. 'You can't catch it just like that.'

Lee followed their conversation like a tennis match, her head turning from side to side.

Tel said, 'We shouldn't be talking about this stuff in front of her.'

Lee said, 'No, this is interesting. It's grown-up stuff. No one ever lets me talk to the grown-ups. It's all "Here's some money to go and buy yourself some sweets." Did you go to prison, too?'

Tel looked up at the ceiling and laughed. 'Borstal.'

'That's a kind of junior prison,' she said.

'I suppose.'

'Why did you get sent there?'

'Breaking and entering.'

'What does that mean?'

'I broke a window and entered a building.'

'That doesn't sound very serious.'

'That's what I thought. But the beak didn't agree. It wasn't my window or my building.'

'The beak?'

'The law, the judge.'

'Are you an alcoholic?'

Tel's eyebrows went up. 'Who told you?'

'I heard the other man telling you.'

Tel plucked at his sleeve. O'Grady thought that he'd probably never been asked before.

'Well,' said Tel eventually. 'It's what I do for a living, I suppose.'

'What, drink?'

Tel laughed. 'Well, I don't do much else.'

'Do you like doing it?'

'I'd be lying if I said I didn't, otherwise why would I do it? You don't feel very good when you wake up, but that's as bad as you feel all day.' He looked at O'Grady. 'We shouldn't be telling her any of this. We're setting a terrible example.'

Lee shook her head. 'One of the really boring things about being a child is that grown-ups always think you don't understand. We all know that Sandra Green's dad's an alcoholic – she's a girl at school – and if you do it up the bum you get Aids.'

O'Grady looked at her. 'When I was your age I used to think you got babies by two of you pissing in a pot.'

'You didn't believe that, you never did!' She squealed in disbelief and slapped the top of the table.

'It's true,' said O'Grady, and Tel looked at him askance.

'"It's only human nature after all,"' Lee recited, '"for a boy to take a girl behind the wall, and pull down her protection and plug in his connection, it's only human nature after all." Didn't they teach you that?'

'Where I grew up they were still figuring out how babies got made.'

She was enjoying herself, O'Grady could see. He was anxious again, and felt bad about letting everything unravel.

In spite of having slept all the time they were out, Shaughnessy complained of feeling exhausted.

'We should be thinking of making a move,' said O'Grady.

'Ready when you are. Good lunch?'

'Fair enough,' replied O'Grady.

'Fish and chips all round?'

'We're that predictable, and the girl had an ice cream.'

'This time tomorrow we'll be bathing in ice cream if we want,' said Shaughnessy.

O'Grady found it hard to look him in the eye and went outside, where he found Tel on the front steps smoking a cigarette.

'When we make the swap, keep your eyes skinned,' O'Grady said. 'There's a gun in the glove compartment.'

'I'm not up to this,' said Tel.

'Sure you are.'

'My ring went years ago. The other night at your place I was a joke.'

O'Grady hoped Ronnie would have the decency to get the girl off the scene first.

They sat waiting in the car for Shaughnessy. The girl had gone morose again. He had told her that he'd prefer them all to stay on, which was true, but he could see she didn't believe him.

Shaughnessy was taking his time. O'Grady would have been happy to wait for ever, but after five minutes he reluctantly got out and went back.

As he moved inside he could see Shaughnessy still in the glassed-in room, lying on the lounger.

Even before he stepped into the room, he knew something was wrong, except wrong was not quite the word. Shaughnessy looked quite peaceful, staring sightless at the horizon. It seemed altogether natural that he should slip away before the trouble started. O'Grady was even a little jealous.

He went back and told the others that Shaughnessy wasn't up to the journey. Tel, thinking he was malingering, wanted to go and sort him out.

'Leave him be,' said O'Grady, starting the car. 'We'll come back for him later.'

They left in silence. O'Grady could see the girl in his mirror. Soon she seemed to be asleep, her head on the armrest. Tel sat in the front, staring hard. O'Grady drove, counting off the white lines on the road. He waited until he was sure Lee was asleep before telling Tel about Shaughnessy.

Tel grunted. 'Are you sure he wasn't just lying there with his eyes open, pretending? I wouldn't put it past him.'

The rendezvous was the service station at South Mimms, on a big roundabout where two motorways joined. The girl was to be handed over in the restaurant and the money change hands, all in the open.

O'Grady was surprised by the size of the place. It was like its own self-contained little island with a petrol station, shops, cafés and even a hotel, and all very busy. He was sufficiently disorientated to wonder if the people milling about didn't live there all the time and he had stumbled across some lost colony. In the main building the neon lights turned everything stark and bleached, and their skin took on a waxy and transparent appearance, making them all look ill. Everything seemed to be happening half a beat too late, as though it was four in the morning, except it wasn't dark.

They joined the queue waiting for food. O'Grady looked around the crowded dining area for any sign of Ronnie, not that he was expecting him yet, as they were early. The girl ordered fish and chips again, and a glass of milk. O'Grady decided he wasn't hungry and only had coffee. Tel said that what he really wanted was a proper drink, which they didn't have.

They waited an hour, the girl growing more bored, sprawled sullenly across the table, hand propping her head. She was still chewing yesterday's gum and had given up checking the entrance. After a while she grew fractious and looked accusingly at O'Grady. 'I told you he wouldn't come, right at the beginning.'

'Maybe he got delayed by the weather.'

'It looks fine enough to me,' she said.

The child was starting to irritate him. When she repeatedly put her finger in her mouth and made popping noises he asked her to stop. Soon afterwards she began kicking the table leg instead.

It turned dark outside and after another half-hour O'Grady decided they were too conspicuous sitting there. The room was much less crowded. Everyone else had stayed twenty minutes, eating and leaving. No one else was waiting. There was nothing to wait for. He also saw there were cameras filming the room, which meant someone was watching them. They would be better off waiting in the car, moving it to a space where they could see the people going in and out. When O'Grady told them of his plan the girl grew panicky, thinking he secretly intended to drive off and not wait. He felt sorry for her being let down by Ronnie.

They found a space about twenty yards from the entrance. Lee insisted on sitting in front and fiddling with the radio, chopping and changing between stations. No one had anything to say. It was as if they had gone beyond waiting, and were all stuck.

Tel went off to buy cigarettes and came back with Dunhill, a surprisingly fancy brand for him, O'Grady thought. He stood outside the car smoking and O'Grady got out and asked for a cigarette.

'You don't smoke.'

'I'm thinking of starting again,' said O'Grady.

The cigarette tasted just how he remembered, after the first foul-tasting drags, bitter and sweet at the same time, and addictive.

Tel said, 'It'll be closing time soon.'

They exchanged looks. It was clear that Ronnie had stood them up.

'What are we going to do?' asked Tel.

O'Grady said he could try calling Spain. They pooled their change and he called international directory enquiries and wrote down the number with a pen bought from the shop. There was no answer.

Back outside Tel was still smoking. O'Grady could not think of anything to do except go back to Ronnie's and keep calling Spain. Tel shrugged and said OK, as if that was the problem solved.

'Give us ten minutes,' he said. 'I'm just going to nip into the hotel for a quick one, then we'll go.' Sensing resistance, he emphasised that the evening was a write-off. Nothing would happen now. 'Go on, just the one. Let's all go, why not?'

'Five minutes, no more,' said O'Grady. 'We'll wait.'

'Always knew you were a gent,' said Tel with a wink. 'See you later, champ.'

O'Grady watched him walk away, pigeon-toed, and got back in the car.

'Where's he gone?' the girl asked grumpily.

'To get a drink.'

'Are you sure this is the right place?'

'Sure.'

'Then why isn't he here?'

O'Grady sighed. 'If I could answer that, we wouldn't be sitting here.'

'What *are* we waiting for?' she asked plaintively. O'Grady had no answer to that.

He gave Tel fifteen minutes, then told the girl they would have to go and fetch him.

'He's not coming back,' she said, sounding quite definite about it.

O'Grady had guessed as much. When Lee refused to get out of the car they rowed. O'Grady could see why she was angry, but that didn't stop him getting annoyed in return, slamming his door when he got out.

The hotel turned out to have no bar and the receptionist had not seen anyone answering Tel's description. There was nowhere in the service area that sold alcohol, she told him. He thanked her and left.

Back in the car they bickered about Tel going off. 'I told you he wouldn't come back,' she said.

'And now you're stuck with me,' O'Grady said, slamming the transmission into reverse.

They drove back to Ronnie's place in silence. He supposed he would have to hand the girl back to Trevor and quietly disappear. He had no energy for anything else and, as for the money, that was looking more and more like a mirage.

He took the precaution of parking some distance from the house and hiding the car off the road. The girl grumbled about having to walk the last part, complained about her shoes getting muddy, and then of the cold.

When a dark shape suddenly crossed the road ahead she gripped his hand in fear. 'What's that?' she hissed.

'Only a fox,' said O'Grady, guessing, more scared than he wanted to admit.

As a precaution he kept the house lights off while they fetched the key to the stable padlock. He rehearsed what he would say to Trevor, and the girl, come to that. She was bound to be difficult.

He opened the top half of the stable door. Inside it was dark. Apart from the pony, which snorted at him, there was no sign of movement. He wondered if Trevor was lying in wait for him up in the loft. He could not think what to do. In the end they went back to the house for a torch. O'Grady anxiously climbed the ladder to the stable loft and shone the beam around the bales of straw.

He didn't see it until he had given up and was about to go back down. The torch, because of the way he was holding it, shone up on the ceiling, and he saw where Trevor had kicked or punched his way through the plaster and lathe and created a space large enough to escape through.

O'Grady climbed slowly back down.

'Trevor's not there,' he said to the girl. 'He managed to get out through the roof.'

'Oh' was all she said, seeming to accept his explanation as satisfactory. But soon afterwards she was crying, her tears silvery in the moonlit sitting room.

O'Grady had failed to get her to sleep upstairs. She had insisted on waiting up, crying silently and turning away when O'Grady spoke to her. He tried to reassure her by stroking her hair and she turned on him, lashing out, screaming at him to fuck off, and that she didn't care if anyone heard her language. She struggled and shouted so much he had to grab her and put his hand over her mouth to shut her up.

'I don't know what's going on any more than you,' he said. 'But it's not going to help if we start fighting. Do you understand?'

She nodded and when O'Grady took his hand away she bit it, making him bellow, which made her laugh.

'There, we're even now,' she said and in her look of spiteful triumph O'Grady saw her father.

They didn't speak after that and a while later he saw she was asleep. O'Grady sat in the dark, expecting nothing. Tomorrow would be another day and there would be another day after that, and whatever he did would make not the slightest difference to anything, unless he shot the pony and the girl and then himself.

He realised how ground down he was for even entertaining the thought. He tried to imagine a situation where he might manage to pull everything together at the last moment – in the nick of time, as Uncle Harry had been fond of saying. It would be good to live in a world where all his accounts were settled – with Molly and Lily and Ronnie, and the girl safely returned, and whatever else it took, instead of everything sliding away sideways as it always did.

At one point he thought someone had come for him when he saw a movement outside on the far side of the garden, and his heart leaped into his mouth, just as in the saying. Then he saw it was a fox, perhaps the same one they had seen before, moving across the lawn, and stopping to stand there a long time, seeming to stare directly at him. Something took hold of his hand. When he looked down he saw it was the girl, half asleep. She pointed at the fox, which was lit clearly by the light of the moon, bright enough to cast a shadow. Then it was gone and she went back to sleep without a word.

O'Grady had already sensed the first of the dawn, in the faintly emerging outline of the trees and in a turning of the dark sky to a paler grey, when the phone rang. He answered it on the second ring.

'Let me speak to Lee,' a woman said.

'She's asleep,' he answered and threw in a dig, adding that Lee was upset at not being collected.

The woman called him scum. He rode the insult and asked if he was speaking to Rusty.

'Who the fuck is Rusty?'

'Ronnie's wife,' said O'Grady, less certain.

'I'm his wife and I'm not Rusty.'

The girl was awake now, watching.

'Take down these instructions,' said the woman. She sounded nervous and irritable.

O'Grady still had the pen from the service station, and took down what she told him.

'It's too isolated,' he said when she was done. 'I'd be mad.'

'I'm not here to negotiate,' the woman replied. 'He's on his way.'

O'Grady tried to remember if the woman he had thought was Lee's mother had sounded anything like the one on the phone, but it was too long ago.

'Now put Lee on,' she said.

O'Grady handed the phone over.

'Oh, hi,' said Lee coldly. 'I'm fine, thanks. We went to the sea-side yesterday.'

The woman spoke at some length and Lee stuck her tongue out.

'We were waiting all last night. Where were you?'

The woman carried on and Lee slowly pressed her finger on the receiver, cutting her off.

'Why did she have to phone?' she asked looking at O'Grady.

When the phone went again, she put her hand on the receiver to stop him picking it up, and said, 'You know where we're going?'

O'Grady nodded and she said, 'Then leave it.'

The phone rang a long time until she picked it up and cut it off, and after that it didn't ring again. O'Grady didn't know what to make of her behaviour. The child was turning out the most complicated of the lot.

They arrived as it was getting light. Neither of them talked about the phone call or its implications. The landing strip was only a few miles from Ronnie's house, a private club for light aircraft, which from the road looked little more than a farmer's field and a couple of Nissan huts. O'Grady presumed Ronnie would be flying over from one of the Low Countries.

He drove past, not slowing down. There was a wood at the end of the airstrip. After a few hundred yards he found what he was looking for. There was a track among the trees and he turned down it and pulled up.

'What's going on now?' asked Lee.

'I want to take a look and check no one else is around.'

'Why can't anything be simple?' she said with an air of exas-peration.

O'Grady thought of the woman on the phone. 'It is simple. I'm going to take a look and then it's goodbye. You can't get much more straightforward than that.'

The girl gave an exaggerated sigh and folded her arms. 'Well, hurry up, please. I'm waiting.'

O'Grady closed his door quietly, so the sound would not carry, and set off through the wood. They were fir trees, planted far enough apart for him to be able to see some way ahead. Soft earth deadened his footsteps. He walked for about five minutes. The wind sighed in the top of the trees. Once he had to stop to catch his breath and a sharp, needle-like pain drove through him, and he felt his eyes widen as he gripped a tree to steady himself. But a moment later he was fine, moving carefully, sensing someone up ahead.

He was about fifty yards away when he saw them, more as a block of something darker among the trees than a specific outline. He moved cautiously forward until he could see two men and a car hidden under the trees, about twenty yards ahead. O'Grady was confident they would not turn round because they were watching their front. One of them had a walkie-talkie because once or twice O'Grady heard the crackle of static. He couldn't make out the men properly beyond them both wearing parkas and one having light hair. The fair one was smoking. The car looked like a Sierra and was dark, either brown or maroon.

He was about to turn and make his way back when he spotted a third man walking through the trees towards the car. It was the peaked cap that first alerted him and made him realise that he had been reading the situation all wrong. These men weren't there for him. They were waiting for Ronnie. They were police and they knew he was coming in. They also seemed pretty confident and not at all cautious, chatting and smoking.

O'Grady saw no point in waiting to see what was going to happen. God knows what he would do with the girl. He was lumbered with her and had nowhere to go, as going back to Ronnie's was out of the question.

She had one more shock in store for him because when he got back to the car she wasn't there. O'Grady was still wondering what to do when he spotted her strolling back down the track.

He motioned to her to hurry up. 'Where have you been?' he asked.

'Where have *you* been?' she echoed.

'Don't slam the door, and hurry,' O'Grady warned her as they got in. He reversed back down the track and swung onto the road without looking, hoping nothing was coming, and accelerated away from the airfield.

'Where are we going?' asked Lee, seeing they were heading the wrong way.

'There's been a change of plan,' said O'Grady.

'I knew this would happen!' she shouted. 'Why can't grown-ups organise anything?'

'There's a Happy Eater about five miles down the road,' said O'Grady. 'We'll have breakfast there and decide what to do.'

With its strip lighting and thin chips and artificially bright colours, the diner felt like part of a new Britain which made everyone look like drifters passing through, and reminded O'Grady in a way of Ireland.

The girl seemed unconcerned about what was going on, irritated, maybe, but not much more, and O'Grady understood that her being messed around in terms of promises and arrangements was typical. He wanted to explain about there being a complication at the airfield, without saying exactly what, but he could see she wasn't interested, probably because she knew she would only be getting another incomplete version of the truth.

'It doesn't matter' was all she said, then added sarcastically, 'I'm sure you'll think of something.'

O'Grady wasn't so sure.

After finishing her food and most of his, Lee announced she was tired and O'Grady told her he had a whole hotel at his disposal.

'I've never stayed in a hotel,' said Lee.

'What, never?'

'Dad always had a house.'

She played the radio while he drove back along the new motorway and then down the A1 and the A5 into London with the other commuters, life feeling almost normal, surrounded by thousands of others driving to work. Cricklewood was snarled-up and he cut round the back and down Willesden Lane. He wondered what people would make of them, driving along together in their smart dark-blue Mercedes. He passed Tommy Doyle's and, sure enough, there were two cars in the drive and even a glimpse of Tommy coming out of the house.

The hotel felt strange and empty to O'Grady, like something from a long time ago.

'We can stay here until we sort you out,' he said.

Lee started crying again. He sensed she was disappointed by the place and she'd had something much fancier in mind. She was right. It was barely a hotel, just rooms. He didn't know how to cope with her being upset except to blame himself. He rang the Spanish number again. There was no answer.

'We'll keep trying.'

He managed to persuade her to sleep for a couple of hours and got her to go to bed. While she was resting he sat in the front room where he had said goodbye to Kathleen.

In the end he fell asleep, too. He woke up to the sound of a car door slamming, with no idea of what time it was. Down in the street a black cab had parked and Molly got out while the driver unloaded her luggage. It was a bright spring day with a blustery wind and a cold blue sky. Molly back. O'Grady didn't know what to think.

She was standing by her luggage in the hall, sorting through letters when he came downstairs. He wondered how he was going to explain the child or the bullet hole in her mirror.

'What's the matter with you?' asked Molly.

'Why have you got a suntan?' he asked.

'Because I was in Florida.'

'Florida!'

'Yes, Florida.' She looked at him as if he was slow to catch on.

Because he had never asked, O'Grady had assumed she had been in Ireland. He had to say, she was looking extremely well. She was doing her hair a different way.

'Who on earth is that?' demanded Molly.

It was Lee standing at the top of the stairs, wrapped in a blanket, still half asleep and blinking at Molly in surprise.

They told her everything in the end, more or less, leaving out Trevor and the details of Lee's abduction and Shaughnessy's death. O'Grady was pleased with his account, thought it almost worthy of Shaughnessy in that he more or less believed it himself. He told Molly that they had gone to meet Ronnie on account of collecting some money he was owed, but Ronnie hadn't shown up. Ronnie was also supposed to come and collect Lee and they had spent the last two days unsuccessfully looking for him. Because no one was answering the telephone at the house in Spain, they had decided to come back to Kilburn until the matter was sorted out.

'Isn't that about the sum of it?' O'Grady asked Lee, who nodded convincingly. He hoped Molly would not ask why Lee, according to his version, was apparently running around unsupervised.

Molly spent most of the time listening with one hand to her breast and her mouth open with surprise. 'Well,' she said when O'Grady was done, 'I've never heard such a story in my life. What on earth did you think you were doing putting a child through all of that?'

Lee shrugged and said, 'We had fun.'

O'Grady thought he wouldn't have put it quite like that but was glad that the child was happy. Most of the time he had no idea what she was thinking.

But nothing in their story matched the surprise Molly had in store for him. She was moving to Florida, she announced, and had already made the down payment on a motel.

'You've bought a motel in Florida!'

She had and she was already well in with the local church, which was run by a Father Garcia. She said that she preferred Spanish priests, on the whole. They were more passionate about their religion.

'Whatever next?' asked O'Grady. 'You'll be taking up the tango.'

'Maybe I will.'

O'Grady had thought Molly seemed strangely unconcerned about what he told her. Now he understood why. She was gone already, moved in her head. She seemed oddly high, frisky even. O'Grady wondered if she had been drinking on the plane and that, with her jet-lag, was causing her odd behaviour.

He left Lee watching cartoons on television while he went out for an *Evening Standard* and some comics for her. There was nothing about Ronnie being arrested. It was always possible that he hadn't landed. Ronnie's sixth sense had always been very good.

He then told Molly he had to go out for a few hours but would be back later in the afternoon.

Molly looked at him. 'What on earth is going on?'

'Nothing. It's being sorted out. Once the girl has been returned, everything's done.'

'And what's the matter with you?'

'Nothing.'

'You're sweating and you're as white as a sheet.'

'It's just the end of the 'flu I was telling you about.'

'And what's that hole in my wardrobe mirror? I'm not blind, you know.'

'Molly, I promise you, it's all nearly over.'

He said goodbye to Lee. She asked where he was going and if she could come and he said it would be better if she stayed with Molly and kept trying the number in Spain. She looked disappointed, as though he was letting her down, and O'Grady in turn could not work out why he felt so sentimental about leaving her.

He drove back the way he had come. The Mercedes still had half a tank of petrol. Driving up Willesden Lane he passed Tommy Doyle's again, saw the two cars in the drive, and without stopping to ask himself why pulled in and rang Tommy's bell. Tommy came to the door himself.

'Well, blow me down' was all he said by way of greeting. 'What brings you round?'

'I was just passing and thought I'd drop by to see how you were. I'm not stopping.'

'Come in, anyway.'

Doyle waved O'Grady into the hall. Doyle looked prosperous and his house had everything a man could want. He was wearing a silk shirt, his trousers had pleats and his shoes shone. He had made himself into everything that O'Grady was not.

'Is that your Merc outside?' asked Tommy.

O'Grady said it was, because any other explanation was too complicated.

'I'm thinking of getting one myself. So how have you been?' Doyle looked at him, slightly puzzled, as if trying to work out why O'Grady was there.

O'Grady shrugged. 'I was driving past. I'm thinking of going away. To Florida, maybe.'

Tommy stared at his shiny shoes and said, 'I've got so much money I don't know what to do with it and I'm bored out of my mind. Bored by my wife and bored by my children and the people I work with. Is any of it worth a candle? Florida, you say? Maybe I'll see you out there. I wouldn't mind a fresh start myself, footloose and fancy-free. I always had half an eye on that sister of yours. She was better looking than she ever let on. Mind you, the only arms that held her were the arms of Christ and there's nothing you can do when you're up against them.'

'Well,' said O'Grady awkwardly, 'I only stopped by to say hello.'

'Take care of yourself, now,' said Tommy, sticking his hands in the pockets of his expensive flannels. 'You look like you could do with a spell in the sun.'

'That's right,' said O'Grady. 'Well, so long, then.'

Tommy came outside and watched O'Grady getting in the car. The asphalt of the drive had the same white flecks as the house in Totteridge.

'What does it do to the gallon?' asked Tommy.

O'Grady had no idea. 'It's pretty good,' he said vaguely, not understanding why he felt so bucked by his little talk with Tommy.

Tommy was still standing in the drive watching as he left, with the same puzzled expression O'Grady had noticed earlier.

He drove back to Ronnie's and parked some distance away and walked through the woods, getting muddy shoes, until he had a view of the house. There were several cars and a van parked outside, and what looked like a lot of official business going on, with boxes being taken from the house and stacked in the van. Not police, O'Grady decided, but nearly police; probably Customs.

He went back to the car and scraped his shoes before getting in. The effort made him breathless. He contemplated the wisdom of what he was about to do, and shrugged. As Tommy said, none of it was worth a candle.

The way the man behind the post-office counter stuck his hands straight up in the air when he saw the gun was almost comic. He was Indian, elderly, with gold-rimmed spectacles. His wife wore a sari. O'Grady remembered them being excessively polite from his previous trip. He had noticed then from the sign on the door that they shut each day for an hour's lunch but had thought nothing of it at the time.

He had waited until a couple of minutes to one before walking in. There was one elderly biddy at the counter fussing over her stamps. O'Grady hung around looking at tins, remembering buying the orange juice and odds and ends for the girl on the first night, waiting for the woman to go, praying she would leave before anyone else came in, and hoping that the trouble he was having breathing was nothing more than nerves. He had at last seen the old girl out, flipped the sign on the door to closed, dropped the lock and turned, with the gun in his hand, pointed at the wife, who was behind the shop till.

'Move over to the counter,' he said.

It was at that point that the man had put his hands up.

'Let's do this quickly and nobody will get hurt,' said O'Grady, looking at the man. 'You know why I'm here and you know what to do.'

'We are just a sub-post office,' the man said, sounding regretful, and O'Grady interrupted, saying he didn't have all day.

He walked out with a plastic carrier bag full of notes. He wasn't even sure if that was all the money that had been in the place or if the man had fooled him. The man and his wife had looked almost sorry for him, O'Grady thought, sensing his desperation.

Nobody saw him go. He had locked the couple in the storeroom to give himself time to get away, apologising for doing so. 'I know you're both gentle people,' he had said. 'And I would not be doing this unless I had to.'

He drove fast back towards the city, pulling over and stopping after ten miles, to count the money. The amount made him cry. Everywhere else it was lunchtime, he thought, remembering the people he had driven into the city with that morning. Maybe he would offer to take Molly and the girl to Tony's steakhouse for dinner, and by then things would feel normal again.

The gates to the Totteridge house were open and several cars stood in the drive. O'Grady drove in and parked, walked to the front door and rang the bell, which was eventually answered by an oriental-looking maid with limited English. She seemed not to know who Lily was and O'Grady wondered if Lily was gone already.

'My daughter,' he repeated for the fourth or fifth time.

'Mistake,' the woman kept answering, wagging her finger.

'No mistake. Lily.'

He changed tack and asked for Keith and was told in more or less straightforward English that he was in the studio and not to be disturbed. O'Grady then showed the maid the money in the bag.

'This is hers.' He was speaking loud and very slowly trying to make himself understood.

The sight of the money brought a degree of understanding to the situation. 'Ily asleep. No disturb,' the maid said. She mimed a balloon around her stomach.

O'Grady didn't get it until the maid said, 'Baby.'

'Baby?' repeated O'Grady.

The maid nodded vigorously. O'Grady felt dizzy. Now her last call made sense. That's what she had been referring to.

'I'm her father,' he said weakly.

Once that was established, the maid agreed to fetch her.

Lily came down wearing a sumptuous-looking man's dressing gown. She seemed neither pleased nor not pleased to see him.

'I just heard the news,' he said.

'Does Keith know you're here?' Lily managed to sound both bossy and distracted. Her face was puffy and O'Grady wondered if she was doped up on something she was taking for the pregnancy. He knew nothing about these things.

He shook his head. He could not find the words and stared at the hall's expensive wooden floor, uncomfortably aware of smelling rank from all the sweating he had been doing.

'I came to give you this,' he eventually said. 'It's not as much as I was hoping but I promised you something for your birthday.'

Lily peered into the bag and shook her head slowly. From her gesture O'Grady knew she had made her peace with Keith, and it was his baby she was carrying. His own offering wasn't even pocket money to them.

'We're getting married,' she said.

He offered her the bag again. 'Buy something for the baby.'

'No, honestly. We don't need it.'

'Take it anyway.'

She shook her head. 'You better go now,' she said.

His goodbye was clumsy. He didn't know what to say and Lily wasn't any better in spite of her efforts to act the lady of the house.

'Look after yourself then, and the baby,' he finally managed.

He leaned forward to kiss her on the cheek but she turned away and O'Grady realised then that Maggie had been right all along. Selfish Lily had turned out to be not worth the bother. She was, after all, his own flesh and blood.

After that he drove. Faced with the choice of turning north instead of going back into the city, he went up the A1, wanting to put miles between himself and everything that had happened, before returning. There was still plenty of time. The car held rock steady at ninety. At the next service station he would telephone Molly and say hello to the girl. He understood at last what she represented and wished he had realised earlier that she had been a little bit of borrowed time for him. He had not been joking when he told Tommy Doyle about Florida. Florida would be the solution to everything. He decided it was where he had been all those years in America, according to Molly, and now he was going back. Molly might take some persuading but he knew he could win her round in the end. She would be needing a handyman to get the motel started, and, knowing her, would find American men intimidating. As for Lee, he had no one else to spend the money on. Three thousand pounds would get them to the funfair. Molly would be trickier on that, but would eventually give in after complaining, 'Heavens, what would I know about children?'

'It's only for a holiday,' he would insist.

Her saying 'Well, you're getting me on none of those rides' would be her first sign of conceding. And they would, get her on the rides, and she would shout in delighted fright with the rest of them, as the bullet-shaped machines hurled them through the air, and she would be secretly pleased not to be in Florida on her own, and none of them would ever be cold again, and nothing would ever be conditional.

O'Grady would pay for the taxi from Kilburn to the airport, and he and Molly would shed no tears for Kilburn. Lee would travel on the passport she used for Spain. They would be on a package flight just for holidaymakers, waved through the passport desk without a glance. In the departure lounge Molly would spend so long in the duty free that they would almost miss the plane. Later, hurrying down long corridors, full of glassed-off rooms of others waiting, O'Grady would find it hard to grasp the notion of so many people departing at once, but going past the lounge for the flight to Toronto he would get a brief glimpse of Shaughnessy, having pulled off his final trick. And then they would be on the plane, sitting three seats in a row, hurtling down the runway. And then they would be up in the air.

O'Grady checked the clock on the dashboard. There was still time enough, but he knew he ought to think of turning back. He saw a broken-down car on the hard shoulder. His own sped on, seemingly of its own accord. He would turn at the next exit he told himself, and switched on the radio and fiddled with the dial until he found music.

He couldn't understand why everything was getting so dark when it was still so early and wondered why none of the other cars had their lights on.

A song came on the radio. The King.

And then he saw the tunnel ahead.